The Turning Glass

by
Marcia G. Moore

Good Fellowship Press
Salt Water Media

ISBN 978-1-62806-232-8 (print | paperback)
ISBN 978-1-62806-233-5 (electronic | ebook)
ISBN 978-1-62806-234-2 (electronic | ebook)

Library of Congress Control Number 2019910287

Published by Salt Water Media
29 Broad Street, Suite 104
Berlin, MD 21811
www.saltwatermedia.com

Cover artwork by Drew Macko

For Jack

Thank You

I have been working on "The Turning Glass" for a long time, longer, in fact, than the span of years from the beginning of the French and Indian War (1754) to the end of the American Revolution (1783). I may not remember all who helped me with research, direction, encouragement, and by maintaining the pretense that they thought I really was writing a book -- the same book -- year after year after year. I am grateful, nonetheless.

I began this book in the 1980's while we lived in Sleepy Hollow, New York. I was given great assistance from the staffs of The Warner Library, Tarrytown, New York, the Historical Society of the Tarrytowns, and the Westchester County Historical Society. Historic Hudson Valley provided me with invaluable information about 18th Century life and customs as well as a working grist mill, which is the setting for a number of scenes in "The Turning Glass."

The Junior League of Westchester-on-Hudson developed and funded a project to publish a guidebook for the burying ground of The Old Dutch Church of Sleepy Hollow. I was the committee chair. That booklet was the predecessor to "The Turning Glass." Our friends Sylvia and Aubrey Hawes of Sleepy Hollow, New York, have kept us in touch with the preservation and education initiative the League started, now Friends of the Old Dutch Church.

My long-time friends -- Elizabeth Hambley Wilson, Karen Rau Cartwright, Tellie Baltes Dixon, Walda duPriest-Brandt, Linda Smith Faulkner, Polly D. Hanes and Jane Elliott Libby -- have never failed to support and encourage me.

The Highlights Foundation, under the direction of Kent L. Brown. Jr., offered workshops that helped me to actually put together a book. The marvelous author Joy Cowley shared her great wisdom, experience and guidance, and I am indebted to them both.

I am immensely grateful to the Working Writers Forum of Easton, Maryland for their optimistic, if quixotic, view that I could indeed write this book. Thank you, Laura Ambler, Linda Fritz Bell, Bill Brashares, Mala Burt, Brent Lewis, the Rev. George Merrill, Anne McNulty and Gerald Sweeney. Suzi Peel brought her excellent editing skills to the manuscript, and made it a polished, correctly punctuated document.

The legendary Sleepy Hollow artist, Drew Macko, created cover art that matched exactly the visions of the Hudson River Valley that I've seen in my mind for all these years.

I have been blessed with an extraordinarily supportive family. My brother-in-law, Dr. Richard S. Moore, an authority on 19th Century American literature, provided many helpful suggestions to transform a 21st Century writer's story into a tale of two hundred years ago. He also kept a watchful eye on my use of commas.

Our children, John Christian Moore and Emily Patten Moore, now grown and parents of their own, most certainly inspired the brother-and-sister bonding and bickering of which, as an only child, I had no experience.

Jack, my beloved husband of 50 years, is a great proofreader, as well as a long-suffering visitor to 18th Century historic sites where I gathered research. He is my editor, agent and publisher, as well as the love of my life.

The Turning Glass

– Chapter One –

The world turned upside down that summer of '76, but we paid little heed. We dismissed each jolt – first the warships, then the raids, then the killing – as a singular stroke of ill fortune. The time would come when we would ask, "How was it all upended?" But not in summer of that year. We were intent upon the matters of our lives.

Papa tended our farm, two hundred twelve acres of fields, pasture and woodland overlooking Hudson's River just north of Tarrytown. Mama dispatched her domestic duties with a frugality of time and effort, so that she could escape into her beloved books. Mama always did prefer paper people to those of flesh, bone and a contrary nature.

Indeed, my brother Brom was the only one of us concerned about the massive British fleet gathered twenty miles to our south in New York Harbour. Brom was sixteen, at the age when he felt keenly the yoke of oppression upon his neck. In addition to the usual injustices imposed by his elders, Brom chafed at the despotism of King George III, whom he blamed for his own sorry circumstances.

And I? I had turned fourteen that spring. When I laced my stays, my waist no longer fell in a straight line from my bosom. My flowering womanhood was chiselling the childish roundness from my face. I cannot say what I was then. I can tell you only what I was not.

I was not the eldest child. After my baby sister was born, I wasn't the only girl or the fairest one. People would say what a beauty Elizabeth would become. They never said that of me.

I was not a flaxen-haired coquette like my distant cousin Laney Van Tassel. I was not slight in stature – *petite*, she would say – like my friend Amy Requa, and I lacked her ease of manner – sauciness, if truth be told – amongst boys we'd known all our lives.

I wasn't learned like Mama, although she'd had a score of years more than I to cram all manner of knowledge into her head. Worst, I was altogether wanting in the cleverness and craft of my cousin Rachel Van Tassel.

Rachel was the daughter of Papa's oldest brother, *Oom* Willem, and she was ten months and six days older than I. In her opinion, her greater age entitled her to vast superiority and sway over me. Rachel was vexed that I had blossomed and she had not. She blamed me for this upheaval of the proper order of events.

Rachel was not bookish in the way Mama was, or even schooled like Brom and me. Rather, she possessed a native cunning. Although she had never heard of an Achilles' heel, Rachel could find its exact location in each person she encountered.

To Rachel's perverse delight, Mama's Achilles' heel was Rachel herself. Mama did not trust Rachel one iota. She suspected that that whey-faced chit with a perpetually smug demeanour led me into mischief just to bedevil her. Yet Mama could hardly tell Papa that his brother's daughter was a jackanapes. She couldn't forbid me to keep company with my own cousin.

Mama had to settle for stern lectures following our misadventures. That was her term for Rachel's tangled plots, many of which ended badly. In this, Rachel could cause me anguish as well, for Mama was as skilled at extracting information as any dungeon-keeper of yore.

Tirelessly, relentlessly, these adversaries warred for control over me: Mama, to guide me to becoming her model of a proper young lady, Rachel to goad me into straying from it. I think now that their efforts were intended to confirm their own utterly opposite manners of living. If I did as one of them did, I supposed, that would mean she was right.

I didn't know that then, of course. Most times, I felt like one of the oysters Brom and I collected at the edge of Hudson's River. Mama or Rachel would try to pry me open while I shrank inside my shell. I longed for them both to leave me alone. I yearned to possess one small, grainy pearl that was mine only.

Such was the state of affairs when I met Hulda. I saw her perhaps a half-dozen times and we never spoke of weighty matters. Still, she was of such importance to me that I would tell her story, for it is my story as well.

Hulda was never one to take an interest in the trivial. I suppose that is why I never learned her family name, or if, indeed, she had a husband, brothers or sisters. To Hulda, such details were of no consequence.

To our neighbours in the environs of Tarrytown, they mattered very much indeed. In the manner of country folk, they took measure of a person by kin and by residence. Hulda's living alone caused pursed lips and raised eyebrows. Her choice of dwelling place caused first a horrified silence, then a vigorous wagging of tongues. Hulda was said to live deep in the little hollow behind the church, a known gathering place for evil spirits. No one had actually set eyes upon her home, but all knew that no one with benign intentions would live there.

As the good folk pondered Hulda's peculiarities, they came upon another appalling truth: No one knew where she had come from. Some said Bohemia, and the few who admitted to conversing with her said she spoke in a Germanic tongue. No one could say for certain when she had arrived. She had just appeared one day, a tall, robust woman of perhaps forty years, in an oft-mended faded grey gown that was likely her only garment.

The gossips at once divined the meaning of her presence: Hulda was in league with the Devil. She had been sent by him to wreak destruction on the people of Tarrytown. The whole countryside was warned about the malevolent powers of the *vreemdeling*, the foreigner. There was not a thunderstorm, a sickly babe, a broken wagon wheel that did not bear her evil mark.

Then, there was the shocking happenstance observed by Cornelius Van Vliet, father of the unlucky Jost. In his sloop on Hudson's River one day, Cornelius spied a rude vessel rowed by native people who were thought to have long since disappeared. The sight of bronze-skinned savages was astonishing enough, but among them, Cornelius swore, was a boy of perhaps ten years. The boy was half-clad in the manner of his companions. That was how Cornelius saw the lad's pale skin and hair the colour of straw.

It took no time at all to deduce who the boy's mother was – it was Hulda, of course. His paternity was a knottier problem – could he be one of the men in the boat? The Prince of Darkness himself? It was hard to say which was worse.

Ours was the only household, I think, where Hulda's name had never been spoken. Mama didn't much chum about with flesh-and-blood people. She never learned any of the local news. So I had never heard of Hulda until I met her one sunny afternoon in June. The occasion, of course, was yet another misadventure.

After years of experience with Rachel's ill-conceived designs, you might think that I would have learned to spot them at a distance. I did, in a way. When it seemed that I had swallowed a very large stone, I knew that things were about to go awry.

That day, a boulder was indeed in my belly, for Rachel's idea was even more foolhardy than usual: we would spy on my older brother Brom as he went to pay a visit to our cousin Laney Van Tassel, the most beautiful young lady in the colony of New York.

In those days there were as many Van Tassels in Tarrytown as cornflowers in a meadow. Laney was our fourth cousin, I believe. We had the same ancestors some generations back.

Mama had unwittingly aided Rachel's plan by sending us off to pick berries. So, a short time after, Rachel and I found ourselves on the Albany Post Road. We intended to hide until Brom passed, then follow him at a distance. As we walked, Rachel studied the landscape.

"Sarah, those rocks are perfect. Brom will never see us spying on him," she declared. "Climb up there."

I looked where Rachel pointed. Leafy shadows danced on a stone ledge at the side of the road, presenting a benign view, even a pleasant one. To reach it, though, we'd have to make our way through a patch of sticky brown brambles. Then we'd need to hoist ourselves up a rough rock crag that was higher than a ceiling and covered with moss, as well.

"Climb up there," Rachel repeated. "You're such a giant you'll not need to reach far."

Rachel knew my height embarrassed me. She was likely to bring up my other weak spots too. I had many more than two Achilles' heels, and Rachel knew them all.

I said, "We told Mama we were going to pick berries."

Rachel drew circles in the dusty road with the toe of her black leather shoe as she contemplated her next thrust. "You're just a coward," she announced at last. "Tom Buckhout said…"

"What did Tom say?"

Rachel couldn't hide a triumphant smirk. "I promised I wouldn't tell," she said piously.

I chided myself once more for having revealed to Rachel that Tom was the object of my amorous fancies. Of course, she prized such knowledge. She could turn it to a cudgel to beat me.

After a while, I said, "Brom's probably not going to Laney's. He's likely going to Storm's Tavern."

"I'd quite forgot," Rachel said. "Brom *would* have to make up a false story. Your mama is a Tory. She won't give him leave to go to the tavern."

Mama was English, and she was indeed a fervent Tory. She had forbidden Brom to go because Storm's Tavern was known to be a hornets' nest of rebellion against His Majesty King George.

Was there no end to Rachel's prying and prodding? A tear sprang to my eye, though I strove to hide it.

Rachel was still tracing circles with her shoe. "You're a Tory, too," she announced, glancing at me. She simpered and affected Mama's English way of speaking. "I day-ah not displease my ma-MAH. *Boo hoo hoo...*"

I leaped over the ditch at the side of the road and strode to the cliff. "You climb up there," I told her. "You're smaller and easier to lift." I guided her shoe into a crevice.

"Ow! These thorns are dreadful!" Rachel batted at the brambles that snagged her green calico skirts.

"Reach up," I told her. "There's a handhold if you stretch a bit."

"You aren't pushing hard enough."

I wedged my shoulder beneath her as she struggled upward.

"I'm nearly there." Rachel reached her arm over the ledge and took hold of something.

There was a sound that could have been dry leaves crunching. But it wasn't quite like leaves.

"Aah!" Rachel reeled backward and lost her footing. From the corner of my eye, I saw an odd-looking bundle tumble off the ledge.

Rachel came bumping down the rocks in a whirl of calico and white stockings. It happened so fast I couldn't get out of her way. We landed with a thump in the underbrush. I was pinned beneath her.

Rachel was screaming. It wasn't one big scream but a series of little "Ow-ow-owws!" It sounded as if she wanted to say something but she couldn't get her breath.

I'd had the wind knocked out of me, too. Rachel's cap had come off. Strands of her light-brown hair were in my mouth. I tried to wipe them away.

The bundle had landed a small distance away in the tall grass. It looked to be an untidy ball of rope, about the size of a cooking pot. The ropes were grey and brown. All were woven in a curious criss-cross pattern.

"Rachel, what...?" I tried to push away her flailing arms.

"St-ing! St-ing!"

There was that strange noise again. Now it was more like a buzz.

Rachel's arm hit me in the throat as she tried to push herself away. I glimpsed a puffy pink circle just above her wrist.

"Sting! Ow!" Rachel tried to roll away but she didn't know which way to turn.

The knot of ropes began to move. Over and under and round, they were coming loose. Some of the ropes were as thick as the lines on *Oom* Jan's boat. Some were more the size of the reins on Pegasus' bridle. The ropes were snakes.

Rachel had stopped screaming. She clutched her wrist and gasped for breath.

One snake had a peculiar handle on the end. It looked to be made of a kind of shell. The handle began to clatter. There was a chorus of clattering.

The snakes were rattlesnakes! They had been on the ledge when Rachel put her hand there. There could have been half a dozen of them. I couldn't count.

The boulder in my belly rose to my throat.

One snake raised its head, rolled itself into a tidy coil and looked straight at me. Its head was flat and its eyes were the very grey-brown hue of its skin. The pupils weren't round like a person's. They were slits, scarcely bigger than the eye of a darning needle.

I stared back. My mouth was open, but I wasn't uttering a sound.

The snake flicked its tongue, a narrow black ribbon that some-one had snipped in the middle. It came closer without seeming to move at all.

Several other horrid heads rose from the tangle. They swayed round each other, vying for a better view of me.

The nearest snake was no more than an arm's length away. I could see its nose, or rather, the hideous little holes where its nose should have been. An illustration from one of Mama's books flashed through my mind: Hydra, the snake monster of Greek myth. When one of Hydra's heads was cut off, two grew in its place. This snake had the same gaunt face and lifeless eyes. It meant to kill me. I was certain.

Two other snakes – one the size of a stout walking stick – had twisted themselves free of their companions. They glided toward us without making a sound.

With a mighty effort, I pushed Rachel aside and rolled away. I scrambled to my feet. I seized Rachel's good arm and dragged her a few paces.

The nearest snake was poised in the grass. It watched my efforts with the same pitiless stare. My breath was coming in great, heaving gasps. I realized that if the snake struck now we couldn't get away.

Rachel tried to sit up. When she saw the snake, she began to keen, a high-pitched moan that didn't rise or fall or stop.

The snake's eyes seemed brighter, and I thought I saw a spark of interest. I wondered if snakes could hear. Then I wondered if anyone else was nearby, if they would come to our aid. Where was Brom? He was likely to pass by at any moment.

I seized the basket we had for the berries and I brought it down with all the force I could muster. I hit the snake midway between its head and tail. It leaped from the blow, then opened its mouth to show pointy fangs the size of my teeth.

I struck a second blow on the snake's head. And another. At last, it tired of the fray. I balanced the basket in my hands and held my breath as it moved slowly off, doubling back upon itself as it went. It gave me a baleful stare before it slithered under some leaves.

Then I looked at Rachel.

– Chapter Two –

"Rachel! Are you all right?"

The instant I said it, I could see that she was not all right, not in the least. Rachel lay curled on the ground, clutching her wrist. Her eyes were closed. Little brown burrs clung to her skirts and bodice. Her sleeve was torn and one shoe was gone.

One of those snakes had bitten her. Maybe more than one.

I turned to look at the great writhing heap. Oddly enough, the snakes weren't coming after us. Indeed, they seemed to have lost interest altogether. One by one, they were slipping away.

Rachel gagged and tried to vomit. She strove to say something, but her words burst from between heaving breaths.

"I'll run home and fetch Papa..." I began.

"Don't... leave... me..." Rachel's face was pale as ash.

"Can you get to the road?"

Her reply was a high-pitched wail. I put my arms beneath her shoulders and dragged her through the underbrush. As we reached the road, she collapsed in the dust.

Desperately, I looked round. Someone had to come by soon. The Albany Post Road was no country lane. The post-rider cantered through with saddlebags bulging with mail, and farmers drove their wagons filled with grain to Philipse's Mill, which we had just passed.

Anybody headed for Storm's Tavern had to go by this very spot. But it was plain that we couldn't wait for long.

I tried to remember what I knew of snakes. Papa said to stay away from them, even the skinny striped garter snakes that my little brother Thomas liked to catch. "Mean as a snake," he reminded us, was no idle saying.

The lump on Rachel's arm was now the size of an egg, and it looked as if it were about to burst through her skin. Two bloody dots were in the centre.

"I'm... going... to... die." Rachel was inclined to exaggerate but I thought that in this instance she might be right. She was quaking so hard that it looked for all the world as if a snake were wriggling beneath her skin.

I was trembling. Likely the snake had bitten me, too. Its poison was running through me and that was why I was shaking like Rachel. Rachel and I would die right there on the Albany Post Road. When they had found our corpses, nobody would know what had happened. Tom Buckhout would be stricken with grief when he realized he'd never see me again. He would die of a broken heart.

Before my morbid fancies could transport me further, I spied a woman striding briskly down the hill from Tarrytown. She wore a faded blue bonnet and she carried a basket. I judged her to be about the same age as Mama. As she came near, I noticed that her loose-fitting grey gown had been mended in many places.

The woman set her basket on the ground and knelt beside Rachel. "*Liebchen! Was ist los?*"

"Snakes," I managed to say.

The woman frowned in puzzlement. I realized that she had spoken in a foreign tongue. Then I realized I'd not seen her before and I thought that was odd. In those days, there were few strangers in these parts.

I tried to recall the Dutch word for 'snake,' but she wasn't speaking Dutch. I imitated a snake: I took my hand and made it 'bite' my other arm.

"*Ach! Die Schlange!*" The woman grasped Rachel's arm, a good deal more deftly than I had. She pulled away Rachel's torn sleeve. The angry red lump was turning purple. The woman clucked and uttered some words I didn't understand.

She turned to me and said something like "Oondsee?" I thought she was asking if I'd been bitten, too. She inspected me. "*Nein*," she said firmly.

Rachel moaned. With snakebite, I thought, you didn't die all at once. It probably took a while.

The woman got briskly to her feet. She pushed a lock of greying hair back under her bonnet and turned to me.

"*Die Schlange*," she began. She took her arm and clamped it with her other hand as she had seen me do.

"Snake," I said.

"The snake." She pondered her words for a moment. "The snake...bad?"

I was inclined to reply that no snake was a good one, but I thought she was asking if it were poisonous. "It was a rattlesnake," I answered. I wagged my finger and made clicking sounds.

"*Ach! Nein!*" The woman rummaged in her pocket. In the Dutch fashion, it hung from a cord round her waist, and was made of brightly coloured patchwork.

Rachel watched through swollen red eyes as the woman drew out a small knife with a pearl handle. She struggled as the woman tried to take her by the wrist.

I said, "She's trying to help you, Rachel. I think she means to draw out the poison."

The woman agreed. "The poison. Out."

Rachel wailed, "I'll bleed to death...and die!"

The woman straightened up. "Not die!" she snapped. She motioned for me to take Rachel's arm.

Rachel clawed at me with her free hand, but I was a good bit bigger, and I had the advantage of being on my feet. I caught her arm, turned to the woman and nodded.

She made two small precise cuts, right over the dark bloody dots where the fangs had pierced Rachel's arm. She bent her head and for a moment I thought she was looking closely at the cuts she had made. Then she pressed her mouth to them.

Rachel shrieked, "She's killing me, Sarah! I'm dying right now!"

I got a firmer grip on Rachel's arm. "She's drawing out the poison. Be still."

The woman lifted her head and turned away. She spat into the road. She smiled at us, and I could see a bit of blood on her teeth.

She took a large, fuzzy comfrey leaf from her basket and rubbed it between her fingers. She laid it across Rachel's arm and pressed it into the wound. "Keep like so," she ordered.

She got to her feet and looked about. "Where...the snake?" It came to my mind that she was pleased to have learned a new word.

I pointed to the ledge. "They were up there. They fell when Rachel...There was this terrible squirming tangle..."

The woman thought this over. "The snake. You scare."

That snake had more than scared us, I assure you. But that was not what she had meant.

"The snake. There." She nodded at the ledge. "The snake... sleep. Rachel *und*..." She looked at me and I realized that she expected me to tell her my name.

"Sarah."

"Rachel *und* Sarah. The snake. Wake up." She opened her eyes wide and jumped back as if she'd been startled.

We had frightened the *snake*! I was irked at this outlandish notion.

"We didn't see it up there," I protested.

The woman chuckled and I flushed with embarrassment. "You

need..." She thought for a moment. "You better see."

I was not of a mind to continue this perplexing conversation. Rachel sat slumped in the road holding the comfrey leaf to her arm.

The woman seemed to understand. "The Rachel house. Where?" she asked.

"Just across the Saw Mill River, ma'am," I answered

"I help."

At this announcement Rachel began to cry more noisily than ever.

The woman nodded and said, "I go." She picked up her basket.

I curtseyed as Mama had taught me. "Thank you for helping us, ma'am."

The woman smiled again and the blood was gone from her teeth. Her blue eyes crinkled at the corners and I thought it could be said that she was almost pretty.

"Rachel. Sarah. *Ja*," she said.

We watched until she had crossed the bridge by Philipse's Mill and disappeared round the back of the old stone church.

I asked, "Who was that woman? I've not seen her before."

Rachel's eyes rolled heavenward and I thought she was going to faint.

"That was Hulda," she gasped. "Hulda the Witch."

"She was altogether pleasant and helpful!" I exclaimed. "Why do you say she's a witch?"

"*Everybody* knows she's a witch. Everybody in Tarrytown. Everybody in the colony of New York."

Rachel gave me the smug look that often accompanied her sweeping proclamations. I noticed that the conversation had revived her.

Rachel went on, "She was mumbling and I know it was a spell."

"You just said she was from a foreign land. No doubt she was speaking her native language."

Rachel ignored me. "We went to pick berries. The snake appeared and then the witch. And that, Sarah, is no happenstance."

When Rachel acquired an opinion, she held it fast. She was not swayed by logic or reason. It was of little use to argue with her. And then, I wasn't certain that Rachel wasn't right.

– Chapter Three –

Three days passed before Mama summoned me to explain what had happened with Rachel and the snakes. I was glad for the time to ready an explanation, but Mama's skills were such that I knew that, in the end, she would ferret out the true story.

I was tired of being prodded and probed. Tired of Rachel, who could worm through a crack in my composure, tired of Mama who could deftly twist an opening into the thoughts that I wanted to keep to myself.

With this latest occurrence, I could see that it was all Mama's fault and I was of a mind to point that out to her. If Mama hadn't given Brom permission to call on Laney, Rachel wouldn't have got the idea to spy on him. If Mama hadn't told us to pick berries, Rachel and I wouldn't have encountered the snakes. If Mama ever bothered to chat with our neighbours, she would have learned about the witch. She could have warned me about Hulda.

Mama herself was the true problem, and I believed her English descent to be the cause. Mama was born in Connecticut, where her family had settled 150 years earlier. But it seemed that the longer the Seaburys lived in America, the more English they became.

Brom asked me once if I didn't think it odd that Mama had married a Dutch farmer like Papa. She'd moved away from her English family and her English friends to a place where English people were scarce. Then she kept to herself as if other peoples' Dutchness or Frenchness would rub off and tarnish her. Brom was right. It was indeed peculiar.

Mama did not look like any of the other women, either. She was very slender, and her hair and eyes were dark as ravens' wings. When Papa stood next to her, the top of his head was level with her ear.

Mama kept a garnet necklace and pearls and even a bracelet of emeralds in a carved wooden box in her bedchamber, but she never wore these remnants of her former life. By far her dearer possessions were her books. Her father, a sea captain, had given them to her. Those much-read leather volumes, their pages edged in gold, were my treasures, too. My favourites were stories of gods and goddesses, heroes and monsters in ancient times.

From all her time spent reading, Mama had learned much about character and motive, not to mention plot. She loathed Rachel and was greatly aggrieved that an ignorant, impertinent wench should be vying with her – indeed, besting her – in the war for influence over her daughter.

Mama was in the faded green velvet armchair by the sitting room window. She put down the book she was reading a bit reluctantly, I thought. She studied me through her spectacles. "You may help with the mending as we talk, Sarah," she said.

Mama acted quite as if she were granting me a privilege, allowing me to darn socks. And a talk! The misadventure with the snakes had happened the day before yesterday, and I had no relish for recounting it yet again.

There was another matter as well, although I would have been hard-pressed to name it. The truth was, I didn't want Mama to know about Hulda. I couldn't have said why.

Mama looked at me over the tops of her spectacles. She began, "How is it that you and your cousin" – when Mama was truly angry she couldn't bring herself to say Rachel's name – "encountered snakes?"

"It's summer. Snakes are out." I rummaged in the sewing basket. I hoped that Mama would see the indisputable truth in my reasoning and leave it at that.

"Where were these snakes?"

"On a rock ledge." I took a white cotton stocking and examined a hole in the heel. "You sent us out to pick berries," I added, remembering my resolve to speak up about Mama's part in this unhappy episode.

Mama frowned. "Berries don't grow on rocks."

"We had to climb over the rocks to get to the berry patch."

Mama looked at me over the top of her spectacles. "It seems to me, Sarah, that whenever you and Rachel are together, you are caught up in some distress. I think Rachel plans misdeeds."

"She surely didn't plan to be bitten," I pointed out.

"Sarah, you have been taught to use sound judgment and..."

"I couldn't just leave her there. Rachel might have died!"

"That is exactly what I am saying. Rachel gets herself into ghastly predicaments and she draws you in as well." Mama regarded me with sombre brown eyes. "Sarah, you must think and act for yourself, like the young lady you are now. You must gather the courage to resist Rachel's trickery."

Rachel called me a coward for balking at her "trickery" and Mama was calling me a coward for going along with it. Now my eyes were welling with tears. Maybe Mama would think I was remorseful and stop asking questions.

Of course, Mama knew there was more to the story. "After Rachel was bitten, what happened?" she continued.

Across the room, my baby sister Elizabeth started to fuss. I jumped to my feet to fetch her. "I helped her to the road," I said.

"Did you fetch assistance from Philipse's Mill?" she prodded.

I lifted Elizabeth from her cradle. "Rachel didn't want me to leave her."

"Someone must have come by to help you." Mama took Elizabeth and prepared to nurse her.

I studied the hole in the heel of Brom's stocking.

"Did someone come by?"

"A woman."

"A woman? What was her name?"

"Rachel said it was Hulda."

"Is this Hulda from here?" she asked.

"Rachel said she lives in that little hollow behind the church."

Mama grimaced at this disclosure. "But where does she come from?"

"I don't know." I put my hands under my knees and swung my legs. "It was lucky that she came by. She had a basket with some leaves and roots."

"Sarah, young ladies sit still. Was this person a cunning woman?"

I folded my hands in my lap. "I think so."

"And how did she treat the snakebite?"

"She made little cuts in the wound with a knife. Then she put her mouth to the wound and Rachel thought she was biting her…"

I had revealed too much. Mama's eyebrows soared nearly to the ruffle on her cap.

"…But she was drawing out the poison. Then she spat the poison in the road." I took a breath.

Mama's eyes widened. "She *what*?"

"She spat…"

Mama waved her hand to silence me. The image of Hulda smiling through bloody teeth sprang to my mind.

Mama pursed her lips to keep her outrage from escaping. She

said, "Sarah, I believe that you know what is right."

"I remembered to thank her!"

Mama patted Elizabeth before she went on. "You must not let your cousin lure you into wrongdoing."

For an instant, I was relieved. Mama was going to say once again how I had to think for myself and then the lecture would be over.

Mama added, "By now you should know the sort of person one must avoid."

I looked down at my mending and nodded meekly. She was going to tell me to keep away from Rachel and then I could go.

"I expect that you will not encounter that unfortunate woman again."

I stared at her, open-mouthed. "I...I thought the woman did a good deed," I managed to say.

"Sarah, I believe that my meaning is clear: I forbid you to see that woman again. If you do, you will remove yourself at once. You will not speak to her."

With Elizabeth still in her arms, Mama got to her feet. "Why, it's nearly time for tea," she said. "Off you go then, Sarah. Your papa will be home soon."

The creaking of wagon wheels announced Papa's return. He and Brom had taken a load of wheat to Philipse's Mill. All of us knew that when Papa went to the mill, he was likely to come home with presents for us from the market sloops at the dock.

"Papa! Papa! What did you bring me?" I could hear Thomas shrilling as he danced around the wagon.

"The ships today had a trinket for only Sarah," Papa replied. "I am sorry, *Olykoek*." "Doughnut" was his pet name for Thomas.

Papa had a trinket for me. I wondered what it was. Of late, it had been hard to predict. Last winter, he had brought me a length of fine green velvet ribbon, but the next time, my gift was a doll. It had a head of painted china and a blue satin gown, but I hadn't played with dolls for two years, at least.

"There you are, *Puffertje!*" Papa padded into the parlour in his stocking feet. His blue eyes shone with excitement. "Now. Which pocket?"

I was Papa's "little cinnamon cake," and of course I was supposed to guess in which of Papa's pockets the present was hidden. I was also supposed to pretend at first that I didn't see the small round bulge in his brown leather vest. I thought myself far too grown-up for such foolery but I did want to see what he'd brought.

I pointed. "There!"

Papa drew out a piece of glass the size of an egg. The surface was of triangles no bigger than Baby Elizabeth's thumbnail.

"I've never seen the like!" I exclaimed.

"Look closely now, *Puffertje.*" Papa held the glass to the window and at once little pink and yellow creatures flew out. They danced on the whitewashed walls and across the red and blue Turkey carpet. He turned the glass and the creatures curtseyed and bowed.

"I see things I never knew were there!" I exclaimed. "Let me try!"

I held the glass to my sleeve and the embroidered flowers bloomed and withered. Mama's candlesticks of heavy English silver became eight instead of two, then four, then none at all. A host of Sarahs smiled back at me from the looking glass. All of us were framed by rainbows. It crossed my mind that with this glass, I could become so beautiful that Tom Buckhout would at once fall in love with me and propose marriage.

I was the only one of us four children who looked like both Mama and Papa. Brom was a younger version of Papa – fair-haired and sturdy. Thomas had dark eyes like Mama, and like her, he didn't have a pinch of spare flesh. Elizabeth had inherited the Van Tassels' flaxen hair and blue eyes.

I was neither fish nor fowl, as Grandmother Seabury had once remarked. I had brown eyes like Mama, but my brown hair had golden lights. I was tall like Mama, but I had Papa's sturdy build. Both Mama and Papa assured me often that my demeanour was quite pleasing. More pleasing to God, and therefore to them, they hastened to add, were an affable nature and a kind heart. Of course, I did not believe them.

I was at the looking glass when Brom stormed in. Verkenner, our old hound who was forbidden to be in the parlour, ambled after him and collapsed on the carpet in a puddle of black, white and tan.

Brom threw himself into Mama's red silk chair and stretched out his long legs. He hadn't scraped the mud from his shoes.

"Look, Brom! Papa gave me a magic glass!" I had been trying of late to imitate Brom's world-weary demeanour, but I was too excited.

Brom scoffed, of course, but he rose to snatch the glass from me. "Sarah's nose is as big as Hook Mountain," he announced.

"Give me back my present!"

Mama had come into the parlour holding Elizabeth. Thomas was with them. Mama nudged Verkenner with her foot. "Off you go then," she said. Verkenner shuffled into the kitchen.

"A prism!" she exclaimed. "Why, Peter, what a cunning present! Wherever did it come from?"

"It was on a market sloop from New York Town," Papa told her.

"Did my prism come from across the sea?" I imagined a voyage from a land with oracles and goddesses who could see everything, just

- Marcia G. Moore -

as in Mama's books.

Brom made a sound of disgust. It was halfway between a snort and a guffaw and it was intended to point out what a simpleton I was. He added, for good measure, "Nothing comes from across the sea any more, Sarah. Not with the British Navy bottling up New York Harbour."

Mama set Elizabeth in her cradle and straightened up to her full height. "Those ships are there to protect the loyal subjects of His Majesty King George," she said crisply.

Papa took his long clay pipe from the wooden box on the mantel. "They're there to remind those *zots* who are thinking of making war not to be so stupid."

"They're there because we chased them out of Boston!" Brom shouted. "We've shown King George that we won't endure tyrants here any longer!"

"Where are the tyrants? I don't see any tyrants." Papa tamped tobacco into his pipe.

Thomas tugged on Mama's skirts. "Who's King George? Mama, who's King George?"

Mama said, "King George is our ruler. He guides and protects his subjects in England and other places, too. He gives us laws to keep us safe and free..."

Brom cried, "*Free*! That shows how muddled the British are! Elijah says..."

"Time for your chores, Abraham." Papa called Brom by his full name only when he was truly irked. "Take Verkenner. He will listen to your speeches."

Thomas shrilled. "Papa! Papa! Who is king here?"

Papa beamed at his younger son. "Why, you are king!" he exclaimed. He sat and patted his knee. "Come, sit on your throne, King *Olykoek*." He turned to Mama. "We Dutch folk have good sense," he reassured her. "These foolish troubles will not come here."

– Chapter Four –

The skies glowered but no rain fell. The chickens were listless, the cows were skittish and the copper rooster wind vane atop the barn spun aimlessly. All of us were snappish and fretful – at sixes and sevens, Mama said.

On other farms, in other houses, this dispirited weather was no doubt blamed on Hulda. In our home, she had not been mentioned since the day, a fortnight past, that Mama had told me to stay away from her.

Mama could not stand sentry over my thoughts, so I did think of Hulda. I went over our encounter over and over in my mind. I tried to recall something seen or said that would support Rachel's view that Hulda was a witch, or indeed, Mama's opinion that she was to be shunned.

I pondered how Hulda had seemed not at all surprised to find Rachel and me in that dire predicament. Had she foreseen it? Had she *caused* it? How did she come to have a comfrey leaf – just the right remedy – at hand? What was she muttering as she examined Rachel's snakebite? I remembered, too, how her eyes crinkled as she smiled.

I had always found the most vexing member of my family to be

Thomas, and during those unsettled days he tried my patience all the more. In addition to his squirming, his tattling and his endless questions, he had found a new way to bedevil me.

Thomas had become a king. Ever since the day when Papa had brought me my prism, he had worn a pewter bowl on his head for a crown and had carried a stick for a sceptre. His robe was one of my old aprons tied round his neck.

I was the only one who did not find this to be amusing. Mama and Papa pretended to obey his frequent commands to serve him a sweet or to fetch his spinning-top. Even Brom enjoyed the joke. It gave him opportunities to point out how King George behaved like a five-year-old.

One afternoon I was at the woodpile gathering sticks for kindling when I spied Thomas running through the apple trees in our orchard. I hoped he would not see me, but of course I was unlucky.

"What ho, minion!" he cried, as he came up to me. To him, everyone was now a minion. He was like King George, I thought sourly.

"You're t'posed to bow down." Thomas grinned and displayed the gap in his front teeth.

I pulled a small branch from the woodpile and shook off the cricket that clung to it. Thomas whacked my shoulder with his stick.

"Ouch!" I considered whacking him back but Mama refused to let Brom or me lay hands on him. Seething at the injustice of it all, I bundled the kindling into my apron and walked back to the house as he danced round me.

"Off with her head!" he shrieked, using another kingly phrase he had learned. "Off with Sarah's head!"

After I brought in the kindling, Mama bade me to call Brom and Cousin Dan from the barn. Papa had invited Dan so Brom could spend time with "a fine young Dutchman." I suspected that he did not tell Mama that his true purpose was to keep Brom away from rebels and troublemakers, most of whom he believed to be English.

I was sure that Mama didn't tell Papa that she trusted Dan no more than she did his younger sister Rachel.

"Brom and Dan," I called, stepping over the threshold and blinking, as my eyes grew used to the dim light. The cows were in the pasture but their warm, earthy smell lingered. I peered about at the dusky wooden stalls and the dirt floor. A tidy row of rakes, shovels and scythes hung from wooden pegs.

I heard Verkenner's tail thump against the floor. He lay at the foot of the ladder to the hayloft and he wagged his tail to greet me.

"Whoooo looks for youuuuuuu?" It was Brom. He was imitating a barn owl. I heard Dan cackle.

"Oh, there you are," I said. "Mama said she wants you to..."

"This is the terrible barn owl." I knew Brom was squeezing his lips together to sound like an owl.

"I'm coming to get youuuuuuu!" This "owl" was Dan. He was not nearly as good as Brom, but he had not had the practice.

Everyone in the family, and clearly "family" included cousins, knew that I was wary about the barn. When I was six, I had been climbing the ladder to the hayloft when a barn owl had flown at me in a rush of white feathers and fierce yellow eyes. I had been so frightened I fell off the ladder and had the breath knocked out of me.

Now, I marched over to the ladder and began to climb. I heard the boys scrambling in the hayloft. The ladder tipped backwards. I jumped off and caught it before it hit the ground. Verkenner yelped in astonishment as his resting place was disturbed.

Dan's grinning face appeared, and I remembered how much I hated him. I was also struck at how Rachel took after him. They both had mousy brown hair, squinting grey eyes and mouths set in permanent sneers.

Brom leaned over the edge of the loft. He was holding a sheaf of papers. Dan grabbed the papers and tried to stuff them into his shirt. "She's a spy," he told Brom.

I thought it likely that Rachel's brother would view all sisters as spies and tattletales. Luckily, Brom came to my support. "You can show her," he assured Dan. "She won't tell."

Of late, Brom's view of me had shifted – sometimes. In place of the bothersome little sister, he now saw me as an ally of sorts in his battles with Mama and Papa. Some months past, Brom had discovered that both were simpletons whose sole intent was to cause him misery. Both were thoroughly wrong in their thinking, of course, and Brom saw it as his duty to point this out.

Dan grudgingly produced a leaflet. It was the length and breadth of a book, but it was thinner and not bound in leather or cloth. I couldn't make out the printing on it.

"Let her come up and we'll show her," Brom said to Dan. To me, he added, "It's all right. The owl's not here."

I climbed to the loft, settled myself in the hay and smoothed my striped linen skirts. "What is it? Where did you get it?"

"Elijah," Brom said.

"That fellow at the mill?"

"Do you know him?" Brom asked.

I shook my head. "What's he doing at the mill?"

"He helps Ceaser grind the grain."

"Is he African, too?"

"No. He comes from Peek's Kill."

Dan held the leaflet just beyond my reach.

"*Common Sense. Written by an Englishman,*" I read.

Brom took the pamphlet. "It's about how ridiculous it is to have a king."

I put out my hand. "Let me see."

"Girls got no business with '*Common Sense.*'" Dan snickered as Brom handed me the booklet.

I glanced through it before I gave it back to Dan. "Read me something you think a girl could understand," I snapped. Dan couldn't read English well and I felt not at all guilty about reminding him.

Dan said to Brom, "What about that old king? William Something?"

"Do you mean William the Conqueror?" I asked.

Brom found the passage. "Here it is. It says that "The first king of England's present line was a Frenchman and...""

Dan was amazed. "He wasn't *English*?"

"No, he was French," Brom and I said together.

"The king we have now isn't English," I told them.

"Sarah's right," Brom said. "George the Third's family is German."

Dan curled his lip in scorn. "Can't see why English people keep him on then. Dutch people wouldn't be such *zots*."

"Dutch people are the *zots*!" Brom cried. "They pay English taxes without a word of protest."

Dan retorted, "English people are Tories like your mama. Why, they lick the king's boots and thank him for the privilege."

"The colonists who are fighting for our liberty are English," I reminded him, using an argument Papa often made. "George Washington! Thomas Jefferson! Sam Adams! There's not a Dutchman among them!"

I rose to my feet and shook the hay from my skirts. "I'm supposed to tell you that it's time for dinner. And Dan, I forgot to ask how Rachel is faring."

He narrowed his eyes. "Good as she can. Gets bit by a snake and a witch. All your doing."

"My doing?" I stopped as I was about to descend the ladder.

"You and the witch. Plotting together."

"I never saw that woman before!"

"Witch put a spell on you to help her hex Rachel. Sarah got Satan to bite Rachel," he explained to Brom, who was staring at him in astonishment.

"How did Sarah get Satan to bite Rachel?" Brom managed to

ask.

"Devil turns himself into a snake. Even you know that."

Brom said, "I thought the snake was up on some rocks."

"Sarah knew the snake was there."

My voice was rising. "I did *not*..."

Dan pointed an accusatory finger at me. "She made Rachel climb up on the rocks. Wouldn't go herself."

Brom was still mightily puzzled. "But why would Sarah want to cast a spell on Rachel?"

Dan's mouth widened in a gleeful grin. "She's a spy. Had a plot to spy on you. When you were going to see Laney."

I protested, "We were not spying! We were going to pick berries!"

Brom snatched a handful of hay and began to tear it to bits. He was so furious he couldn't even look at me.

"Brom, listen." I put my hand on his arm but he brushed it away.

"Tell you one thing," Dan said. "That witch is a spy, too. Like your sister."

Brom was as confused as I was. "You mean that woman? The witch? The one who's quite mad? How is she a spy?"

"She said it." Dan jerked his head toward me. "The witch is German. Like your English king."

– Chapter Five –

Dan's visit was on Midsummer Day, an occasion Mama marked by laying branches of the birch tree over our doors. A long-ago Scottish ancestor believed that birch boughs, displayed at the summer solstice, warded off ill fortune.

"Why, this is a glad season," I said to her as I stood on a footstool and placed a leafy branch upon the lintel. "Daylight well past teatime. No cloaks or heavy woollens. Of what evil need we be wary?"

Mama thought a moment before she replied. "The birch reminds us that the solstice is the day the Earth turns toward winter. We must not be lulled into thinking that summer will last, or that evil spirits don't lurk on warm days."

As I huddled in my bed that night, I reflected ruefully that Mama's jaundiced view was in fact the wiser. Evil spirits abounded, none worse than Dan! It was small consolation that I had managed not to cry in front of him.

I began by berating myself, of course. I should have known that Rachel would invent a tale that twisted the truth like a skein of yarn. I should have guessed she would turn things round so that I was to blame. I should have told Dan that *he* was under a spell to have spoken such outrageous lies. Remorse and spite coursed through me in equal measure. I sniffled, then sobbed, into my blue-and-white checked linen pillow-bears.

Yet that was not the whole of it. Something was altogether out of tune. Perhaps the wamble in my belly meant that my monthly purgation was upon me. I had not yet experienced it enough times to know.

I sat up and peered through the shutters. The half-moon scurried between the clouds, giving just enough light through the shutters to see my prism next to the candlestick on my bed-stand. I took the prism and turned it in my hand. The enchanted pixies hid inside.

Straightaway a horrifying thought came to me: The odd occurrences had begun that very day that Rachel and I met Hulda. Indeed, snakes were out in summer, but a nest of rattlesnakes, lurking on a ledge? I had never before heard of such a calamity.

Then there was the matter of Hulda. She had appeared almost at once to aid Rachel in her distress. How did Rachel come to climb the rocks when I was supposed to have gone? I had told her to go. Perhaps I was under the witch's spell, as Dan had claimed.

Shortly after, Papa had brought the prism home. Indeed, the prism itself was most peculiar. Papa was as practical a Dutchman as ever lived. He had never before given such a frivolous bauble.

I ran my thumb over the prism's tiny triangles. *Hulda* had given me the prism. She was trying to get me in her evil grasp. She had put a spell on Papa so he would buy the prism. Perhaps she had even conjured it. Surely that was what had happened, for no one knew where the glass had come from.

As for Mama's command to avoid Hulda, why, that was beginning to make sense. Mama had figured out that Hulda was a witch, just how, I wasn't certain. Or perhaps Mama didn't know. Maybe Hulda had sent some message to draw Mama into thinking she needed to make jam the day she sent Rachel and me to gather berries. Maybe Hulda had conjured the snakes, as well. And what had Mama said about the prism? She'd said it was 'cunning.' We'd all thought she meant 'fanciful,' but maybe she meant 'deceptive.'

"You better see." That was what Hulda had said to me. I thought that she meant that I must see more clearly, but perhaps she wanted me to see matters as a witch might. She had put a hex on me so I would do her bidding.

As I set the prism back on the table and sank into my featherbed, I thought she might be warning me. I had *better see*. Yes, that must be it. I had better see how Rachel turned things round. I had better see how Mama insisted that her opinions were right and that everybody else must think as she did. I had better see things for myself.

In the days after Dan's visit, matters were strained between Brom and me. He didn't speak to me, but that of itself was unremarkable. That Mama and Papa wouldn't notice was not unusual as well. So, I was not certain that Mama knew that Brom and I were at odds when she bade me go to the far cornfield to fetch him. More likely, she gave no thought at all to my sensibilities.

The field sat atop a rocky bluff overlooking Hudson's River. In just the last week, the stalks had brought forth ears, wrapped tightly in green husks and tipped with tassels of brown silk. Papa was pleased that in his domain, all was in order.

I waded through the knee-high grass and saw Brom sitting under the sycamore tree at the edge of the field by the river. I had not announced my approach, of course. I had reached the great tree, with its thick mottled brown and white trunk and leaves like waving hands, before he noticed I was there.

"Look," he said.

A monstrous ship was gliding up the river. It made no sound as it came nearer, veritably slicing the landscape in two. The bowsprit jutted from the ship quite as if it were a haughty nose in the air, and it was half the length of the vessel itself. The green river waters backed away as it advanced.

The ship had a long black hull with a yellow stripe round it. Along the stripe, a dozen square black eyes watched in an unblinking stare. Three masts held a giant spider web with three men, no, four, caught in its lines.

"Look there," said Brom. "There's another one."

A second ship was creeping up the river, blotting out the houses of Nyack Village as it passed. Four smaller vessels followed, looking for all the world like ducklings scurrying along behind their mother. A white-sailed market sloop scurried past, heading for the harbour. Alongside the British ships, it looked no bigger than the toy boat Papa had whittled for Thomas.

Brom shaded his eyes. "Those are British men-o'-war. The big one over there is HMS *Phoenix*. The smaller one is *Rose*."

"What purpose have they here, save to terrify us?" I demanded.

"They're guarding the river."

"Guarding from farmers who don't give a fig who rules them? From merchants and tradesmen who pay their taxes and keep the peace? The British must be utterly mad."

Brom said, "Our country's fate will be decided here, on Hudson's River. Sarah, where are the two centres of revolution in the colonies?"

"Why, Boston, I think. And Philadelphia." I was gratified when he nodded.

He went on, "Suppose you wanted to travel from one to the other. How would you go?"

"Across Hudson's River," I said. "But couldn't you go by sea?"

Brom snorted at my ignorance. "With ships like those guarding the coast?" He went on, "Suppose you are General Howe, and you want to move troops and munitions from British bases in Canada?"

"You'd go down Hudson's River," I conceded.

"If the British are masters of this river, they shall win our revolution," Brom said. "They'll cut our colonies in two, as neatly as slicing an apple. Then they will finish us."

I looked out upon the Tappan Zee. That three-mile-wide bulge in the mighty waterway at once took on an ominous aspect. The very stillness seemed to hide roiling currents beneath the surface.

I whispered, "Those ships are like that dreadful Greek beast with the hundred eyes! Argus! They're watching us!"

Brom stepped to the edge of the bluff. "Those are gun ports. Every one of those "eyes" has a big gun inside."

"They might shoot you!" I pulled him back behind the tree and pointed at the ship. "There. Under *Rose's* bow. There's some kind of animal."

"That's the ship's figurehead. It's the British lion."

"It's sticking out its tongue," I said, and then I remembered. The silent glide, the staring, lifeless eyes – the ships were like snakes. They were just like rattlesnakes – cold-blooded and bestial. Those ships meant to wipe us off the face of the earth.

- Chapter Six -

Mama believed that misfortunes came in threes. Of course, the encounter with the snakes was one. The arrival of *Phoenix* and *Rose*, those horrid ships lurking on the river, was the second. The third one I couldn't have guessed, since it had happened only once before. Grandmother Seabury was coming to visit.

I had recollections of a frosty old lady, clad in black and looking for all the world like a scornful crow. I supposed that Grandmother must have servants, for she had commented several times that Mama had not been brought up to toil like a common wench. Of course, now Mama did have a servant: me.

I'd taken the Turkey carpet outside to beat it with a stick to get out the dust. I polished the silver candlesticks, rubbed beeswax into the furniture, and gathered fresh pine boughs to lay in the fireplaces. Then Mama set me to weeding the kitchen garden. She had spied a stray clump of purslane and said that Grandmother Seabury would surely notice it.

Mama came out to inspect my work. "Mind the thyme," she said.

I sat back on my heels. "It's not midmorning yet."

Mama smiled for the first time since Grandmother Seabury's letter arrived three days ago. "The thyme," she said. "It's between the parsley and dill."

On a whim, I picked a sprig and handed it to Mama. "You can

use this for our dinner," I told her.

"I suppose I could," she replied ruefully. "It's said that thyme gives one courage."

"Do you need the thyme to help you get along with Grandmother?" I asked. I wondered how I could not have seen before that Grandmother's visit must be as disagreeable for Mama as for the rest of us. Maybe that was why she had married Papa and come to live near Tarrytown.

Mama said, "You must pull out that dandelion, Sarah."

I looked at the perky little yellow flower with jagged leaves. The name came from "*dent de lion*," the French words for "tooth of lion." It seemed to me that a plant with such a clever name shouldn't be torn out like a common weed.

I thought of Hulda. I asked, "But isn't dandelion a useful plant? Don't you use it to make tea for bowel distress? Or fever?"

"No one here has bowel distress. Pull the dandelion out now, please."

Mama watched as I twisted the flower and leaves from the stem. She didn't see that I'd left the root in the ground. The dandelion wasn't gone at all. You couldn't see it, but it was there. It would grow back.

Shortly after noon, we heard a horse and carriage coming down our lane and we lined up outside in our roast-meat clothes to greet Grandmother Seabury. Elizabeth had a long white organdie gown and bonnet, and Papa, Brom and Thomas were wearing coats over their waistcoats, and linen shirts and breeches. Their hair had been tied back in cues. Papa complained about the discomfort of such clothing on a hot day. Brom, of course, gave a speech about the hypocrisy of pretending this was our common dress, and that our daily labour was accomplished by phantom servants.

"Next, you'll be making us wear wigs," he told Mama.

Thomas' crown, robe and sceptre had disappeared into the kitchen cupboard. He kept asking for them, but Mama assured him he looked very regal just the way he was.

Mama's gown was of green silk, and I had my favourite gown, of rose-coloured linen with lace-trimmed petticoats. My cap was trimmed with the same lace.

An African man was driving Grandmother's shiny black carriage. After he brought the horses to a stop, he jumped down and opened the door for Grandmother and Aunt Charlotte, Mama's younger sister.

Grandmother Seabury had not changed one whit. She was dressed in black and the lines round her eyes and mouth were set in an expression of disdain.

"It's a sorry day when an old woman must make a perilous journey to see her daughter," she said as the man helped her from the carriage. "Charlotte, my cane!"

A cane with an elaborately carved ivory handle appeared. Then Aunt Charlotte squeezed through the carriage door. She was short and mousy and very fleshy. It was hard to believe that she and Mama were sisters.

Mama took a breath. "Mother, we are glad to welcome you. Charlotte, you are looking well." She and her sister embraced briefly.

Grandmother leaned on her cane and peered up at Brom with flinty grey eyes. "Abraham. I've not got used to that name."

"I'm called Brom," he corrected her. He and I exchanged glances.

"Why, I'm surrounded by Biblical figures." Grandmother pronounced it "figgers," in the English fashion. "I shan't need to read Scripture today. And who is this tyke? Thomas?"

Thomas frowned. "I'm a king," he informed her.

We all were relieved that Grandmother didn't hear him. "The last time I saw you, Mary, this lad was in dresses."

"I believe that was several years ago," Mama replied smoothly. "This is Elizabeth, our new little one."

I couldn't imagine that such a rosy blonde cherub couldn't charm even Grandmother, but she said, "Why, Mary, you keep producing little strangers. Small wonder you're too busy to pay me a visit."

So far, Papa and I had been the only ones to escape notice. Of course, my reprieve didn't last. Grandmother said, "Mary, you should put a brick on that girl's head. If she gains more height, she'll never get a husband."

I thought of several tart replies but of course I didn't dare say them. Mama was watching, and I curtseyed as she had taught me. For all that Grandmother didn't like us, I wanted to show her that we had good manners.

Mama said, "Come inside, Mother. You and Charlotte must refresh yourselves after your journey." She held out her hand but Grandmother ignored it.

"I've learned to manage without you," she snapped as she hobbled toward the door.

Papa said to Grandmother's driver, "You will have food and drink. The horses, too." He nodded at Brom. "Help this man loose the harness. *Olykoek*, you will come with me." He took Thomas by the hand and set off for the barn.

Brom whispered to me, "Did you notice? Grandmother didn't even speak to Papa! She acted as if he wasn't there!"

I knew that Mama was anxious to find out why Grandmother Seabury should have made this trip, a half-day's journey from her home in the southern part of Westchester County. I also knew that she wouldn't ask, for it was sure to bring more sharp words.

Grandmother seated herself on the red silk divan in the parlour. Aunt Charlotte took an armchair and I was sent to fetch a pitcher of watered-down cider flavoured with nutmeg. Mama set Elizabeth in her cradle and sat down, too.

After I served the cider, I retreated to a rush-seat chair in the corner. I vowed to keep my hands folded in my lap and to never, never swing my legs. I was still vexed at Mama for being unfair about Hulda, but I wanted her to be proud of me.

Grandmother examined her glass before she raised it. "God Save the King!" she declared. Mama and Aunt Charlotte answered, "God Save the King!" I raised my glass but I didn't say anything. I didn't think that the King should be saved if he was going to send monstrous ships to frighten us.

Grandmother set her glass on the table next to her chair. She snapped open her silk fan, which was black, of course. She waved it a few times before announcing, "I've come to say good-bye, Mary. I shan't see you again."

Maybe Grandmother was going to die soon. I tried to feel sorry.

Grandmother said, "I'm leaving my home. I shan't live amongst barbarians."

"Barbarians?" Mama asked. She rocked Elizabeth's cradle with her foot. I sat up straighter in my chair.

Grandmother looked about as if she expected savages to come leaping though the parlour window. "Look what they did to poor Samuel!" she exclaimed.

I knew what was coming next: A recitation of the outrages suffered by The Reverend Samuel Seabury, Mama's cousin. He was an Anglican clergyman and a staunch defender of King George. The previous fall a pack of rebels had looted his house and threatened his family. Then they had dragged him and two other Tories off to a prison in Connecticut. Almost every time Mama and Brom got into a dispute over politics, Mama held up Cousin Samuel as an example of what happened when a mob took the law into their own hands.

"All of them were released," Mama said. "The other two…"

Aunt Charlotte chimed in, "Nathaniel Underhill and Judge Fowler. Isn't that right, Mother?" She finished her cider and looked hopefully at the pitcher. As I got up to fill her glass, I saw that Mama was pursing her lips.

Mama went on, "The other two renounced their King to save their own skins. I'm glad we Seaburys are made of sterner stuff." She leaned over to smooth Elizabeth's coverlet. "Has Samuel been plagued again by rebels? Have you?"

Grandmother snapped her fan shut. "I shan't wait about to have some rebel rat stick a bayonet in my face, thank you. Samuel says he cannot serve God and King in such a brutish place. We're all going to live under the protection of His Majesty's soldiers. So, Mary, this will be our last farewell. Unless you come with us, of course."

I had been thinking that it must be a pleasure for Mama to converse with people with whom she agreed, but I was taken aback by Grandmother's last remark. From the look on her face, so was Mama.

For a moment, it was so quiet that I could hear the clock on the mantel. Its slender black hands crept over its pale face. The ornate brass pendulum swung. Something was wrong, though. The pendulum was out of rhythm. Then I remembered. Mama had told me to wind the clock with the brass key that fitted into a little hole on its face. I'd forgot. The clock was running down. The pendulum was slowing. The hands were hesitating before they lurched forward. I wanted to jump from my chair to set it right but I didn't dare to draw attention.

Aunt Charlotte leaned forward and her chair creaked. "Do come with us, Mary," she said. "There's a place just south of New York Town, Staten Island, I believe. There are many of us Loyalists there. Cousin Samuel says we'll be out of danger until the rebellion is put down."

"I can't just leave!" Mama exclaimed. "My family..."

"Your mother and your sister are your family," Grandmother told her.

"My children..."

"You may bring them, if you like," Grandmother said.

"But Peter... our farm..."

"I'd think that by now you would have had your fill of that Dutch bumpkin." Grandmother shook her head and the black ribbons on her bonnet squirmed. She looked like Medusa with her hair of snakes. And she had just called Papa a bumpkin. I was altogether stupefied.

Grandmother pointed her closed fan at Mama. "The source of all this misery is because your father treated you like the son he never had. He had you learning Latin and reading those ancient thinkers. 'A woman shouldn't be concerned with such things,' I told him. 'It makes for a wrinkled brow and contrary disposition.'"

I thought that Grandmother Seabury was both wrinkled and contrary, for all that she hadn't studied the classics.

Aunt Charlotte's chin wobbled as she nodded. "That's right. We used to call you 'Mary, Mary, quite contrary.'"

Grandmother Seabury paid no heed to the interruption. "He even encouraged you to debate with him. Then he died before he could taste the bitter fruits of his folly."

"What bitter fruits?" I blurted out the question before I realized I mustn't speak unless spoken to.

Grandmother Seabury turned her icy blue glare on me. "Why, you don't know the family history, do you, girl? Your mother was quite the rebel, but I'd almost brought her round to her senses after her father died. She was betrothed to a fine English gentleman. Then she ran off with a lout so she could work like a dog and raise a litter of mongrel pups. One simply cannot comprehend..." The snakes on Grandmother's bonnet wriggled again as she shook her head and sighed.

It took me a moment to grasp Grandmother's meaning: Papa was a lout and we children were half-breed dogs! In all my life, I'd not heard such an insult.

Before I realized what I was doing, I jumped to my feet. "Papa is *not* a lout!" I said to Grandmother in a voice that was so shaky I didn't recognize it. "He's a farmer and he's kind and good and he loves us and he knows how to read!"

To my amazement, Grandmother laughed. She sounded like a rusty hinge on a door but that was probably because she didn't laugh often. "I see you've raised a brood of rebels just like you, Mary." She wagged her fan at Mama. "The apple doesn't fall far from the tree."

I felt the blood rising to my cheeks. "We're not mongrel pups! We're people! We're not English and we're not Dutch. We're..." I strove to think of what we were. "We're Americans, and we're not going to tolerate you any longer!"

Mama's voice was low. "Sarah, please restrain yourself."

"We're not going to tolerate your simpleton king, either!" I wasn't sure how king George got into the argument but it seemed fitting.

Mama had risen from her chair and had me by the arm. "Sarah, that will be all," she said. "Go to the kitchen, please, and see if the mutton is done. I believe it's nearly time for dinner."

Grandmother let out another rusty-hinge laugh. "Take my advice, Mary. You should take a stick to that girl. Beat some obedience into her."

I struggled free from Mama's grip. "I'm not 'that girl!'" I shouted. "My name is Sarah. Sarah, as in the Bible!"

– Chapter Seven –

Grandmother's driver was sitting on a bench by the kitchen table. He wore a bright blue coat and red waistcoat with pewter buttons. I wondered if he dressed like that every day.

He seemed startled to see me, and altogether chary, as well. Small wonder he was frightened, if Grandmother Seabury was his main acquaintance with people here.

He gestured toward the barn. "The mahn say I be here," he said. I thought he was explaining that Papa told him he should wait in the kitchen.

I went to the fireplace and turned the spit. I took a long fork and pierced the mutton. Clear juices ran into the dripping pan set beneath it. I should tell Mama the roast was done, but I couldn't go back to the parlour.

I looked round at our efforts to cook a special meal: a chicken pie topped with golden pastry, potatoes, carrots and beans from our garden, a tender spoonbread and raspberries with cream.

The last course had only sweets, of which English people were very fond. Mama wouldn't let us eat many because our teeth would rot. I had forgotten to look at Grandmother's teeth, but I didn't think she showed them, even when she made that sound that was supposed to be a laugh.

Mama had made an English pudding called a trifle, and doughnuts, which were everyone's favourites. *Puffertjes* sprinkled with cinnamon and little round cakes called *koekjes* were my contributions.

I asked the man, "Are you hungry?" I made eating gestures with my hands. "Would you like to eat? We have so much food here."

I took a pewter plate from the cupboard and served him a generous portion of chicken pie. Then I gave him some vegetables and spoonbread.

"Thank'm."

"My mama and I worked so hard to make a dinner for that horrid old woman who doesn't deserve bread and water," I told him.

He hesitated and then began to wolf down the chicken pie.

I had wrestled the leg of mutton off the spit when Papa, Brom and Thomas came in.

"Where are your good clothes?" I asked.

Brom said, "In the barn. We won't be *macaronis*, even for Grandmother."

"What are these *macaronis*?" Papa asked.

"Fops. Dandies," Brom explained. "What happened to dinner?"

"Grandmother will not be dining here today," I said grandly. "So, gentlemen, allow me to help you to a slice of mutton."

"Poor Mary." Papa didn't seem surprised at my announcement. He sat down next to Grandmother's driver. Brom took a big spoonful of the beans and passed the bowl and Papa cut up a piece of mutton for Isaac. I took a helping of chicken pie and sat down with them.

We were enjoying Grandmother's dinner when Mama appeared. "I came to tell you that Mother and Charlotte are leaving."

Papa nodded. "*Ja*, Mary. Sarah told us."

Mama looked about and evidently concluded that she was not going to reckon why we were savouring the dinner intended for Grandmother Seabury. She said, "You must come and say goodbye. Sarah, you must apologize to your grandmother."

"No! I'm not sorry!" I put down my fork and met Mama's eyes

defiantly.

Brom looked at me in amazement. "What did you do?"

Mama answered, "Sarah was quite saucy to her grandmother and she needs to ask forgiveness."

"Grandmother should ask forgiveness of us!" I cried. "She said we were mongrels. She said Papa was..." Papa was looking at me with great concern. I couldn't tell him Grandmother said he was a bumpkin and a lout. "She was a dreadful, rude old woman."

Brom laughed. "It must have been quite a row. Sorry I missed it."

Papa turned to me. "Sarah, you must ask your grandmother to forgive you."

"I'm not sorry!"

Everyone had stopped eating. They were all watching me.

Papa signed. "*Puffertje*, we must do some things that we don't want."

Brom pushed himself back from the table. "The damned English insult us and then expect us to apologize. Hurrah for Sarah, I say!"

I gave him as much of a smile as I could manage.

Papa said to Brom, "That's *genoeg*. Your mama is having a hard time. You must not add to it." He sighed and shook his head. "Sarah, please say to your grandmother that you are sorry."

"No!"

"For your mama."

For Mama! Mama was always lecturing me to stand up for myself, but when Grandmother said mean things about us all, she was as quiet as a churchyard. I shook my head.

"For me, then, Sarah. Please." Papa reached across the table and patted my hand. "Will you, then, *Puffertje*?"

I sniffled as I nodded.

Mama arose from the table. She looked very tired. "That's it, then. Now you must all come and say goodbye."

Papa speared a piece of mutton and put it on the driver's plate.

"Toby here is hungry," he told Mama. "They'll go after he's finished his dinner."

Toby brought round Grandmother's carriage and we were all lined up again.

Mama nudged me. "Sarah has something to say to you, Mother."

I was looking down so that Grandmother wouldn't see the tears in my eyes and think I was truly sorry. I searched my pocket until I found my prism. I closed my fingers round it and squeezed hard. "I'm sorry, Grandmother," I murmured. I kept my head down but I looked at her.

Grandmother was smiling. It was not a false smile, like her laugh that wasn't a laugh. I saw her teeth between her thin old-lady lips. They were a bit crooked, but they weren't rotted at all. "You're the likeness of your mama, child," she told me.

Brom stepped closer to me and touched my arm as Grandmother patted Elizabeth and Isaac on their heads. With Brom and me, she had to settle for patting our shoulders because we were so much taller than she was.

When she got to Papa, I was holding my breath.

"Peter," she said. She extended her hand and Papa took it.

Grandmother embraced Mama. She said, "I have one last thing to say, Mary. Your stubborn independence may cost you dearly."

"We're safe here, Mother," Mama answered. "This isn't like the lower part of the county. Lord Philipse will protect us."

"Hah!" cried Grandmother. "You haven't heard that that traitor George Washington has ordered Lord Philipse's arrest. No one will be safe until that Washington fellow has been strung up on gallows!" She turned to Toby. "Help me in."

Aunt Charlotte stood on tiptoe to kiss Mama's cheek. "Goodbye, Mary," she whispered. Her chin was trembling.

Grandmother rapped on the roof of the carriage with her cane. "Drive off," she ordered.

"We could have stayed for some teacakes, Mother," I heard Aunt Charlotte complain.

Grandmother didn't answer. As Toby slapped the reins and the carriage began to roll, I could see that her head was bowed. She was holding something in her hand. It was a handkerchief. A white hand-kerchief.

"Don't worry, Mama," Brom said when the carriage was out of sight. "The militia will protect us. I'll join up and see that the British..."

"*Niet spreken!*" Papa ordered. He added in a softer voice, "Mary, you are right. We are safe. No one is making trouble. Come with me to the sitting room. Sarah will fetch you a plate of dinner. Thomas, go with your sister. She will give you *koekjes*."

As soon as we were in the kitchen, Brom grabbed my arm. "Grandmother must have been horrible! What happened?"

I looked at the remains of the feast. A few bits of pastry clung to the chicken pie dish. The mutton had grown cold, but I put a slice on a plate with some spoonbread and raspberries and cream. Mama favoured raspberries. Perchance she would eat them.

I told Brom, "We heard about Cousin Samuel again. Grand-mother and Aunt Charlotte are moving with him to an island south of New York Town where there are lots of Tories. She wanted Mama to go with them."

Brom put down his fork. "Mama and not us?"

"We were allowed to go, but not Papa."

"Why not Papa?"

I didn't answer. I was glad to be getting out of the kitchen, if only for a moment. I handed Mama the plate and she thanked me, but I could tell she wasn't going to touch it.

Brom had moved on to finishing the potatoes. Thomas clamoured for *koekjes*, and I gave him some and shooed him out the door.

Brom asked again, "Why couldn't Papa go?"

"She didn't say."

"I'll tell you why," said Brom. "It's because Papa isn't good enough for them. That's just like the English. They're think themselves better than anyone else." He took a mouthful of spoonbread.

"She did say good-bye to Papa," I reminded him.

"That was charitable. And now you're standing up for her."

"I stood up *to* her."

"You said you were sorry." Brom pulled the spoonbread closer. "*You* apologized after *her* rudeness. That's precisely the hypocrisy we're rebelling against."

"I said I was sorry only because Papa asked me." I took a bite of cold carrots from my plate.

Brom mimicked Papa's accent. "*Ja*. Anything not to make a fight."

"Brom, I think Grandmother loves Mama and she's sad about how things have turned out. She doesn't think she's ever going to see Mama again."

"She's only sorry because she doesn't have Mama under her thumb."

"She did say Mama was a rebel."

Brom struck the table with the palm of his hand, and the raspberries jumped in their bowl. "Now that is proof of how addlepated the British are."

I pushed my plate away. I didn't tell him about Grandmother's smile and how her teeth weren't brown and ugly the way I thought they'd be. I didn't tell him about her white handkerchief.

– Chapter Eight –

A week after Grandmother Seabury's visit, our household was still out of sorts. Mama kept to her closet. Papa and Brom were glum, Elizabeth was fretful and Thomas was even more vexing than usual. Brom had told him that kings were fond of torturing their subjects, so he went about threatening to chain us and hang us by our feet.

I was glad to see Amy Requa and Jemima Van Wart coming up the lane.

"We're going to visit Rachel," Amy told me. "Could you come with us?"

I was not at all certain that I wanted to see Rachel, but I did want to escape our house. "I'll ask Mama," I told Amy.

She asked, "Do you think that Brom would come, too?"

Amy had favoured Brom for as long as I could remember. The walk to Rachel's house would offer the chance to display her considerable charms: a well-moulded form, glossy black curls peeping from beneath her cap, dark eyes enhanced by thick eyelashes and dimples she showed all the more in the company of young men. Amy's Protestant forebears had escaped from papist France a century before, but she had inherited the French custom of turning every discourse to the subject of love. At least, that was what Rachel said. Small wonder the boys flocked round her.

I liked Amy, but in truth I was envious of her easy manner round boys. That was no doubt because she had four older brothers and no sisters. They probably spoke pleasantly and offered Amy compliments, while Brom saw it as his duty to insult me as often as possible. That was but one more way in which my life was unjust.

I told Amy, "He's in the far field. It would take too long to fetch him."

The cicadas whined in the oak trees along our lane. A portly red cardinal hopped about. "Irked! Irked!" he complained. That was just the temper I was in.

I said, "Mama's mother came to visit last week. Since then, everyone has been grumpy."

Little white butterflies danced among the daisies at the side of the road. Mama said that butterflies were handkerchiefs that pixies wave. I thought of Grandmother's white handkerchief and felt even more dismal.

Jemima kicked a pebble at a fuzzy brown caterpillar that was meandering across the road. Of my companions, she was indeed the most unfortunate. Her freckled flesh was stretched taut over her frame. She had inherited the red hair of her Van Wart kin, but in Jemima it was the hue of dull copper. Her lips were so thin as to be nearly invisible.

Jemima said, "I never had a *Grootje*. I don't even have a mama anymore."

"You have a new mama and a new brother and sister," Amy reminded her.

"Yes, and they're always grumpy."

I kicked a pebble, too. "I wish I were free to do as I pleased."

"Like Marie-Louise Storm," Jemima said.

Amy exclaimed, "Marie-Louise hasn't a proper gown. Her hair could be a nest for the birds. How will she ever make some man a wife?"

"Not everybody is a wife," I reminded her.

"Households must have wives. Children must have a mama," Amy declared. "It's fun being somebody's wife and having babies."

I told them, "Maybe I won't be a wife. Maybe I'll go off on an adventure."

"That fellow at the mill – Elijah – wants to go across the sea," Amy said. "He had to leave his home on a creek near Peekskill. He behaved in a dishonourable manner with a *mademoiselle*. But, Sarah, I have a secret for you. It is about Tom Buckhout. He was with my brother Gabriel."

"That's not a proper secret," Jemima said.

Amy's eyes shone. "This is the secret, Sarah: I told Tom that you favour him."

"No! You didn't!"

What a fool I was to have confided in Amy, who was known to chatter. What must Tom think? He would know I was a ninny and a forward ninny, to boot. I remember Brom's contempt for the Van Vliet sisters, who pined publicly over young men. People would make jokes about me, too.

"What did he say?" asked Jemima.

"He did not quite *say*," admitted Amy. "But when I spoke Sarah's name, he smiled in that way that he does, you know."

Of course I knew. I pictured Tom's ruddy hair, his sleepy green-brown eyes and one side of his mouth turning up more than the other when he smiled. No doubt he'd smiled only because he thought I was a simpleton. Of all the misery I had endured of late, this was the worst. I was glad when we came to the rough-hewn wooden bridge over the lazy little Saw Mill River. We were nearly at Rachel's house.

A question that Brom and I had debated for years was which ancient monster of fable Rachel's mother, *Tante* Gertje, more resembled. I said Charybdis, because although she appeared to be an ordinary Dutch housewife, she snarled and snapped and tore to bits anyone who crossed her path. Brom insisted she was Scylla, the monster who swallowed ships whole. That would account for her wide girth, he said.

I wasn't surprised that when *Tante* Gertje opened the top half of the Dutch door, her mouth was turned down and her eyes were squeezed between her brow and her cheeks as she scowled. The scowl deepened when she saw me. I wondered if she intended to tear me to bits or to gobble me whole.

"Where is Rachel?" Amy asked.

Tante Gertje motioned toward the sitting room, but she blocked my way. "Come with me, Sarah," she said.

I followed her nervously into the warm, spacious kitchen. *Tante* Gertje had been baking. A sweet, buttery smell mingled with the aromas of roasted pork and bread.

Tante Gerte disappeared into the cold room behind the kitchen and returned with a green pottery pitcher of cold cider. I was relieved. She'd asked me to the kitchen to serve the cider and a plate of *koekjes*.

Tante Gertje set the pitcher on the wooden table and shook her fist at me. "*The wicked go astray, speaking lies. Their poison is like the poison of a serpent*," she intoned.

I'd not heard that particular verse, but I had no doubt that it came from Scripture. *Tante* Gertje read the Bible so much she knew great chunks of it by heart. There was seldom an occasion for which she didn't have at hand a passage of holy writ. This verse managed all at once to include snakes, poison and lies. I knew that I was the wicked person.

I took the *koekjes* and cider and hurried to the sitting room.

Rachel was seated at the spinning wheel. Her injured arm was wrapped in linen bandages, and she had turned back her sleeve so that all could see them. When I greeted her, she looked away and didn't answer. Jemima shrank from me as I passed the *koekjes*, and Amy gave me a sad smile. They all watched as I put down the plate and took a seat on a bench by the window.

I cleared my throat. "Is your arm healing, Rachel?"

"She is recovering from the snake-bite," Amy answered.

"But the witch-bite was worse," said Jemima.

"We were lucky that woman happened by," I said.

"*The vile person speaketh villainy,*" Rachel proclaimed.

Now she was quoting from Scripture. I wished I'd stayed at home.

Rachel went on, "I'm talking about you, Sarah. You're a vile villain."

Amy told me, "Rachel said that you and that woman…"

"The witch," Rachel interrupted.

"The witch. You and the witch plotted together. She says you're a witch, too. You caused her to be bitten by snakes." Amy leaned forward. She had little frown lines round her dark eyes.

Rachel stepped on the treadle and the spinning wheel began to go round. She said, "I knew it was evil to spy on Brom, but Sarah said we must."

Jemima asked, "Why did you want to spy on Brom?"

"Brom is sweet on Laney Van Tassel," Rachel told her. Her foot kept a steady beat on the treadle.

"Brom is sweet on *Laney Van Tassel*?" Amy was much more dismayed by this news than about my plotting with a witch. "Did the witch know of this?"

"Of course. She keeps company with the Devil. He told her to wait for Sarah to lead me into their trap."

Clearly, that was the moment I should have spoken, but I had no notion where to begin. I jumped up and fetched a pair of metal cards and tufts of grey-and-white wool from a basket in the corner. I began to comb the wool with the cards to clean out the dirt.

Jemima peered at Rachel. "How did the Devil poison you?"

"He was the snake, of course," cried Rachel.

Amy took a bite of *koekje*. "This one you say is a witch, Rachel. It is that woman who lives by herself, no?"

"She doesn't live by herself," Rachel replied. "She lives with the Devil way up in that odd little hollow behind the burying ground. In fact," Rachel paused for breath. "They made a child together."

Amy's eyes widened. "A child with the Devil? But how... I wish to say..." Amy's English was too limited for her to continue further. She delivered a lengthy query in French, accompanied by a waving of her hands.

"I have proof of their coupling," said Rachel. "There's a boy who lives with the savages. He's part savage, but he has light hair. The witch is his mother."

Amy asked, "Who is his father, then? Perhaps it is one of the natives."

Rachel gave her a withering look. "Of course it's the Devil. No one would..."

She searched for words and finally settled on a Biblical phrase. "No one would lie with a savage."

Jemima bit her thumbnail. "I was thinking about that woman," she said.

"The witch," Rachel corrected her.

"I had measles and somebody left a jar of marigold tea on the stoop. The tea was to help my sore eyes. We thought it might have been left by the... the witch. The same witch that you saw."

"You drank the tea," said Rachel.

"Well, yes," Jemima admitted. Her thin face was so red that I could barely see her freckles.

"And now you're under her spell," Rachel declared.

Jemima began to sob and Amy jumped up to console her. "You are the one under the spell, Rachel. Since the snake bit you, you are full of the poison."

Rachel eyed Amy in the way that a fox might size up a particularly feisty rooster.

Then she said, "There was *Mevrouw* Storm, Marie-Louise's mother. She was always sickly but especially so with the baby coming. Just like so..." Rachel snapped her fingers. "The witch was at the door. She had a jar of a horrid green potion. *Mevrouw* Storm drank it and she died two days later."

"You said she was sickly," Amy reminded her.

"The baby died, too," Jemima added.

"Yes, and it was a blessing. He had a red spot on his back in the shape of a hoof. The devil's cloven hoof." Rachel was veritably gloating.

Amy shook her head slightly. "Spots on the skin are not the mark of the Devil. My brother has such a mark."

Rachel was twisting strands of wool. "Jost Van Vliet," she said. The way she said it, the name sounded quite like the tolling of a bell.

"He had that terrible accident at the mill," Amy said. "But what has that to do with...?"

Rachel gave her a quick, triumphant smile. "Dan dared him to find the witch's house and bring back something as proof he'd truly gone there. That was the day before the *accident*." She smiled mournfully. "Now you know the evil Sarah has brought upon me."

The treadle kept time, the wheel went round and the bobbin spun merrily as it collected the finished yarn. I felt the burning in my nostrils that meant I was about to cry.

I raked the wool though the cards. Specks of dried mud and nettle flew out. I didn't want Rachel to see me crying, but of course she did. They all did.

Rachel pointed at me. *"Repent, and turn your face away from all your abominations."*

"Sarah's turning away her face," Jemima observed. "Are you repenting, Sarah?"

Rachel bowed her head. "Let us pray to the Lord to make Sarah repentful. She kneweth not what she diddest."

Amy put down her *koekje* and shut her eyes. Jemima watched me from behind her folded hands.

"I pray thee, Lord, forgive the wickedness of that sinner Sarah. She has sinned snakily. She was befooled by the Serpent but I ask you to forgive her. Just as long as she's sorry. Amen."

"Amen," Jemima repeated. "Are you going to forgive her, Rachel?"

Rachel gazed heavenward. "Who can forgive sins but God alone? But there is something Sarah can do to prove she's repentful."

I put my hand in my pocket and took hold of my prism.

"Sarah can make sure the witch never harms anybody again. She can find out exactly where the witch's house is. Then we can drive her away."

Amy finished her *koekje*. "If this witch has so much power, she will know why Sarah is there."

Jemima shuddered. "Her eyes are like Sarah's glass. They see little bits of everything at once."

"*Taisez-vous*! She is listening!" Amy rested her chin on her hands as she thought the situation over. "Sarah must pretend to ask for something. *La magie* to make Laney Van Tassel go away? No, it must be something good. Sarah can ask the witch for a potion to make Rachel beautiful." She laughed.

Rachel glared at her. "This is not a matter to laugh about."

Amy studied me. "Sarah does not need to be more beautiful. Perhaps not so tall. Or perhaps the witch could find her a tall man."

Jemima blinked. "Rachel, you said that's what Jost Van Vliet was going to do: go to the witch's house. Something terrible might happen to Sarah."

"Sarah's a witch, too. She won't be harmed," Rachel assured her airily.

"I'm not sure that the woman is a witch..." I began.

Rachel managed to cut me off and ignore me all at once. "If she's not a witch, then Sarah has nothing to fear." She rose slowly to her feet. "It's settled. Sarah will go to the witch's house."

"Sarah will go to the witch's house," Jemima echoed.

Rachel yawned. "I must rest now. You must go."

Rachel's mouth was smiling, but her eyes were flat and cold as a snake's. Rachel wanted something dreadful to happen to me, just like Jost Van Vliet. If nothing happened, that would prove I was a witch, too.

- Chapter Nine -

Papa, Thomas and Verkenner were sitting on the kitchen stoop as I trudged up the lane.

"You have been gone a long while," Papa said. He didn't call me *Puffertje*.

"I was visiting Rachel." I looked at the house. "Where is Mama?"

"She is *ziekelijk*." She is lying down. Your brother is doing your chores for you." Papa sounded altogether weary.

"I'm not so very late. I can do them." Now Brom would make me do his chores. I would have to rake out the pigpen and maybe even butcher a sheep.

Thomas straightened his pewter-bowl crown. "What ho, minion!" he shrilled. "You have been very, very bad. I sentence you to be chopped into little bits."

"That's *genoeg*, Thomas," said Papa. "Go now. Help Brom with the chores."

I knew that I was in for a lecture. Papa's lectures weren't as long as Mama's and didn't require as much nimble thinking. I was wary nonetheless.

"Sarah, your mama is having a bad time. You must not be thinking only of yourself. You must be thinking how you can help your family."

When did they ever think of me except when a chore was to be done? I didn't think I had tears left after that horrid afternoon at Rachel's, but my eyes filled.

Papa was distressed, as he always was when one of us was unhappy. "Now, *Puffertje*, I know you are sorry."

As I turned and ran for the barn, he called after me, "There is no need for you to cry over your chores, *Puffertje*. Brom will have finished them by now."

Brom was in the loft, pitching down hay for the cattle stalls and singing a tune he had learned of late, *The World Turned Upside Down*.

"Goody Bull and her daughter fell out. Both squabbled and wrangled and made a great rout..."

When he saw me, he aimed a forkful of hay in my direction. I ducked just in time.

"Where've you been, Sarah? Did you squabble with Goody Bull?"

"I've not seen Mama since morning. Did you do the milking yet?"

"I have enough chores of my own, thank you. Thomas fed the pigs. A fitting enterprise for a king, don't you think?"

I'd have laughed had I not been so miserable. "I had quite an ordeal. I paid a visit to Rachel."

"And how is Fish Lips?" Brom had given that name to Rachel for her wide mouth, which was perpetually puckered in an expression of distaste and suspicion.

"Rachel told Amy and Jemima that the witch and I plotted to put her under an evil spell."

"What witch? That German woman?" Brom tossed a last forkful of hay and climbed down the ladder. "Why'd she say that?"

"Rachel was bitten and I wasn't."

Brom pushed back a lock of his blond hair. "Then shouldn't Rachel be under the evil spell?"

"That's what Amy said."

I fetched a bucket. Milky, our calico cat, appeared at once. As I sat on the milking stool and drew on Anke's teats, streams of milk splashed into the bucket. Milky rubbed against me, purring. She waited to lick milk from my fingers with her rough pink tongue.

"Amy quite fancies you, you know," I told Brom. That should pay back Amy for tattling on me to Tom.

To my amazement, Brom coughed and looked altogether pleased. He asked, "Gabriel Requa's little sister? With big brown eyes?"

"The very one," I said.

"I'm glad she took your part." Brom took up his pitchfork and began to toss hay into the stalls.

"Rachel said that I'm a witch, too. Then she prayed for me and said I could make it up to her by going to the witch's house. I think she wants me to come to harm."

"If I were the snake that bit Rachel, I'd worry about my bodily humours."

"Do you think I should go to the witch's house? Rachel said that I must find it so we can drive her away."

Brom thought this over. "This is one of Rachel's malicious plots. Don't go."

"That's what Mama said."

"Did you tell Mama about Rachel's plot?"

"No. Mama said I mustn't ever have anything to do with that 'unfortunate.'" I wrinkled my nose as I mimicked Mama's highborn accent.

"Well, if Goody Bull told her daughter not to go, that's the very reason you should." Brom leaned on his pitchfork, and I could tell that he'd stopped making jests.

"Sarah, do *you* think you should go to the witch's house?"

"I don't know that she's a witch."

"Then you need to see for yourself." Brom grinned and I understood why Amy was sweet on him.

The next day, Mama was still indisposed – and by that, I mean she was not disposed even to rise from her bed. She bade me fetch her Homer's *Iliad*, a worn volume bound in green leather with gilt-edged pages. Of course, she told me to mind Elizabeth.

I, too, was indisposed, or at least of a peevish humour. I was still upset by Rachel's insistence that I visit the witch – and also by my own meek acquiescence – but I was more greatly irked at Mama. She was no better than Grandmother with her high-handed commands to servants! What gave Mama the right to lie abed as I took over her household duties? Did anyone consider that perhaps I might prefer to be reading, as well?

In this temper, you may guess that the first thought that came to my mind was a visit to the very place I'd been forbidden to go. So, after brewing a pennyroyal tea to ease Mama's digestion, I picked up Elizabeth and set out for Hulda's home in the hollow. I considered leaving the baby at home, but then my absence would be more readily discovered.

I headed south along the Post Road, all the while trying to invent a plausible story should someone I knew encounter me with my baby sister and report it to Papa. I had read enough to know that it was just such a triviality that foiled many a plot.

I came upon Philipse's Mill, which was busy that fine summer morning. Ceaser the miller was outside the old grey wood building, helping to unload great round bushel baskets of winter wheat from a farm wagon. The wooden mill wheel was rumbling round, sending out foamy ripples that rocked the market sloop at anchor in the river. Another sloop was at the dock behind the mill. I could see its mast poking above the mill roof. It must be waiting to take on the grain that was being ground. Then that grain would sail down Hudson's

River to New York Town. Maybe it would even cross the ocean. For an instant, I was tempted to stop and watch, and to ponder my dismal life in a rustic backwater. But that would increase my chances of being seen.

Next to the mill was the plain white stone house that the first Lord Philipse, a very rich Dutchman, had built nearly a hundred years ago. His descendants had removed themselves downriver to a fine brick mansion where they put on more British airs than King George himself. Grandmother Seabury had said that General Washington had ordered Lord Philipse's arrest. I wondered if that were true.

The first Lord Philipse had also built the little stone church across the road from the house and mill. Behind the church was the burying ground. The dusky red tombstones were lined up in rows: father beside mother, old folks on the end and babies in between, the same way people sat in church. I hoped that families got along better in Heaven than here on earth.

Just before the bridge, I turned onto a seldom-used footpath that went round the church and down along the riverbank.

That odd little river valley had a fearsome reputation long before Hulda dwelt there. When we were children, we were forbidden to venture into the rocky ravine. All manner of *spooks* and demons lay in wait for us, our elders said.

So the hollow was a tempting place indeed. On Sundays, between morning and afternoon church services and after the customary midday picnic, little boys dared each other to cross the rushing stream and their older brothers found secluded places to profess their affections to young ladies. *Tante* Gertje's insistence that the Devil did his most dastardly work on the Sabbath served merely as enticement.

But that was the Sabbath. This was mid-week, and the nearest human was out of sight and likely out of hearing as well. I descended the rocky embankment warily, balancing Elizabeth's warm weight against my shoulder.

Although it was near midday, the sun's rays hadn't reached the hollow. Perhaps they never did. Perhaps the chill I felt was because I was hard by the brook. It would be exaggerating to call such a small stream a river.

Yet – and here was an oddity – once the Pocantico left the hollow and passed under the Post Road Bridge it indeed became a river, so placid and deep that great boats could sail on it.

I glanced back at the church, but the grey stone building had vanished altogether. I'd not gone more than fifty paces, but already I'd ventured so deep into the hollow that its craggy sides had closed round me. I heard not a bird nor a squirrel, nor even a droning bee. This must be what it was like to be dead and buried, I thought.

"*The Lord is my shepherd,*" I whispered. "*Yea, though I walk through the Valley of the Shadow of Death...*"

The Valley of the Shadow of Death! I would wander here forever. Elizabeth and I would die and turn into ghosts. No one would ever know what had become of us. Rachel would be sorry she'd been so mean, Mama would be sorry she made me mind the baby and Tom Buckhout would realize too late that I was his true love.

A ragged splotch of red in the stream caught my eye. It looked like a bloodstain and it was racing merrily toward me on the swift, shallow water. I yearned to flee, and for an instant, I almost did. The bloodspot drifted closer and I saw that it was a maple leaf. But it was odd that in high summer a leaf had turned red and fallen.

I picked my way along the path, and may I say that 'path' was a generous description. It was a scarcely distinguishable ribbon of stones and damp earth that passed through a thicket of laurel. The laurel had sent forth one sad pink blossom, a season too late, I observed. A crouching fox turned out to be a large stone as I grew near, and the sleeping bear was but a rotted log.

Elizabeth murmured and moved her head in her white linen bonnet. She'd drooled on my gown. I told myself I'd best stop being such a coward and find the witch's house straightaway.

A few barren hemlocks had pushed through the mossy earth and were making a feeble attempt to reach the sunlight far above them. One had fallen at a rakish angle; a remaining upright branch gave it the look of a clock with hands askew. It came to me: in this hollow, nothing marked the hour or season. It was quite like being in a dream. Familiar things appeared to have gone awry and it was very, very quiet.

I shivered, and Elizabeth raised her head from my shoulder and opened her eyes. She had inherited Papa's fair complexion and placid demeanour, but she had Mama's instinct for knowing when something was amiss. Now, she knit her small brows together and her little pink lip jutted out. I recognized the signs of a gathering tempest.

If the baby and I left directly, we could be home before Mama… Mama! What would Mama say if she discovered I'd not only disobeyed her but also taken the baby with me to this forsaken place? The ensuing inquisition might as well take place in the Tower of London.

But why was it always my duty to mind the baby? Mama was the one who "kept producing little strangers," as Grandmother Seabury said. Let Mama care for them.

Elizabeth was trying to chew the white linen of my sleeve. She was getting hungry. I should have brought the rag dipped in sugar-water that Mama gave her when she needed to be calmed.

I must leave at that very moment. Rachel would jeer, but I could invent a story. I needed only to turn and walk the way I'd come. No, I had come a good distance. I should keep on. Perhaps I was close to the witch's dwelling.

I reached into my pocket to touch my prism. It wasn't there. I'd intended to bring it with me for luck. As I shifted her weight to my other arm, Elizabeth began to cry. Great crystal tears formed in her blue eyes and ran down her chubby cheeks.

"Sh-sh-sh." I jiggled her but she cried all the harder.

Maybe she would be quiet if I gave her a sip of water. I stepped carefully across mossy rocks to reach the brook. As I bent to dip my hand in the water, I slipped. I thrashed about to regain my balance and Elizabeth tumbled from my arms. She landed in a muddy patch of moss. At that instant, I didn't think to thank Providence that she hadn't fallen into the river and been carried away. I did recall some long-ago warning about the Pocantico's treacherous behaviour.

I could see that the baby hadn't been harmed, but merely offended. Her shrieks echoed off the hollow's rocky walls. I offered a finger for her to chew, and I felt the jagged edge of a tooth on her lower gum.

The thought crossed my mind that I was surely better off without the company of a screaming, bedraggled baby. I looked about for a place to leave her. I could visit the witch and retrieve the baby on my way home. Elizabeth couldn't tattle on me.

If I set her between the roots of that oak she couldn't roll away. Then I saw the slender stem with clotted red leaves twined round the tree. Poison ivy.

"We need to find water," I told Elizabeth, surveying her muddy gown as I lifted her. "The brook's altogether too risky. There must be a spring nearby."

I looked round at great brown drifts of last year's fallen leaves. Then I spied a little stripe of green ahead and hurried toward it. The stripe was a line of skunk cabbage and indeed a thin stream of water was trickling through it. It must have come from a spring on that little hill rising from the hollow. I gathered my skirts, balanced Elizabeth on my hip and began to climb. Brambles tore at my ankles and I suspected that all manner of crawly things hid in the leaves, but I pressed on.

Someone had set stones round the spring, making a wall to hold in the water. I dipped my hand and put a wet finger in Elizabeth's mouth. She sucked hungrily and again I felt the newly-cut tooth.

There was a tug on my sleeve. I started and nearly dropped Elizabeth once more.

"Is good you come," said Hulda the Witch.

– Chapter Ten –

Hulda held out her arms for Elizabeth. She gave me a rueful look as she saw the baby's wet, muddy gown, but she smiled into Elizabeth's tear-filled eyes.

"*Liebchen, Liebchen,*" she cooed. "I am..." She made rolling gestures with her free hand.

"You're happy to see us?" I asked hesitantly.

"Ja. You come." She tapped her head. "I know why."

Hulda had known all along about Rachel's plot. Now she had Elizabeth in her clutches. Mama was right that Rachel got me into the most dreadful predicaments.

At the thought of Mama, I remembered my manners. I curtseyed.

Hulda nodded approvingly. Then she said, "The *Liebchen* sick. Make better."

"What does that word mean, '*Liebchen*'?" I asked.

"The good word. Sweet. So," she asked. "What is wrong?"

"She is getting teeth." That truly could be a reason for visiting Hulda. Maybe she would forget about Rachel's spiteful scheme.

Hulda put her finger in Elizabeth's mouth. Not the teeth." She pronounced the word carefully. "It is..." She rubbed her middle.

"The stomach? How do you know?"

"With the teeth, the crying is *Wah wah, wah*. This crying –*Waaaaaaah-*

hhhh! - is the, the *sto-mach*. The house." She pointed. "We make better."

You could never have seen Hulda's home from the path below,
and you could scarcely see it even from the spring because it was
nearly hidden by the garden round it. Hulda carried the baby, and I
followed past heads of fat green cabbages, wispy green carrot tops and
beans winding round poles made from tree branches.

There were vervain and boneset. I saw bee balm, with its slender
leaves and curly purple flowers and a little round feverfew bush with
spicy-smelling flowers that looked like daisies. Tall stalks of pink and
white hollyhocks jostled each other for space in the sunshine. I spied
orange marigolds and I remembered Jemima's measles. I wondered if
Hulda brewed her healing tea from such flowers as these.

Hulda's dwelling could not be called a house. Indeed, even
cottage was too generous a description. It was a small, rude shelter framed by bent saplings lashed together and covered with great
patches of tree bark and a flourishing honeysuckle vine. A rocky embankment covered with dense green alder bushes provided the back
wall. The alders rustled slightly as I approached. A branch snapped:
a squirrel or rabbit, I supposed.

I had to bend to get through the opening that served as the en-
trance, and it took my eyes several moments to become accustomed
to the gloom. Benches of bound-together branches along the walls
must have served as seats and sleeping pallets, for they were covered
with folded blankets and the hide of an animal, a deer, I supposed.
A sizable oak stump with two smaller stumps provided a table and
chairs of sorts.

There was no hearth or fireplace; rather, a shallow pit in the centre had charred logs and an opening in the roof directly above it. A dark iron kettle hung over the pit, suspended from three stout sticks. A weathered rifle rested on a pegged board was nailed to the sapling frame. A half-woven basket was in a corner, and there was a narrow wooden shelf crowded with odd little jars and vials. Sweet-smelling plants hung to dry from the ropes strung cross the ceiling.

There was but a single object that I took to be of a civilised origin: a chest of drawers made of ruddy walnut wood. Hulda opened the top drawer, rummaged among the contents and brought out a folded white cloth.

"That linen is too fine," I exclaimed, peering at the embroidered flowers. "You mustn't..."

"No use here." Hulda pointed round at her primitive abode. As expertly as Mama, she set Elizabeth down on the blankets, whisked away the wet clouts and gown. She probed Elizabeth's stomach with a gentle finger.

"Ja, the bad wind," she said, clucking as she swaddled the baby with the linen. She took one vial from the shelf and put it back. She opened another and tapped a few seeds onto the table.

"Fennel," I said, recognizing the dark, sweet scent. "We use this to make pickles."

"Ja." She drew a knotty orange root from a jar. "This one you do not know: the gin-ga. It comes on the boat. From the small lands in the sea."

"Ginger?" I asked. "From the Indies?"

Hulda nodded. "The In-dies, ja. Gin-ger..." Hulda pronounced it as I had. "Good for the bad wind. Ach! And the one more: chamomile." She peered at me. "You know the chamomile?"

"We make a tea from the flowers to calm ill temper and to bring sleep."

I leaned over and breathed in the same grassy scent that Hulda herself had about her. I recalled the day she'd treated Rachel.

"How the friend, the snake friend?" Hulda asked suddenly.

Clearly, Hulda had divined my thoughts. As I began to stammer a reply, she said, "The pine. Good also for the snake."

I was relieved to have a new topic of conversation. "How did you learn about remedies?"

Hulda shrugged. "I learn in *mein heimatland*. The flowers grow there. They grow here." She scooped water from a great earthenware jar and poured it into the kettle. She motioned to me to fetch some twigs for kindling.

"How is the Mother?"

"My mother?"

"*Ja.* The... *Schwester*?"

"Elizabeth is my sister," I told her. "We have the same mother."

Hulda seemed pleased that I'd understood. "So. The mother is..." She coughed and put her hand to her forehead.

"She is *ziekelijk*," I told Hulda. Perhaps she knew the Dutch word for "sick."

"*Krank!*" cried Hulda, nodding vigorously.

"Yes. *Krank.* Sick," I said. "But how do you know?"

"I see."

Mama had hardly left her bed since Grandmother's visit. Hulda couldn't have seen her, unless, of course, she indeed possessed the occult powers Rachel insisted she had. The suspicion did indeed cross my mind.

"*Schwester... Die Milch...*"

"Mama's milk is sour because she's ailing. That caused Elizabeth to have the bad wind."

"*Ja, Liebchen.* You see now," she said. Hulda's smile was winsome and warm.

∞

Brom caught up with me on the Post Road.

"The warships are gone!" He shouldered an imaginary gun and aimed at an oak tree. "The damned British have finally seen that they're not welcome here."

"You haven't been in a fight with them, have you?" I studied him for signs of a scuffle.

"They sneaked away before we had a chance to fight them."

I shifted Elizabeth to my other arm. The tea Hulda had made from the fennel, ginger and chamomile had sent her straight to sleep. "Did the ships go back to New York Town?"

"Actually, they went upriver, to Haverstraw Bay and perhaps as far as Peek's Kill. Elijah says good riddance to them."

"I thought Elijah was from those parts. He should be concerned for his family."

Brom scoffed. "The British are bullies. They think they can scare us with their big boats."

"What were you doing at the mill?" I asked

"Looking for you. Mama thought you'd be down at your rock by the river. You weren't there, so I went to the mill. Where were you?" His eyes widened. "You went to see the witch! And you took the baby! What happened?"

"Elizabeth had…" I started to say 'the bad wind' "…discomfort in the stomach. Hulda made her a remedy."

"Ummm." As I had hoped, Brom was satisfied with the explanation. "What's the witch like?"

"It's strange. When she looks straight at me, she's quite fair. Then she turns her head and her nose is too big and she's homely. It's like our looking-glass, Brom. You know how the glass is bumpy and when you look from a certain place, your features change?"

"Ummm," Brom said again, and I realized he hadn't passed as much time before the looking glass as I had.

"She seemed to see into my thoughts." I paused. "I was thinking about Mama and straightaway Hulda mentioned her. She knew Mama was ailing because Elizabeth was, too."

Brom appraised me with serious blue eyes. "You're a patriot, Sarah."

"A patriot? How does paying a visit qualify me to be a patriot?"

"You're free and you're brave. You're not bound by nonsense rules made by silly people."

I smiled at the compliment, although I never would have called Mama silly.

"Brom, can you carry Elizabeth? She's very heavy."

Elizabeth awakened as Brom took her from me. He tossed her in the air and caught her, although Mama had often warned him not to. Elizabeth crowed with delight.

– Chapter Eleven –

Mama looped a white linen cravat round Brom's neck and tucked the ends into his dark blue waistcoat. "Why, you look smart as a carrot," she told him gaily. I was accustomed to Mama's being of a far more affable disposition with Brom than with me. Nonetheless, I was irked.

We were waiting on the stoop for papa to bring the wagon round. I had been pinching my cheeks to make them rosy so Tom Buckhout might think I was almost as pretty as Laney.

Brom noticed. In those days, he alternately tormented or confided in me and I never knew which it would be. That day, unluckily, it was the former.

"That won't help, Sarah," he said. "You'll need to visit *the witch* again. Ask *the witch* for a spell so you won't be so ugly."

At the mention of "witch," Mama at last turned to me. She said sternly, "Sarah, you recall that I have forbidden you…"

I was saved by Papa's arrival. "*Haasten zich!* We must not be late!" he said, clapping his hands together.

Mama turned to him. "Now is it the Word of the Lord you're anxious to hear, Peter? Or is it news of the livestock?" She was in a rare affable humour. I watched her warily. In such spirits, Mama was a spinning weathercock, liable to turn in a trice.

Papa turned our wagon off the Post Road and guided our old

brown draft horse Pegasus up the knoll. The stone church, a little white bell tower perched atop its angled Dutch roof, was open for Sabbath services. People were waiting outside.

Amy and Jemima came rushing over. "Did you make a visit to the witch?" Amy whispered. Her dark eyes were wide with concern.

I slid down from the wagon. "Shh! Mama will hear you!"

Amy took my arm and we walked round the church. "Did you visit the witch?" she asked again.

Tom Buckhout was standing under an elm in the graveyard. He was with Samuel Youngs. I paused by a weathered red tombstone and tried to think of something to say if Tom should come over.

Jemima blurted, "Did you ask her to cast a spell on Laney Van Tassel?"

At that instant, Tom saw me. He tilted back his head and looked at me through half-closed eyes. He gave me the smile that showed his top teeth on one side. In truth, it was more a grin, rakish, knowing and full of mischievous intent. Surely he wouldn't have smiled that way if he were completely smitten with Laney. On the other hand, perhaps the smile meant he felt sorry for me because I was such a fool.

"Sarah! Make attention!" Amy had a way of translating phrases word-for-word from her native French. The boys thought it charming.

"Yes, I went to see her," I answered. Tom and Samuel were walking toward the church.

Amy looked worried. "You did not ask for a spell to make Laney go away? I know I said at Rachel's that you should ask for such a thing, but I was joking."

Jemima asked, "Were you even thinking of Laney? Because the witch can see inside people's heads. She can tell what they are thinking."

Hulda did know when I was thinking of Rachel and of Mama. I tried to recall if Laney had crossed my mind. "No," I told them. "Why?"

The old bronze bell in the steeple clanged to let us know the service was about to begin. As I turned to go in, someone took my elbow.

It was Tom! I jumped in fright and felt my face turn crimson. Perhaps he was going to tell me that he didn't want a child like me besotted with him.

"Scared you?" he asked, giving me another crooked grin.

"N-no."

I was thinking I'd never stood so close to him. He smelled of leather and salt, and there was a mole on his cheek that you couldn't see from a distance. His eyes... they were different colours of brown and green. There I was, fidgeting and stammering. I was such a dunce.

"Sarah, I was going to ask you..." That was the first time that Tom had spoken my name. "Could you, uh, go walking before the afternoon service?"

"W-walking? W-where?"

Tom looked surprised. "Oh... you know. Maybe down by the river." He nodded toward the hollow and favoured me with another showing of teeth.

I was the biggest fool since... well, maybe ever. When a boy asked you to go walking, it meant he wanted to be alone with you. He would hold your hand and likely try to kiss you. Now Tom would know nobody had asked me to go walking before. He would probably have a turn of heart and ask another girl.

Behind Tom, I saw Brom. He was simpering and gesturing at me and Amy was giggling at his antics.

"There you are, Sarah." Mama appeared beside me. She was wearing the same green silk gown she'd worn for Grandmother Seabury's visit. Except for the Anglican prayer book she carried, Mama looked entirely as if she were about to take tea with King George. She said, "You must take charge of Thomas whilst we are in church." She sounded even more embarrassingly English than usual.

Thomas flailed and kicked as Mama tried to make him take my hand. "You can't make me! I'm a king!" he shouted. "Off with your head!"

Tom looked perplexed at this untidy scene. He fled though the heavy wooden door into the church.

Of all the horrid, dreadful, calamitous disasters! Just when Tom had asked me to go walking with him, which meant he must have liked me a little. But he didn't like me now and he would never, never ask me again. Nobody would. I would be a spinster forever, like Aunt Charlotte.

Straightaway I laid the blame at Mama's feet, which that morning were encased in dainty green slippers with little curved heels that made her even taller. She had intruded at just the wrong moment, and worse, she'd veritably screamed that she was English. Tom probably knew that Mama had put those notions of being a king in Thomas' head. Now he surely thought I was a Tory, too. It was so unfair.

I seized Thomas by the ruffle on his shirt and dragged him into church. "And don't you bite anyone," I warned him.

Thomas was widely known to be a rascal. In fact, he was ofttimes presented as a model of a child reared by an Englishwoman: he was utterly unruly, saucy and given to loud displays of displeasure. Once, when *Tante* Gertje called him an insolent pup, Thomas straightaway had dropped to his hands and knees and bitten her on the ankle. Brom and I had not aided Mama's reputation by snickering.

Dominie Ritzema, a substantial silver-haired man wearing his long black pastor's gown, issued the call to worship, and we stood to sing the opening hymn.

"*We gather together to ask the Lord's blessing,*
He chastens and hastens his will to make known.
The wicked oppressing now cease to be distressing..."

Oppressing was one of Brom's favourite words. He bellowed the next line with such enthusiasm that Mama nudged him.

"*Sing praises to His name for he forgets not his own.*"

Dominie Ritzema climbed the circular staircase to the pulpit. He gazed sternly down upon the congregation and began to read from the Holy Scripture. Papa shifted his weight and Thomas squirmed. Mama opened her *Book of Common Prayer*. She'd never learned Dutch well enough to understand the service.

Tom was three rows in front of us. His reddish-brown cue curled down over his shirt and light brown waistcoat. I imagined how it would be if his arms were round me, and then I remembered that would never happen now. I made one little sniffle that nobody heard.

I stared at the back of Tom's head, trying to make him like me again and take me walking. If Hulda could delve into people's minds and turn their thoughts, perhaps I could as well.

I glanced through the open door. In the grove of hemlocks across the river, I glimpsed something that looked altogether like Hulda's blue bonnet. I leaned forward so I could see better and at once felt Mama's hand on mine. When I could sneak a look again, the bonnet had disappeared.

As we filed out into the midday sunshine, Rachel sidled over to Brom. "I heard that you're hoping to capture Laney Van Tassel," she said. "You're too late. She's been captured."

Was Laney betrothed? My first thought was relief that now Tom could not court her. I'd told myself to avoid Rachel, but I followed her down to the millpond. I asked her, "Who is it? Who is Laney going to wed?"

Rachel ignored me for a moment. Then she sighed and gazed out over the water. "I said she was *captured*."

"She was captured by the British!" added Jemima, who had hurried over with Amy.

"By the British? But how did she meet...?" Laney must be betrothed to some British man. I couldn't imagine how Brom would take the news.

Amy guessed what I was thinking. She cried, "No, no, no!" She is not going to be married. She was captured. By British soldiers. That is why I thought you had asked the witch to make her go away."

"But she's over there," I said. Laney was walking near the white stone house by the mill. Her head was bowed and her friend Annetje Martling appeared to be consoling her. "Where was her father?" I asked.

"The British carried him off to prison in New York Town," Jemima said. "He'll probably die there."

The sun danced on the millpond and I shaded my eyes with my hand. "Tell me what happened," I insisted.

"I am faint." Rachel pointed to her arm and sank down into the grass. We sat, too. Rachel fanned her face with her hand. "Those horrid British ships have been poking round here for some time now..."

"Brom says they're gone," I put in.

Rachel was annoyed at the interruption. "As I was *saying*, those ships kept sticking their long pointy noses where they had no business – right in front of the Van Tassels' house."

Amy added, "Each time that they looked at the river, there were those terrible ships. They could not see across the river the view they'd seen all their lives, for all those..." She drew masts and spars with her hands.

Jemima shivered. "The worst thing was, the Van Tassels couldn't sleep at night, for those nasty ships hard by their house."

Rachel corrected her. "The worst was when *Mynheer* Van Tassel was coming back from the privy. He saw men on the deck pointing at him. 'Why, I'll not be watched by some *verdoemd* Englishmen!" he cried. That was when he went in the house and got his big goose gun. He waited until the tide turned and the ships swung close to shore. When a soldier got within range, he shot at him."

My jaw dropped. "He shot a British soldier? On a man-o'-war?"

"He shot a hole in... one of those pieces of cloth." Amy waved her hands in a billowing gesture.

Jemima bit her fingernail. "*Mynheer* Van Tassel didn't harm anyone. The British were mean to come and take him away."

I asked, "Did the soldiers come ashore?"

"Well, of course," said Rachel. "*Mynheer* Van Tassel didn't row out to the ship and ask to be taken prisoner. That was when the soldiers ransacked the house and barn."

She continued, "Laney's mama and aunt set upon them with mops and brooms. Dinah the serving-maid chased the soldiers, too. She was swinging a shovel and shouting an African war cry."

I asked, "Where was Laney?"

"I was getting to that directly," Rachel said. "The soldiers cut down the hams from the smokehouse and cleared out the chicken coop and..."

"They were dragging a cow down to their boat," Jemima put in bravely.

Rachel continued, "Then one of them found Laney. She was in the root cellar hiding amidst the potatoes."

I couldn't stifle a small cry of mirth. A dank cellar was clearly no place where the dainty Laney usually passed time. Jemima and Amy giggled, too.

Rachel gave us a dark look before she went on. "The soldier slung Laney over his shoulder like a sack of flour. He began to carry her off."

"She was kicking and screaming!" exclaimed Jemima. "Can you imagine how terrible...?"

Amy showed her dimples. "It might not have been so terrible if he was *beau*."

I tried to picture the scene. "Did they take her away?"

Rachel said, "He tried, but her mama and aunt beat him with their brooms. Dinah whacked him so hard that he dropped Laney. So they let her go and they left, but not before they set fire to the house."

We were all silent for a moment. I thought I should get my hat. The sun on the water hurt my eyes. Jemima spotted a ladybug crawling across her skirt and flicked it away.

"No, no, no!" Amy exclaimed. "It is bad luck to hurt a *coccinelle*."

Rachel said, "If I were you, Amy, I'd be frightened. You live by the river, just like Laney. The British are likely to burn your house, too."

"Sarah lives by the river," Jemima pointed out.

"The British don't harm Tories," said Rachel.

Jemima argued, "But they might not know Sarah's a Tory."

"I'm not a Tory!"

Jemima bit her fingers again. "I've been thinking about Laney. It must be very hard for her to be so beautiful."

"It was hard for Helen of Troy to be beautiful." Everyone stared at me, so I explained. "Helen was a queen in long-ago Greece. She was the most beautiful woman in the world."

"A beautiful queen?" Amy was intrigued. Jemima was perplexed and Rachel looked impatient.

"Helen was captured like Laney," I went on. "A prince called Paris carried her off to his home in Troy. Her husband the king got together an army and attacked Troy to get her back."

I left out the part about a Greek god shooting Helen with a magic arrow so she'd fall in love with Paris and run off with him willingly. That might have sounded like witchery.

Amy leaned forward. "Did the king get her back?"

"He did, but Troy had a big wall around it, so the Greeks couldn't get inside. Then they thought of a trick. They built a big wooden horse and hid their soldiers inside. They left the horse outside Troy's walls and when the Trojans pulled it into the city, the Greeks jumped out and opened the gates so all their soldiers could come in. They destroyed Troy."

Amy was speechless but Rachel scoffed, "Sarah's talking foolery again. There's nothing like that here."

In my mind's eye, I saw the great wooden beast coming into the city. Its painted eyes stared and its carved tongue lolled from its open mouth. It glided silently and the Trojans weren't sure what to make of such an oddity. But I knew, and I felt a tremor of the coming destruction. Rachel was wrong that there was nothing here like the Trojan horse. I'd seen the British ships.

– Chapter Twelve –

Mama was under a maple tree at the edge of the graveyard. She put down her book.

"Where is your hat, Sarah? Your face is quite pink."

"It's in the wagon. Mama, something terrible happened to Laney Van Tassel and..."

"Sarah, we must have a talk."

"Laney's house was burned!"

Mama paid no mind. "There has been a goodly discussion of witches of late," she observed.

"I'll fetch my hat now," I said.

Mama patted the blanket where Elizabeth was napping. "You may sit here in the shade so you won't need your hat. I wonder where you were the other morning." She didn't raise her voice at the end of the sentence, but it was a question, nonetheless.

"I was at my special place." My rock down by Hudson's River was one of those places. I'd decided that Hulda's home was another.

Mama looked at me, and I recalled what Brom often said: Mama's spectacles made her eyes larger so that she could see into people's thoughts. She asked, "Have you had occasion to see that unfortunate woman again?"

"Well, I, uh..." I should have known Mama was going to plague me about Hulda! I aimed poisoned thoughts at Brom, who'd stirred her suspicions. "Not actually," I concluded.

I could see from her sceptical look that Mama believed me not one whit. I steeled myself for the coming onslaught of questions.

"I saw her the other morning. At a distance," I added. I hoped that statement would explain my hesitation at answering the first question. By then I'd learned there was no way to be truthful and obedient as well.

"I hope you did not speak to her."

"Elizabeth was with me, and then we met up with Brom."

The moment I uttered that half-truth, I realized my blunder. Mama, a talented inquisitor, would surely notice that I'd not actually answered her question. Then, too, I'd opened a veritable Pandora's box of queries: "Where were you when you saw the woman?" "Why was Elizabeth with you?" "What was Brom doing?" She could always confirm my answers with Brom. Depending on his humour, he could rescue me or vanquish me altogether. I eyed her uneasily.

Mama said, "You remember, Sarah, that you are to have nothing to do with her."

By then I was thoroughly tired of the subject. Mama had no right to know everything I thought or did. Brom was right. She was a tyrant, just like all English people.

I said, "Mama, the Holy Scripture said this morning that all of us are equal in the Lord's sight."

Mama sniffed. "We may be the same to God, but surely you can see that some are more... *ill-favoured* than others."

I sat up straight. "Not here, Mama. In this country, everybody's favoured the same."

"Yes. Quite." Then Mama said, "Off you go then. Fetch your father and brothers and don't forget your hat."

Papa and his oldest brother *Oom* Willem, who was Dan and Rachel's father, were over by the wagons. They were wearing round-brimmed straw farmers' hats and puffing placidly on long-stemmed white clay pipes. Isaac was on Papa's shoulders.

I found Brom in the graveyard in the midst of a gathering of men known to be fervent patriots, or traitors, depending on your own view. Dusky red tombstones crowded round them as if they were hoping to hear.

Joseph Youngs, a portly man much given to making speeches, sought to seize control of the discussion. His son Samuel, standing beside him, was tall, skinny, bespectacled, of a pallid complexion, and noted for uttering great wisdom with an economy of words.

The irksome Dan was in attendance, and of course, in any gathering where turmoil might rear its dishevelled head, Isaac Martling was in its midst.

Isaac was the age of Joseph Youngs, or Papa, I supposed, for he was a veteran of the French and Indian War. He had lost his right arm in that conflict, to the tomahawk of an Algonquin warrior, Isaac insisted. A goodly number of our neighbours believed otherwise: an irate farmer whose henhouse Isaac raided had set upon him with a scythe, they said. As the loss of such an important limb kept Isaac from honest labour, he passed much of his time in Storms' Tavern, where he had assumed the role of jester.

I tugged at Brom's sleeve. "It's time for our meal," I told him.

Brom guffawed. "Sarah, why were you staring at Tom in church this morning? Did the witch tell you to put a spell on him?"

"No!"

Dan snickered. "Sarah was spying on Tom." He closed one eye, made a spyglass of his hand and pretended to examine Samuel. The others laughed.

"I thought you patriots would have greater matters to discuss," I snapped. I turned and just in time saw a broken tombstone half-buried in the grass. I was grateful that I didn't trip and ruin my dignified exit.

Brom followed me back to the maple tree. He threw himself down and took a wedge of cheese from our food basket.

"That's dreadful news about Laney," I said, hoping to divert Brom from plaguing me about Hulda.

"What news?" Mama asked.

"The damned British…"

"Brom, mind your language."

"There's no other words for those blackguards! The damned British burned Laney's house and stole all the livestock and provisions. They nearly carried her off, too." He peeled a hard-boiled egg and bit off most of it. "I'd have peppered those scoundrels with birdshot."

Mama said, "Brom, don't talk with your mouth full."

"You'll be an unfortunate," I told him.

Mama gave me the eyes-through-the-spectacles stare again. She said to Brom, "I'm surely glad you didn't pepper them with shot."

I said, "That's what Laney's father did."

Mama was astonished. "Was Jacob Van Tassel shooting at a British man-o'-war? Small wonder they burned his house."

I added, "They took him off to prison. Jemima says he'll probably die there."

Mama removed a winged maple seed Elizabeth was trying to put in her mouth. She said, "I'd say those are Jacob's just deserts."

"Just deserts!" Brom cried so loudly that the women knitting under a tree nearby turned to stare.

Mama said, "There are consequences for those who take the law into their own hands."

"There's no law that the British may imprison us. There's no law that they should burn our houses." Brom's face flushed and voice grew louder as his argument gathered steam. "There's no law that they should even be in our country."

I said, "Mama, we live on the river, too. They might have burned our house."

"They're not going to burn our house," Mama declared.

"The soldiers might have ravished Laney," I added.

Mama was appalled. "Ravish her? Sarah, those men are not godless brutes. They're His Majesty's soldiers."

She opened her book again. Mama always found it easier to consort with people who stayed flat on a page.

"Shall we be crushed under the British tyrant's heel?" Joseph Youngs, a farmer of Papa's age, was shouting from the church steps. "Who here will avenge the atrocities suffered by Jacob Van Tassel?" He wiped his florid brow as he searched for a fitting description. "The Hero of the Goose Gun."

Mama glanced out at the Albany Post Road and gasped as if someone had just stuck her with a pin.

A man on horseback had crossed the wooden bridge and was galloping up to the church. I thought he must be bringing news, but he wasn't a post-rider. I could tell from the lace on his shirt and silver buttons on his coat that he was a gentleman. I'd not seen him before.

Mama was staring into her book but I didn't think that she was reading. She looked dismayed and angry and fearful all at once. I noted that Papa had the same expression.

"Who is that man?" I asked.

"Nathaniel Underhill," Mama muttered.

The man dismounted. With his white wig and tri-cornered hat, I couldn't tell his age, but I thought it to be the same as Mama's and Papa's.

"Go back to your British chums. You're not welcome," someone shouted. Joseph Youngs appeared to know the stranger. "Mr Underhill, what brings you here today?" he asked.

"I am told that *Mijnheer* Van Tassel fired upon one of His Majesty's ships and was taken to prison."

"What business is that of yours?" demanded Samuel.

Mr Underhill scanned the crowd. When he saw Papa, he blinked as if he were confused. "I was concerned about his family... but I see that..."

His words were drowned by shouts of "Tory!" and "Turncoat!" Someone threw a peach and it startled Mr Underhill's horse, a fine bay gelding. The horse pranced and Mr Underhill stroked his neck to calm him.

Samuel called out, "Why aren't you in jail with your crony Lord Philipse?"

Isaac Martling answered for him. "Mr Underhill doesn't care for jails. He's averse to dining on stale crusts and water." Isaac minced to the front of the crowd and pretended to dust something from his waistcoat. Of course, everyone laughed. Even Mr Underhill managed a feeble chuckle.

"That jail in New Haven was a palace compared to where poor Jacob is," cried James. "He's locked up in one of those floating hellholes the redcoats call a prison ship."

Mr Underhill looked flustered, but he persisted. "My only purpose here was to find if the traitor's..."

"We'll see who's the traitor!" Brom shouted.

"...The *man's* family is faring well. It appears I was given the wrong information. The incident..." He chose his words with care, the way Mama sometimes did. "The incident involved someone else."

Oom Willem stepped forward. I was surprised, because like Papa, he was little inclined to be stirred by the passions of politics. "The family is safe in our home. You need not worry."

Laney and her family were staying with *Tante* Gertje and Rachel… and Dan. Brom was bound to be jealous.

I was astonished all the more when Papa spoke up. "We are all well. We do not want those like you here. So go now." Papa put his pipe back in his mouth and fumbled in his vest pocket for his tobacco pouch.

"Don't be so hasty, Peter," Isaac Martling admonished Papa. "Mr Underhill is no Tory. Why, he convinced his jailers in New Haven last year that he's a staunch patriot." He circled round Mr Underhill, who looked as skittish as his horse.

"Here's what I think, lads," Isaac went on. "This Nathaniel Underhill has two sides, like a weathervane. When it suits him to be a patriot…"

"Like when he was jailed last year," someone offered.

Isaac grinned, showing the gap in his teeth where one was missing. "Yes, when he was in jail, Mr Underhill turned about so fast it made your head spin. Why, he crowed for liberty as loud as Patrick Henry."

Isaac paused and shook his head solemnly. "I fear there's another side to him, my friends. Now, that side goes gadding round with Lord Philipse and his pack of minuet-dancing macaronis." Isaac pretended to take a pinch of snuff.

"What we must do is figure out which side is which." Isaac pranced round Mr Underhill as if he were his dancing partner. "By Jove, I have it!" he cried, in an aristocratic accent.

There was a ripple of mirth, and people edged forward in anticipation.

"His front side's the patriot side," Isaac said. "See how cool he looks."

The crowd snickered. Even I could see that Mr Underhill was sweating.

"Where's the other side?" several voices demanded.

"Why, his backside, of course," answered Isaac. "His backside's the Tory side." He walked around the gelding. "Same with the horse," he reported. "Now, this here looks like a Tory rump to me."

"Can't tell one Tory rump from another!" cried Samuel.

Someone else called, "Let's see your Tory side, Underhill. Show us your backside as you leave."

The crowd surged toward Mr Underhill. He vaulted back into the saddle and slapped the reins. The crowd parted to let him go.

Mr Underhill came toward the tree where we were sitting. He reined in when he reached us, but he didn't dismount. He took a deep breath before he said, "I am relieved that you are well, Mary. I am sorry you've chosen not to be with your people."

There was sadness in his eyes I couldn't fathom.

– Chapter Thirteen –

The crowd watched in sullen silence as Mr Underhill's horse clattered across the bridge and disappeared down the Post Road. Then Joseph Youngs waved his beefy arms for attention. He shouted, "We must band together! We must defend ourselves from the... the rapacious, rampaging redcoats!"

Joseph's oratory skills, honed by years of tavern bombast, had the effect I was sure he sought. His listeners, at least the younger ones, were stirred.

"No British boot-licker will invade my home!" cried Brom, heedless of the truth that one such person, Mama, was ensconced in that very dwelling.

"Or my home, either!" Tom yelled.

Joseph beamed. "Now, there are fine young patriots," he said.

Oom Willem stepped to the front of the crowd. "Let us reason, Joseph. Who can defend us from such a foe? These young *zots*..."

Joseph thundered, "Why, the Lord mighty in battle will defend us. You all know the words on the church bell..." He pointed to the little white steeple. "If God be for us, who can be against us?"

I wanted to ask how, if God was going to save the King, as Mama and Grandmother Seabury and Aunt Charlotte hoped, he was also going to help us drive out the King's soldiers. But a Dutchman like *Oom* Willem was not disposed to question the Lord. He retreated, shaking his head.

"Ja! Ja!" The faded blue bonnet I'd spied earlier reappeared as Hulda pushed her way through the throng.

Mama plucked my sleeve. "Is that...?"

"The unfortunate? Yes."

"Sarah, I do not care for your sauciness." Mama craned her neck to see.

"How dare that *vreemdeling* come to the church?" cried Jemima's stepmother.

Mevrouw Frena Romer, James' mother, heaved herself to her feet. "The Lord commanded us to welcome strangers," she said sharply.

Tante Gertje seemed annoyed that someone else was citing Scripture. "He also said, 'Depart from me, ye cursed, into everlasting fire,'" she proclaimed.

People turned to *Dominie* Ritzema to interpret what the Lord meant. Then old Mijnheer Buckhout spoke up. "As all here know, I suffered for many years with stomach distress..."

"That is true, *Dominie*," his wife called out. "This woman brought a basket of dried roots. John chewed them and straightaway he regained his health."

Tante Gertje scowled so deeply that her eyes nearly disappeared. "The devil is come down unto you," she said.

"The devil would not have cured my husband," Mevrouw Buckhout answered. "I see others this woman has helped. When you had headaches, Catherine..." She turned to Mevrouw Couenhoven. "...You sought out this woman for a tea of willow bark. Jacob Acker was relieved of an earache by a concoction she made. Comfrey and rue, I believe it was."

Jacob nodded in agreement. "Joseph, you said that we need to come together to defend ourselves. This woman could help us."

Hulda had understood the talk. She turned to Joseph and asked, "You need the fight? I fight."

Joseph cleared his throat, "You are generous in your offer of help, but..."

"The soldiers come here. I shoot."

"Have you seen soldiers?" Joseph asked.

Isaac Martling cried out in a high-pitched voice, "Ja! I saw them in my pot as I cooked a magic spell."

Hulda said calmly, "The soldiers come. I fight."

Joseph asked again, "Did you see soldiers?"

"Ja!" Isaac sang out. "I take a little snake juice, a bit of skunk stink and whoof! There's a redcoat."

Hulda faced him. "You make the laugh but the soldiers come."

The church bell tolled to announce the beginning of the afternoon service. *Dominie* Ritzema climbed the church steps. The men took off their hats and the women called the children from the graveyard where they'd been playing hide-and-seek.

Tom was standing with Brom and Dan. I tried to catch his eye, but he didn't look my way. How could that Mr. Underhill make so much trouble? He'd spoiled my walk with Tom and Tom would never ask me again. In fact, I spotted him giving Amy one of his rakish smiles. It was so unjust. I wanted to scream and kick a tombstone.

"We've had our fill of *vreemdelings*," Isaac Van Wart was shouting.

Brom agreed. "They are the real enemy, those foreigners. They don't belong here. Drive her out."

"She's a witch!" cried Tante Gertje. "She tried to poison my daughter."

"She's a spy!" Cousin Dan screamed. In the short silence that followed, I looked at Hulda. She didn't understand every word, but she knew that people were turning against her.

"A spy?" asked Joseph Youngs.

"A Tory spy, just like that turncoat Underhill," Dan declared. He folded his arms across his chest.

Brom shouted, "Small wonder she's lurking round here today. She's trying to learn how we're going to fight the English tyrants so she can tell her chum King George."

Mama's mouth was ajar. For a moment I took pleasure in her certain distress that her most-favoured child was leading the verbal assault on the British.

Hulda turned to the dominie and opened her arms in a pleading gesture. I thought she was asking for his help.

Dominie Ritzema cleared his throat. "Does this *vrouw* belong here?" he asked. He added something in Dutch that I thought meant, "Is she a member of this church?"

Several people shouted, "No!"

The dominie looked about nervously. He coughed again.

"Yea, Lord, get Satan behind us," Tante Gertje called out.

"Since God is for us, surely he's against whoever is against us," Brom added.

Dan had broken off a branch from a sapling at the edge of the graveyard. He came up behind Hulda as someone threw a rock. The rock struck Hulda on her shoulder just as Dan hit her with the branch.

Hulda staggered but she didn't fall. Dan hit her again, and several others threw rocks. Hulda began to make her way through the tombstones, shielding her head with her arm. The young men followed her. I realized that I'd stood up to watch and so had Mama.

Brom shoved her roughly. Hulda stumbled and went down behind a red sandstone grave marker. Brom and Dan and a few others closed in on her. They were circling like wolves round a wounded doe, I thought.

"She's bleeding!" someone shouted.

I leaned forward. Mama gripped my arm.

Hulda struggled to her feet. A dark stain was creeping across her bonnet. She gripped the tombstone to steady herself and Dan struck her hands with the branch. He shouted something about disturbing the dead.

Hulda fumbled for her pocket, the one with all the colours, and used it to wipe her bloody brow. Her body heaved with the effort to breathe. She was moving toward the hollow and I thought that she was trying to find her way home.

What if Brom and the others followed her? What if they killed her? I took a small step forward and once more felt Mama pull me back.

But Hulda didn't go toward the hollow. She turned toward the tree where Mama and I were watching. I could feel myself go hot and cold at the same time.

"Go the other way! That's the way to your home," I wanted to tell her.

She kept tottering in my direction. The blows to her head must have made her dizzy. Her eyes were glazed with pain. I was thankful that she didn't see me, and at once I felt a flush of shame.

Hulda was about ten paces away when she stopped. She started to reel backwards. Mama's hand closed like a vise round my arm. "Sarah!" she hissed.

It seemed as if Hulda stood there forever, swaying and nearly toppling over. Her bonnet had come off and hung loosely round her neck. Her light brown hair was matted and black with blood. There was a raised red mark on her cheek where a rock must have hit her. Scarlet spatters dotted her dingy grey gown.

Then, I don't know how, Hulda stopped teetering. She stood straight. She looked right at me. She was pleading with me to help her. She didn't say a word but I knew that was what she meant. She was asking me to come forward and take her arm to steady her. That was all.

I looked at the ground.

– Chapter Fourteen –

The only sounds were the wagon wheels creaking and Pegasus clip-clopping as he pulled us home. No one spoke. We all were lost in our "studies," as Mama called pensive humours.

It took me little time, of course, to lay the blame at the toes of Mama's silk slippers. If Mama hadn't been there, surely I would have gone to Hulda's aid. Why didn't Mama keep her nose in her book, as she always did? Why did she pick today to interest herself in the go-ings-on? Why did she even trouble to go to church, for that matter? She didn't follow the service. She could stay home to read her Bible; in fact, she should heed its very words about aiding the downtrod-den. She certainly didn't stop Brom when he was attacking Hulda. Then why did she keep me from helping her? Mama was just the sort of Pharisee that the Lord denounced, I concluded with no small dose of satisfaction.

Truly, though, it was Brom's fault, as well. He'd stirred up the crowd against Hulda. He'd even pushed her down! That was only because that Mr Underhill had spoken to Mama. Brom had to let people know he wasn't a Tory like Mama. Brom was a selfish fool.

And Tom... the worst was Tom. He'd come up to me right by the tombstone that was smeared with Hulda's blood.

"Sarah," he said, and for an instant I'd thought he was going to say he was sorry we'd not gone walking. "That crazy woman. You don't know her, do you?"

The winged face on the tombstone averted its stony eyes from the bloodstains. I stared at the epitaph:

My cares are past
My bones at rest
GOD took my life
When he thought best.

I hoped God would take me at that very instant. If I were dead and buried, nobody could bedevil me, and everybody would be inconsolable. Tom would never love anybody else. He would be a bachelor all his days.

"Do you know her? That witch?" Tom asked again. "She went over to you. Seemed she was going to say something. I thought you knew her."

I shook my head. I hoped Tom didn't see that I was crying.

Brom broke the silence. "I'm going to join the militia," he said.

"You may put that notion out of your head," Papa snapped.

Mama said, "Brom, you are far too young to consider such a thing."

"I am old enough to know my rights and to fight for them," Brom shouted. "I'm not one of your babies who died."

His words hung over us like a shroud. No one spoke.

You might have counted four Van Tassel children in the wagon that day. There were three more. Susannah was born a year before Brom and James a scant two years after me. A third baby, a boy, left this world quite as soon as he'd entered it.

I'd been six when that little one was born. I remembered the hushed comings and goings of the women who cared for Mama, and

I remembered *Tante* Gertje saying that a skinny English sapling such as Mama would never bear robust fruit.

Papa reined in so hard that Pegasus whinnied in protest. He turned to Brom. "Get out of this wagon."

"I meant only..."

"Go!" Papa ordered. "You will have time to think on what you meant. Do not come home until you tell your mother you are sorry."

"I have new shoes."

"Then your blisters will remind you of how you have hurt your poor mother. Now go before I myself throw you into the road."

As Brom slid down from the wagon, I could see tears in his eyes.

Papa jerked the reins and we started off again. "Perhaps that young zot should join the militia. If the British get hold of him, they'll coddle him far less than we do."

Mama always sprang to Brom's defence, no matter how outrageously he'd behaved. She said, "I think Brom believes that he must prove himself to the other young men, and certainly to Laney. He's quite smitten with her, you know."

"He'll prove himself to be a *zot* if he keeps on with this militia nonsense."

I said, "William Dutcher raised a militia and it came to nothing. After a day or two, the men went home to tend to their farms."

Papa answered, "Things are more serious now, *Puffertje*. Those who meddle where they should not..."

"Like your cousin Jacob," Mama put in. "Shooting on His Majesty's ship! I can't think what possessed him."

"Hmmmmph," Papa said. I was sure he agreed with Mama but he couldn't criticize his kin.

She said, "The ones who truly suffer are his family. What will they do without shelter or food?"

"*Oom* Willem's family has taken them in," I told her. "*Tante* Gertje said the British *zwijn*..."

"The what?" Mama asked.

"The swine. *Tante* Gertje said that the British swine..."

Papa said, "*Genoeg*. We don't need another rebel in the family."

Pegasus came to a stop by the front door. He bowed his head and found a tuft of grass. Papa got down and Thomas jumped off the wagon, raising a small cloud of dust.

"Stay out of the barn," Papa called after him. "Take the little one inside, *Puffertje*." There was something he wanted to say to Mama.

I laid Elizabeth in her cradle and pushed it closer to the window where I could hear them.

Papa said, "I know that you were taught to read books in heathen tongues. You have filled your head with useless ideas from those books. I did not complain when you taught our children in the same way. It is time for this to stop."

Mama said something I didn't hear.

"Do not say again that you will send off my son to a rebel school like that Yale College where the *idioot* English teach their sons to read books that urge them to destroy their very own order of things." Papa paused. "You English sing of the world turned upside down," he said. "Just so. You yourselves have turned it."

Mama replied crisply, "May I remind you, Peter, that you yourself were a rebel once. We both were. In a very serious matter indeed."

The instant I could escape the house, I ran – and indeed, I did run, heedless of my new station as a young lady -- down to Hudson's River. I sank gratefully onto my rock and sought to regain my breath and my composure. It was hard to run with my body trussed up in stays.

The old locust on the riverbank bent its branches round my

shoulders and the leaves whispered soothingly. The river washed gently against the great grey stone. A robin on a low branch tried to jolly me into a better humour. "Cheery cheery cheery!" he called.

Years ago, on pleasant afternoons, Mama would bring Brom and me to this very place. She told us of pixies that played in the tiny pools left in rocky crevices as the tide went out. The three of us hadn't come here since Thomas was born. Mama had a dreadful time giving birth to him. Our circumstances changed after that.

I was the only one of us who continued to visit the rock. It had long since become my place, and mine only. I went there to find solitude, of course, but that day I was also longing for the days when the world rolled round on course. Why, that summer it wobbled so that I was altogether queasy.

I gazed across the river to the wrinkled red cliffs north of Nyack. There was Hook Mountain. At its foot there appeared to be a curved point of land jutting out into the river. Oom Jan, Papa's brother who sailed a market sloop, said there was no real hook at all. It just looked that way. The times I'd been out on his boat, the hook appeared as we moved over the water toward Nyack and disappeared as we turned to sail back home.

I scooted forward so I could look downriver at Kidd's Rock. Boats used the hulking grey boulder as a mark to turn in to Philipse's Mill. Papa said it was called Kidd's Rock because the first Lord Philipse, a Dutchman, used to row out there to do business with the pirate Captain Kidd.

I strove mightily to banish from my mind the image of Hulda, bloody and beaten. But the truth pricked me like a pin: I had shrunk from Hulda because she looked utterly dreadful, bruised and battered with her gown smeared with blood. Why did she come over to stand in front of me, so I couldn't help but see her? Why couldn't she have just gone home? Then I could visit her by myself as I'd done already. I could be her secret friend. It was too hard the other way round, with everybody knowing about it.

"I thought you'd be here." Brom sat down next to me.

I looked out at the river and pursed my lips as Mama did when she was vexed. If I said nothing, perhaps he would go away.

"I can't remain a prisoner of tyrants!" Brom exclaimed.

I was not disposed to hear one more time how Mama and Papa oppressed Brom. "If you join the militia and the British catch you, you'll find out what it's like to be a prisoner of tyrants," I told him.

"You're taking Mama and Papa's part. They don't understand."

"Mama understands that you have to prove yourself to Laney and your friends."

Brom jumped to his feet. "Is that what they think this is about? Proving myself to Laney?"

I asked, "What are you going to do now?"

"What should I do?"

"Go home and apologize."

"*Apologize*? Apologize for what?" Brom was as scandalized as if I'd suggested that he become a British grenadier.

"For talking about our brothers and sister who died. You know that upsets Mama."

"That's another reason I can't go home," Brom declared, ignoring the fact that Papa had forbidden him. "The blatant hypocrisy. The babies who died. Mama uses them as an excuse whenever she wants to keep me from living in my own way."

Brom sat down again and wiped a spatter of mud from his shoe. He said, "When you do a thing you know isn't right, you're being a coward. Like you, Sarah. Apologizing to Grandmother Seabury for speaking up after she insulted us."

The setting sun was an orange arc behind Hook Mountain. At the solstice, a few weeks past, it had set hard behind the hook. Now it was slipping south. One December afternoon the sun would set south of Nyack Village, and we'd wonder how it could have moved all that way without our noticing. I supposed that was how I'd become a coward – by degrees so small I hadn't seen them.

I got to my feet and stepped carefully across the rock down to the river. The falling tide had left a half-dozen pixie pools.

Brom stepped out on the rock behind me. He found a pebble and tossed it in the water. He said, "Don't worry about me. I have a place to stay."

"With Dan?" I tried to concentrate on what he was saying.

"At the mill with Elijah."

"Are you going to work helping Ceaser and Dimond, too?"

"Elijah has bigger ideas." Brom flung another pebble.

"I heard something about his wanting to put to sea. You're not going to put to sea, are you? What about joining the militia?"

"I could do both," he said mysteriously.

"How would you get past the British fleet?"

"Elijah knows of plans."

"How does he know of plans? All those ships are way down in New York Harbour."

"Not all the ships."

"You mean *Phoenix* and *Rose*? They're upriver now."

Brom scanned the horizon. "If they go upriver, Sarah, they'll have to come back down. When they do, we'll be waiting for them."

The sun was gone and the cliffs were in shadow. The wind was rising as it always did just after sunset. Winking fireflies swarmed round us.

"Tide's turned," Brom said.

I remembered: when the tide had gone out as far as it could, when it had drifted past Manhattan Island and out into the ocean as far as it could, indeed it did turn. It began to come back in.

It was rising now. Ripples so small you could barely see them were gliding upriver. By the time the moon rose in the eastern sky over Kykuit's leafy dome, the pixie pools would be underwater.

– Chapter Fifteen –

Moonlight through the shutters on my bedchamber window drew black bars across the slanting walls. The white-faced barn owl was on his nightly hunt. "Whooooo looks for youuuuu?" he taunted the field mice. I fluffed my pillow-bears and pulled my feather coverlet over my head. I thought of Hulda.

That occasion I visited her home, I'd gone because Mama had forbidden me and Rachel had dared me. But that was not the whole of it.

Something had drawn me to Hulda. I didn't think anybody else – at least anybody I knew – had seen it. But once I had seen it, I couldn't go back and pretend I hadn't. Like Grandmother Seabury's handkerchief or Rachel's eyes, it would change forever the way I thought of her.

When Hulda smiled, merry little lines appeared in the corner of her eyes. The years of hardship and weariness vanished and she shone with joy and goodness. Hulda, odd and rude and decidedly unfortunate, was altogether winsome when she smiled.

At that instant, I, Sarah Seabury Van Tassel, resolved to redeem Hulda in the eyes of the people of Tarrytown. I myself would transform her from "pariah," a word I'd learned long ago in a spelling lesson, to "paragon," another word that sounded mythological.

"Indeed, I know her," I'd declare if someone asked, and I would add, "She's a kind, good woman and we are friends."

I wouldn't steal away to her home. I'd just go, and if Mama should ask me where I was off to, I wouldn't weasel my way out with vague half-truths. Once Mama realized that I was right, she'd admire my pluck. She'd see that I was indeed thinking and acting for myself, as she always preached. Why, she might invite Hulda to take tea with us.

I'd convince Jemima to thank Hulda for making the marigold tea for her measles. I wouldn't take any pains to change Rachel's opinion. Likely, I wouldn't have to. Once Rachel realized that everybody else viewed Hulda favourably, she'd keep her opinions to herself. But when did Rachel ever do that? Well, she'd be alone. No one would pay her any mind.

I couldn't just appear at Hulda's cottage, though. I couldn't pretend I hadn't been at the church. She'd seen me. I needed to tell her I was sorry that I saw her being beaten and didn't move to help her. No, that would be entirely awkward. Maybe she hadn't seen me. No, I was sure she had. I would have to bring a gift, something I truly treasured.

"You must have this."

I took my prism from my pocket and tried to dismiss the anguish I felt at parting with my dearest possession. If I gave Hulda my prism, she might forgive me. That was the price of my cowardice.

"It's magic," I said. "Now, see." I held the prism to the dim light. "You turn the glass like so."

We were sitting on the rough wooden bench by the wall of Hulda's home. Her head was bound with a white cloth. There was a yellow stain where the wound had been. Ragged tufts of hair stuck out and I thought that she might have chopped some off so that she could treat her wound. She was wearing the gown she'd worn Sunday. She'd washed it but I could see the brown outlines of bloodstains on the roughly woven grey cloth.

Hulda winced in pain as she raised her arm to take the prism. She said, "You think *der Glas* make better... me?"

"Yes."

"You think I keep *der Glas*?"

"Y-yes." I hoped she'd not noted my quavering reply.

"Glass not mine."

"I'm giving it to you. My papa bought it for me. It was on a market sloop."

"You have now," she pointed out. She raised her shoulders and extended her hands in a gesture of questioning. "Who have before?"

"I-I don't know. It was on a market sloop," I repeated.

"That one still have?"

"Why, no," I said. "Now it's mine. And I'm going to give it..."

"No thing only for one," she said. She set it on the bench between us. "Now I make better. You help." Hulda pushed herself to her feet. "The leaves."

I put the prism back in my pocket, not entirely with regret, if truth be told. Hulda pointed to her basket and to the stout oak stick in the corner that was nearly as tall as she was. She hobbled through the open door. I tried to take her arm but she pushed me away.

"What leaves are we looking for?" I asked as we started down the hill.

Hulda didn't answer. She planted her stick a small distance before her, and then stepped carefully down to it. I could see the beads of sweat on her brow. She eased herself onto a boulder by the stream and watched the water tumble over the rocks.

"Are you thirsty? I could fetch..."

"*Nein.*"

She was clearly not happy to have me with her, but I couldn't leave her here. She could never get back to her home. I sat on a smaller rock and set the basket beside me. "You said at the church that soldiers would come. Are they going to come here?"

Hulda studied the water. "The soldiers here."

"Are they here now?"

"*Ja, Liebchen.*"

I looked about. If soldiers were hiding among the rocks their scarlet coats would surely give them away.

Hulda was enjoying my puzzlement. "You do not see the soldiers." She cupped her hands round her mouth and uttered a loud cry.

A faint "Aaaugh!" came back through the trees.

"The soldiers!" Hulda said triumphantly.

"Not real soldiers," I said. "Magic. How did the soldiers come to be here?"

"There is the old man, the *magic* man."

"Is he Dutch?" I couldn't picture a Dutchman being a magic man, but maybe he was a *spook*. Papa had talked of such.

"*Nein*. His home here." She pointed to a sunny meadow across the stream.

"Is he an Indian?"

Hulda nodded. "He sees..." She tapped her cheekbone. "...Like the hunting bird. One day he sees the soldiers."

"British soldiers?"

"Indian soldiers."

"Indian soldiers are called 'warriors,'" I told her.

Hulda was not at all ruffled by the correction. "These soldiers..." She 'walked' her fingers across her lap and said, "Shh."

"They crept up to attack the old man's village," I translated.

"*Ja*, but the old man sees them. He..." She wiggled her fingers. "He makes the magic. The soldiers come. They go asleep."

"Oh, and they're still sleeping!" I exclaimed. I'd read enough ancient myths to know how echoes worked. "When you shout, you wake them up and you startle them. You don't hear your own voice calling back, but the warriors' cries."

Hulda laughed. Then she flinched. Laughing had caused her side to hurt.

I asked her, "People say in this place there are many *spooks* – ghosts, spirits. How did you come to live here?"

Hulda heaved herself to her feet with great effort. "The leaves now," she said.

I picked up the basket. "What leaves do you need?"

She pointed to the meadow where the old Indian had lived. She planted her stick on the bank and extended a foot over the water.

I cried, "No! Tell me about the leaves and I will fetch them for you." Hulda didn't protest as I helped her to settle herself on the rock once more.

"The leaves in the grass," she said, panting. "They grow first in sun, then in shade."

I looked across the brook at the meadow. "There's a maple tree. Would the leaves grow under the tree?"

"You must look, *Liebchen*."

"Are they big leaves? Plants?"

"Big like so." She spread her fingers wide.

"A vine! Does it have flowers?" I was keen to see this plant.

"The flowers like so." Hulda put her first finger on her thumb to indicate something very small indeed. "The white flowers. The leaves small."

"Is this plant hard to find?"

"*Nein*. It is all round."

I held the basket on one arm as I stepped from rock to rock across the river, and I studied the ground as I walked through the meadow. I wondered if Hulda meant to test me with a riddle: A plant that grew along the ground, not up. A big plant with tiny flowers and leaves. A plant that grew everywhere.

"Do you mean chickweed?" I pulled up a bunch and shook the soil from the roots.

She nodded, so I gathered a dozen bunches more and put them in the basket. Then I made my way back across the brook.

"People say chickweed is horrid. It takes water that good plants need. It grows everywhere, even in the barnyard. That's where chickens eat it."

Hulda seemed offended. "It has the use. Many use. Now I make the..." She rubbed her fingers together.

"A poultice?

"The poll-tise, *ja*. For the hurts."

She made her unsteady way back up the hill and I followed with the basket.

"Do you want me to draw water?" I asked, as we passed the spring. "You can't carry a big, heavy pail..."

I glanced down. There, in the soft earth round the spring, was the print of a foot, a bare human foot. I judged it to be that of a man, for it was large in size.

Hulda knew that I had seen the footprint. "I have the water," she said.

- Chapter Sixteen -

The pigs were jostling each other to be first at the trough. The cleverest ones knew I was bringing them their evening meal of table scraps. As they pushed their long pink snouts into my bucket, they muddied my skirts.

"Shoo!"

The pigs were undaunted. I kicked at them and lost one of the pattens I'd strapped to my shoes to keep them out of the mud.

"You'll all be turned to hams by St. Martin's Day," I scolded them.

"*Puffertje*, do you need help?"

"I'm done, Papa."

"I'm done, too," Thomas said grandly, adjusting his crown. He was grinning so broadly that I could see two new teeth cutting through his gums.

Papa took off his hat and wiped his brow. "Run and find your Mama, *Olykoek*. I must talk to your sister."

I latched the pigpen gate behind me, Papa fetched pails and the milking stool and we went out to the pasture. Milky the cat trotted after us. She watched as Papa set a bucket under Anke.

"You have been gone during the days, *Puffertje*."

Was Papa going to question me about Hulda? I felt a small, nervous jolt under my ribs. Of course, I'd vowed to speak up for Hulda but I hadn't expected the occasion to arrive so soon.

Papa looked up at me. The corners of his eyes had crinkles like Hulda's.

"Your mama says you have been at that place." He pointed in the direction of my rock by Hudson's River."

I breathed easily once more. He wasn't going to ask about Hulda.

Brom had been gone for nearly a fortnight, yet Verkenner was the only one who behaved as if something was amiss. His long hound face drooped to the ground. He sniffed about and I knew that he was trying to find a scent of Brom. Brom's chair had been moved into the corner and we didn't mention him.

I told Papa, "Brom is at the mill."

"The mill? For what is he there?"

I was tempted to remind him that he'd sent Brom away. "I suppose he's with Elijah," I said.

"That young *zot* who wants to put to sea?" Papa was suspicious of people who preferred water to land. He finished milking Anke and we went in search of Beletje. Milky followed us.

Papa said, "It is *zonderling*."

I wondered if he meant how strange it was that Brom had taken up dwelling in the gristmill, or how strange our household was with him gone.

We were at the edge of the pasture. Hudson's River was spread before us like the train of a lady's blue silk gown. It was the hour when the setting sun made a glittering path across the river and the sky was gold and pink and purple. I closed my eyes to fix the scene in my mind. I wanted to see it forever.

"This land is *zonderling*, too, Papa," I told him. "See those cliffs by Hook Mountain? They look as if someone had taken an enormous knife and sliced them as you'd cut a loaf of bread. The top with the trees is the crust and..."

Papa laughed. "You are like your Mama, *Puffertje*," he said. "You see what cannot be seen."

I thought of Hulda and the Indian soldiers. "Perhaps this land is full of such curiosities. Is Holland like this?"

Papa looked puzzled. "Our family has lived here since the days of Peter Stuyvesant. Not one of us has gone back."

"Mama went to Holland once. She sailed to Europe with her father on one of his ships."

"Do not think that I will take you on a ship."

I looked out at the river again. "Papa, what do you think that the first Dutchman thought when he saw this land?"

Papa's gaze travelled to Beletje. "He thought that this land would give good grass for cows to graze on. He thought his *vrouw* could make fine cheese from that cow's milk." He turned to me. "Your brother must come home. It is time to bring in the wheat."

The old wooden mill was dark inside, even though the shutters were open and sunlight danced on the Pocantico River. The great grooved stones that ground the grain were still.

Ceaser the miller came to greet me, "Missy Sarah!" he said, beaming.

Ceaser was wearing his white apron and his hair was covered with a white cap. Other times, he'd been so covered with flour dust from the milling that his deep brown skin looked grey. There was no dust on him that day. There were no sloops at the dock behind the mill, and no farmers' wagons with loads of grain.

"Where is your papa?" Ceaser asked.

"I came alone," I told him.

Straightaway Ceaser recognized the purpose of my visit. "Your brother is not here. All have gone to White Plains."

"White Plains! He's not..."

"No, no," said Ceaser. He searched in his pocket and produced a sweetmeat. "Brom will not join the soldiers, although there is much talk of such. He has gone to fetch some paper to read. He said it was of great importance."

I decided that although I was a young lady, too old for the candies that Ceaser dispensed to all children, I could take one this time. I thanked him.

"You are not busy today, Ceaser," I said after I'd finished the sweet.

"Always I am busy," he answered and I was sure that was true. Ceaser was a slave, but Lord Philipse had entrusted him with the manor's main business. Ceaser oversaw the mill and dock and he kept the ledgers. He spoke English to me, but he conversed in Dutch with Papa, and I'd heard him say words in French to Amy's father. All his words were spoken in musical African tones.

"Is the mill often this quiet?" I asked.

Ceaser was sweeping the floor, although it was already clean. "It is like this most times now."

"Have the British warships stopped the market sloops from sailing?"

"The British must eat, too," Ceaser said.

I wondered if Ceaser favoured the Tories because he worked for Lord Philipse. Papa worked for him, too, but Ceaser was Lord Philipse's property. Lord Philipse could sell him and send him away at any moment. Of course, Lord Philipse would be without a very able miller, and Lord Philipse was now in jail. I wondered if Ceaser knew that.

I looked out the window. Nobody was riding up the Post Road, but a sloop was drifting up the Pocantico River. The boatman was behind the sail, but I recognized *Oom* Jan's sloop, *Zomer Wind*. I hurried down to the pier.

Zomer Wind's yellowed sail slid down the mast and *Oom* Jan's blond head appeared as he gathered in the canvas. He coiled a stout rope and tossed it to me.

I tried to remember how he showed me to wind the rope, no, the line, fast round the big wood pillar, the piling, at the pier. "Around and over and through," he told me, and jumped off the boat as she glided to a stop. "Good work, mate," he said, giving me a hug.

Of Papa's four brothers and three sisters, *Oom* Jan was my favourite. He was the youngest. If you'd stood him next to Papa, you'd know that they were brothers, but *Oom* Jan's nose was sharper and he was a bit leaner. He was married to *Tante* Margaret, who was very pretty and sweet and had hair so red *Tante* Gertje said it must be the mark of the Devil.

Oom Jan looked about. "Where's that Elijah fellow?" he asked. "And where's your big brother, for that matter?"

Ceaser had come onto the dock and he answered for me. "They have gone to White Plains. They will be back." He leaned over to look into the boat. "You have little cargo coming from New York Town," he said.

Oom Jan hoisted a wooden barrel and set it on the dock. "This rum for Storm's Tavern is about the whole of it."

I asked, "Are *Phoenix* and *Rose* harassing market boats?"

He answered, "*Phoenix* and *Rose* are in Haverstraw Bay, Sarah. Our militia is firing on them whenever they get close to shore, so they don't have time to bother us little fellows." He gave *Zomer Wind* an affectionate pat. "Don't you fret, *Zomer*," he told the sloop. "You're as valiant a girl as those fat British hussies."

Ceaser pointed out, "There are many more British ships in New York Town. Did they try to stop you?"

"In truth, it's General Washington who's trying to stop boats. He's set on keeping the British fleet from sailing upriver. He has a contrivance called a "shivers de freeze.""

"Does it make them cold?" I asked.

Oom Jan laughed again. "I suspect you'd get the shivers and freeze if you found your ship sinking."

Ceaser and I looked puzzled, so he continued. "General Washington is nailing old ships together with logs that have iron spikes on them. Then he sinks them. He hopes that the British ships will plow into those spikes and be caught like fish on a hook. Then we can finish them off with cannons from shore."

Oom Jan's eyes turned hard as flint. "River's full of tricks," he said.

– Chapter Seventeen –

Brom had collected a goodly following on his way back from White Plains. Dan and Rachel were in the wagon with him. So were Samuel Youngs, James Romer and Amy and her brother Gabriel. I suspected that Storm's Tavern had emptied and that its patrons had followed on foot, for there were Isaac Martling and a few fellows I didn't recognize. Brom brought the wagon to a halt in the yard between the mill and Lord Philipse's house, and the others stepped down.

"Which one is Elijah?" I asked Rachel.

She looked about. "I don't see him, but there's Tom Buckhout. Laney didn't come with us, so maybe he'll pay some mind to you."

Brom stood in the wagon. "This is it, my friends," he announced. "It's our Declaration of Independence."

"Read it!" several people urged.

Brom unrolled the document and cleared his throat. "*When in the Course of human events, it becomes necessary for one people to dissolve the political bands...*"

Rachel whispered something, but I moved away from her.

"*We hold these truths to be self-evident, that all men are created equal, that they are endowed by their Creator with certain unalienable Rights...*"

Rachel pulled at my sleeve. "What kind of rights?"

"*...Life, Liberty and the pursuit of Happiness.*"

Everybody had a right to life, liberty and happiness. Once, when I was but a tot, the earth had trembled and the glass windows in our house had shaken. I will vouch that it trembled again at the very moment Brom spoke those words.

Brom was reading a list of terrible things that King George had done.

"For imposing Taxes on us without our Consent... waging War against us..."

Each new outrage was greeted with cries of agreement.

"He has plundered our seas, ravaged our Coasts, burnt our towns, and destroyed the lives of our people."

King George must be truly dreadful! I wondered if Mama knew how horribly her monarch had treated us.

"We, therefore, the Representatives of the united States of America, do... solemnly publish and declare, That these United Colonies are, and of Right ought to be Free and Independent States..."

We were free. We were our own country, just like Britain or France. Nobody could tell us what to do any more. It sounded entirely appealing.

Samuel stepped up on the wagon and took the Declaration of Independence from Brom. His eyes behind his spectacles shone with a new light.

"Our Lives, our Fortunes and our sacred Honor." Samuel read the words slowly to let us feel their weight. He said, "We must pledge our Lives, our Fortunes and our sacred Honor as these great patriots have done."

All cheered.

Isaac Martling tried to climb up on the wagon and Brom took his arm to steady him. This was what our new country would be like, I thought. Everybody would help each other.

"Let us raise a cup to liberty!" Isaac cried. He had long ago discovered, I am sure, that proposing a toast provided an opportunity to drink one.

"What shall we drink?" Samuel asked.

"There! On the dock. There's a barrel of rum," shouted Dan.

The men and boys streamed down to the pier. I ran after them.

"That's my uncle's rum," I cried. "He's to sell it to Storm's Tavern."

Isaac guffawed. "Why, we'll save him the trouble of hauling it up the hill, then. We'll drink it here. Who has an axe?"

Samuel found an axe and a wooden scoop inside the mill. Gabriel seized the axe and sank it into the barrel's lid. Brom tried to tear away the splintered wood to get to the rum. As the men and boys thronged round the barrel, shoving and grunting, they called to my mind pigs at a trough. They were quite as mannerly.

"That barrel belongs to my *Oom* Jan," I shouted but no one heard me.

Isaac had never been steady on his feet, an affliction caused more by his taste for spirits than by his missing arm, I always thought. "Let us drink to General Washington!" he shouted. He swallowed a handful of rum.

"To Thomas Jefferson and the patriots in Philadelphia!" James dipped into the barrel as everyone cheered.

I suspected that each of those patriots – John Adams, James Madison, John Hancock, Ben Franklin – would be toasted in turn. I was astonished, then, to hear Brom's salute.

"To Lord Philipse!" he cried.

Although the rum had muddled his companions' reasoning, they seemed to discern that Lord Philipse was not of the same stripe as General Washington. There was a puzzled silence.

"For leaving his property and possessions to us!" Brom shouted. He waved his arm grandly. "All this is ours now."

Everyone brayed approval and crowded closer to the rum barrel.

I made a last try. "My uncle paid for this rum. You're stealing it. From him, not Lord Philipse."

Dan had drunk liberally from the barrel, but he still heard me.

"Run to your friend the witch. Get her to make it disappear."

"We're making the rum disappear quite by ourselves," Samuel observed.

Dan wrested the scoop from Samuel's hand and dipped it into the barrel. As he tilted back his head to pour the rum down his throat, he lost his footing and splashed into the river.

Gabriel cried, "Dan's lost the measure! Now we need drink from the barrel." He came away with rum dripping from his hair. Isaac pretended to lick his face.

Dan floundered in the water, shouting for rescue. I took wicked pleasure that no one hastened to aid him.

"Need a cup," Brom said. "Where's a cup?" His eye fell upon me. "Why're you here, Sarah? Go home." His words were curdled as a potted cheese. He stumbled after me into the mill.

I said, "Papa sent me to fetch you. You're to come home at once."

At first, I thought he'd not heard me. But he said, "This is home. I'm free. Need a cup, Ceaser." Brom spied a tin vessel on a shelf. As he reached for it, a clay jar fell and shattered.

"Mind you, take care, Brom," Ceaser admonished him. "This is Lord Philipse's..."

"No, no," Brom assured him. "This... all ours now." He waved his arms in a gesture I knew usually preceded a speech, but his mouth seemed utterly at odds with his reasoning.

He said, "Lord Philipse is gone. For good and all. We were slaves like you and now we're free. You too, Ceaser... you're free now. Amy!" Brom spied her in the mill yard and made for the door.

Ceaser shook his head. "Saying you are free does not make it so," he said.

Inside the mill, the air hung heavily as wet linens pinned upon a line. I found a shaded bench outside.

"Looking for you, Sarah."

It was Tom. I'd quite forgot he was there. He sat down beside me and stretched out his legs. We both looked at his scuffed black shoes. The pewter buckle on the left shoe was about to come off, but I didn't think I should point it out. I would sound like a scold.

This was the closest I'd ever been to Tom, even closer than at church. He must not think I was a witch or a terrible Tory, after all. But that was because he'd likely been drinking the rum.

He broke the silence. "Good to be free."

I nodded vigorously. "Oh, yes!" Amy said that boys liked girls who agreed with them. Perhaps I should ask him a question. Boys liked to show off how much they knew.

"How is it different now that you're free?" I asked him.

Tom turned the talk with a nimbleness of mind I'd not suspected. "You're free, too," he said.

"No, I'm not," I retorted, dismissing Amy's admonition that men shunned quarrelsome females. I continued, "The Declaration of Independence said all men have the right to Life, Liberty and something else. Oh, yes, the pursuit of Happiness. It didn't say anything about women and girls."

I added, "It said all *men* are created equal. Not women. And it said all men are *created* equal. You might be born equal, but not everybody turns out that way."

From the corner of my eye, I saw Ceaser favour me with an approving grin.

Tom's face flushed, whether from the rum or from annoyance that I was behaving like a harridan, I didn't know. He shifted his weight on the bench, and we both studied his shoes again.

How could I blabber so? A long-ago remark from Amy came to my mind. "*Tu penses de trop*, Sarah," she'd said. I thought too much. My hands were clammy and I tried to dry them on my skirts without being noticed.

Tom took my hand, just after I'd managed to dry it. He asked, "Sarah, can I kiss you?"

Now, I was altogether alarmed and bewildered, as well. If I said no, he would never ask me again. On the other hand, I couldn't say yes. That would make me a loose woman, the kind who didn't wear stays. Mama had warned me about that.

Tom spared me from having to reply. He pulled me closer and put his arm round my back. He drew me to him and planted a kiss on... my forehead.

I had ducked. It was terrible. Amy had once made Rachel and Jemima and me practice kissing our hands so we'd know what to do when a boy actually tried to kiss us. I would never overcome this blunder. I would be an old maid like Aunt Charlotte because nobody would ever want to kiss me again. Certainly not Tom. He was older than I. He must have had some practice kissing.

Tom tilted my chin up and tried again. This time our lips connected. Amy said that how long a kiss was revealed how much a boy liked you, but I forgot to count. Tom's whisker stuck into my cheek, and he tasted of rum.

Tom and I regarded each other shyly. Maybe we were supposed to kiss again but it would have been dreadfully brazen for me to suggest it. As Tom put his arm round me, Samuel burst through the mill door, his hair mussed and his spectacles askew. Just then, I heard the sound of rocks hitting rock and then the shattering of glass. Someone was throwing stones at Lord Philipse's house. There were cries of triumph as windows were broken.

Dan appeared, brandishing an axe. His eye fell on a wooden bench like the one Tom and I were seated upon. Dan raised the axe and laid a mighty blow upon the offending bench. It jumped as it split apart and Dan crowed as triumphantly as if he'd dispatched a redcoat. He ran round the corner of the mill, and I heard more splintering of wood.

It came to my mind that I didn't see Brom. Then I heard James Romer.

"Why, those are piddling efforts, throwing rock and chopping benches," he chided Dan and the others. "We need attack the royalists where they'll truly suffer – in the purse. Let us take down the mill!"

Ceaser hurried by, muttering, "This freedom has gone to their heads with the rum."

Dan ran after him, waving the axe in an altogether savage manner. "Take down the mill!" he yelled. "We'll turn it to kindling for a freedom fire."

I realized that I'd got up to watch and so had Tom. Dan sank the axe into the side of the mill. The sturdy old boards barely budged. Dan looked round.

"The mill wheel!" Samuel cried. "Why, without it the mill is useless." He ran inside, intending to climb to the wheel from the small wooden platform beside it, I supposed. "Give me that," he yelled, wresting the axe from Dan.

As I came round the corner, my heart quite leaped in my bosom. It wasn't Samuel on the mill wheel. It was Brom.

Brom balanced precariously on a flat wooden paddle as Samuel handed him the axe.

"Wood... slippery," he mumbled, trying to gain a sure footing. He took the axe and tried to swing it while steadying himself with his other hand. The axe fell from his hand but caught on the paddle just below where he perched.

The observers groaned.

Isaac Martling called out, "You mayn't wield an axe with one arm. I can tell you as much."

"Give me back the axe!" Dan ran into the mill. "Brom! Let me!" he cried.

"Get away, Dan! Let Brom do it!" Samuel called. Several voices offered besotted agreement.

Dan lunged at the wheel from the window, but Brom was just

out of reach. Brom balanced on one foot as he removed his shoes and stockings. I gasped as he tossed them into the river. Those were his new shoes. I couldn't guess what Papa would say when he learned what had happened.

"Better... barefoot." Brom slipped one foot between the paddles. He demonstrated his surer footing before crouching to retrieve the axe.

There was a mighty rush of water. The roar so startled me that for an instant I didn't know what had happened. A foaming tide sped into the flume from the millpond. The wheel groaned and creaked as it started to turn.

Brom wobbled and fell to his knees. His foot was caught between the paddles.

The wheel gained speed. Inside the great stones began to thunder.

"Brom! Here!" Samuel leaned from the platform and tried to seize Brom's arm.

Brom was writhing as he worked to loosen his foot. He paid no mind to Samuel. Perhaps he couldn't hear him. The wheel lurched slowly round with its prisoner held fast.

Brom clung to the paddles as they turned. His endeavours to free his foot grew feeble as he strove to hold on.

Ceaser appeared. His eyes were wide and he was shouting, "Stop the wheel!" The throng backed away from the great wooden lever. At that instant, I saw that Dan was standing hard beside it. He edged back, a bit reluctantly, I thought.

Ceaser seized the lever and he and James laboured mightily to move it. At last, the wooden gate dropped, water stopped flowing into the flume, and the wheel creaked to a stop.

Although I couldn't see Brom, I knew where he was – at the bottom of the great wheel with his foot twisted between the paddles.

He would be dead like Jost Van Vliet. People would now have two foolish boys to use as examples in their warnings to stay away from the mill wheel. I also had an altogether peculiar sensation. I felt quite as if some force were lifting from me, leaving empty space above. I would be the eldest child now. I wondered briefly if Mama would like me better.

I realized that Amy had slipped her hand into mine. "We must go down to the pier, Sarah," she was saying. "We must..." She began to sob.

I wanted to stay in that small moment left where I didn't know what had happened to Brom, when the world was still the way it would not be again. Amy pulled me toward the steps.

Samuel handed Ceaser his glasses and dove into the water. He was gone for a long moment before he rose to the surface. "Need help," he managed to blurt before diving under again.

James did not hesitate before diving in.

"Dan, he's your cousin, and you're already wet," Gabriel pointed out before jumping in himself. Dan slunk back into the mill and I had a consuming urge to throttle him.

The water was roiled because of the thrashing about underneath. Occasionally, one of the three rescuers would come up to gulp air before diving again. At length, Samuel gasped, "Almost free."

Amy gripped my hand. I realized she appeared to be more distraught than I. We leaned over the edge of the pier.

Brom's head came to the surface. His blond hair was dark because it was so wet. His white shirt billowed round his shoulders as he hung in the water. He didn't move.

"Stand back!" Ceaser was holding a rope sling, the kind that he and Dimond used to lift heavy cargo. He lowered it into the water and Samuel took hold of it. He and Gabriel toiled to lift Brom's limp arm into the sling. James spoke to Brom all the while, although I was certain Brom had been knocked senseless.

He said in a soothing manner, "Now, friend, we're going to lift you from the water. We're going to put your arm like so..."

Brom's body rolled face down. His arms dropped by his side.

"Turn him upright!" shouted Ceaser. "He'll drown if he hasn't yet..."

He saw that I was standing beside him on the pier and let the last of his words fall away unspoken.

Samuel grasped Brom round the chest and turned him once more on his back. Brom looked as I'd seen him at home in his bed. His eyes were shut, his mouth open and he sprawled in utter oblivion. I believed I saw his chest rise and fall, but perhaps it was a vision born of desperation. From somewhere in my mind I pulled out a piece of knowledge that I'd once heard: people could survive underwater for a quarter-hour. I had no notion how long Brom had been trapped beneath the mill wheel.

Gabriel and James managed to coax one arm through the harness, then the other. Samuel slipped a rope round Brom's waist and tied it fast. Ceaser and a couple of the suddenly sober revellers pulled his body toward the dock. Ceaser put his arms round Brom's torso and eased him out of the water. He disappeared inside the mill and emerged with a coverlet of cotton and a pillow-bear that I suspected might be his own. Ceaser laid the coverlet on the pier and motioned to the bystanders to lift Brom upon it. He laid Brom's head upon the pillow and folded the coverlet over him.

"We must strip him of those wet garments," Samuel said. "See, he's shivering."

Indeed, Brom was quaking like a jelly. I thought that must mean he was still alive. I could imagine how mortified Brom would feel to be displayed unclothed in front of a gathering that included his sister, not to mention Amy and other young ladies.

Talking gently, Samuel raised Brom's head and drew his arm from the wet shirt. Brom coughed. Everyone took a collective breath and drew closer. Samuel rolled Brom on his side and began to pound him on the back.

Brom's body flinched with every blow, but otherwise was still. His eyes were closed. At length Samuel stood up and shook his head. He rolled Brom over on his back. Amy was sobbing.

Brom opened his eyes, but I believed it was an unconscious act. The thought raced through my mind that dead people didn't always close their eyes.

Brom gurgled and turned his head. Water and spit leaked from his mouth onto the dock. He choked and spat more water, this time, I believed, with intention. He opened his eyes once more. The blue was shot with red veins but I thought he was trying to see. He took a breath.

"He's alive," whispered Amy. "*Merci, mon Dieu.*"

Brom groaned. For an instant I recalled someone, *Tante* Gertje, no doubt, saying that a dying person groaned at the very instant the soul departed from the body. Then Brom coughed again. He squinted at Samuel and Ceaser, who knelt beside him.

Brom uttered something that sounded like "H-h-hurt," but it could have been but a laboured breath.

I knelt beside Ceaser. "You're hurt, Brom?" I asked, although the reply was entirely obvious. "Your head? Is that what hurts?"

Brom let out another heavy breath that I believed might be his last. Then he said, "F-foot."

We turned to look. Amy screamed.

– Chapter Eighteen –

Ceaser laboured to straighten Brom's swollen, crooked foot. Later, Papa and *Oom* Willem tried to ease the bones apart and to coax them back into place. Mama fashioned a splint. All their efforts were for naught. In one foolhardy show of independence, Brom had consigned himself to a lifetime of bondage. His foot was so twisted that he would never run again. Even walking would require a crutch.

Since we were a family inclined to brood rather than to shout disagreement, not one of us made mention of it, but Brom's prospects had been irrevocably dimmed, if not extinguished altogether. As the eldest son, Brom was intended to take over our farm, to wed and sire a new generation of Van Tassels. It was altogether unlikely that any of that would happen now. Dutch maidens were never so blinded by love that they disregarded the practical. They married men who would keep them housed, fed, attired and busy with a bevy of children.

When Laney van Tassel appeared at our door a fortnight after Brom's accident, I suspect she had no inkling that she had become a sour reminder of a fruit that Brom would never pick.

Laney was accompanied by her friend Annetje Martling. This was utterly unremarkable, as Laney had seldom strayed from Annetje's plump presence even before the attack on her home by British soldiers. Now it appeared the two *meisjes* were permanently tethered.

I wondered about their friendship. Did Annetje suppose that by merely being in the company of the much-favoured Laney, she might improve her own meager prospects? It seemed unlikely, but people were given to all manner of foolish beliefs.

I was astounded to see Laney, mildly pleased to see Annetje and utterly enraged to find that Rachel had tagged along with them. Her customary self-satisfied demeanour was galling. Her eyes set in an appraising squint were altogether vexing. I was anxious to tell that her wicked brother was the very cause of Brom's ruin, but I doubted that I could pluck up my courage.

Brom was recovering on the divan in the parlour. He was cross as a bear, for he was still in much pain. He did not smile even once and offered terse replies to the girls' attempts at pleasant chatter. When Mama appeared and offered refreshments, Brom spoke up that he needed to rest and promptly turned his face to the wall.

We repaired to the sitting room. As I passed a plate of biscuits, Annetje asked, "What are these?"

"Scones," I answered. "My mama made them."

Annetje looked perplexed. No doubt she knew, as did everyone in Tarrytown, that the English were notoriously bad cooks.

"But they are moist and light." Annetje took another bite. "Laney, you must try a 'stone.' Just one. Please."

I set the plate near Laney should she change her mind. I was astonished at the change in her in the weeks since the British burned her house. Her skin was so pale I could almost see through it. Her famous blue eyes had grown while the rest of her had shrunk. Had this near kidnapping by soldiers been worse than had been told? For the first time in memory, I did not want to look like Laney van Tassel.

"All that she's eaten in a fortnight wouldn't fill one plate," Rachel whispered, just loudly enough that Laney heard. Laney offered a little grimace that I took for an apologetic smile.

I was floundering in search of what to say next when Mama appeared at the sitting room door. She appeared to be in one of her rare pleasant humours. As she was inclined to be garrulous, even giddy, on these occasions, I was wary. Thus possessed, she was sure to humiliate me even further.

"I have apples that want peeling," Mama said merrily. "Will you help me?"

Not one of us moved. It crossed my mind that the others might also be suspicious of Mama's unaccustomed affability.

"With apple peels, we can prophesy who your true love is," she persisted.

Rachel beamed as if someone has just handed her a gold piece. "Prophesy, *Tante*, I mean Aunt, Mary?" she inquired sweetly. "Why, is this sorcery?"

Mama beamed. "Most assuredly," she said. I sank straight into a bog of despondency.

Mama set us to work in the kitchen peeling a bowl of greenish-yellow Hightop Sweet apples. "Bigger apples would be more favourable, but we shall make do," she told us. "Now, try to keep the peel in one piece. That is most important."

Laney's knife slipped. "I'm so clumsy," she wailed.

Mama was distressed. "Why, my dear, don't fret so! I shall tell you the magic. Take the peel in your left hand, for it is closer to your heart. Put your hand over your head and wave it round three times."

"Is this the spell?" Laney asked.

Mama nodded. "Now, toss the peel behind you on the floor. What do you see there?"

"It looks like the letter C," I reported.

Mama asked, "Laney, do you know a young man whose name begins with C?"

Annetje cried, "Caleb! Laney loves Caleb!"

Laney blushed and I hoped that Brom hadn't heard. Rachel twirled a peel round her head and tossed it on the floor.

"Perhaps it's an I," Mama speculated.

I could hardly recall an occasion when Mama had been so congenial. She was never so with me, I thought with equal measures of annoyance and jealousy.

"What about Isaac Martling?" I asked, determined to needle both Rachel and Mama with a single jab.

There were groans and the rolling of eyes.

"Isaac Van Wart! But Annetje's sweet on him!" cried Laney. A bit of colour was in her cheeks. "Your mama's magic is fun, Sarah. Now you try."

"It could be an L," suggested Annetje, studying the floor where my peel had fallen.

"I don't know anyone named L," I said crossly. Not one thing in my life was proceeding favourably, not even a frivolous game.

"You wouldn't get a T, Sarah," Rachel pointed out. "Tom's in love with Laney."

Laney seemed truly distressed at Rachel's revelation. She hung her head and buried her hands in her skirts. She looked as if she were about to cry. "Is there more magic?" she asked, glancing at the bowl of apples.

She sounded so dismal that I yearned to comfort her. "I have a prism, Laney. It's a glass that you turn and..." I pulled the prism from my pocket and handed it to her.

Rachel cut in, "Sarah thinks it's magic, but it's not. It's just a glass that bends things so they look different."

Laney held the prism in her palm. "I'd like to look different."

In all my life I'd not been so astonished.

"It wasn't your doing!" Annetje cried.

"There's cider in the cold room. I'll fetch some," I said. Mama had gone to see how Brom was faring. Annetje followed me and watched as I mixed the cider with water and ladled it into pewter cups.

I said, "Of course Laney's grieved about her father and her house. I cannot imagine how dreadful it was to be ..." I bit off the remainder of that sentence. I wondered if the soldiers had dishonoured Laney.

Annetje glanced round before she whispered, "That is not what is dreadful. Her mother blames all their troubles on Laney."

I put down the nutmeg I was grating. "How could she do such a thing?"

Annetje took a pinch of nutmeg and sprinkled it over the cider. "Her mama said the soldiers should have taken Laney. She said that Laney's useless and that it's too bad she's not a boy."

"Is that why Laney isn't eating? Maybe she thinks she doesn't deserve to have food."

"I think it is Laney's small victory," Annetje replied. "Her *Tante* Nochie tries to get her to try just a spoonful of *suppan* or a *koekje*. The more she coaxes, the less Laney will eat."

In the sitting room, Laney inspected her cup of cider before she took a sip.

Annetje said, "I wonder what it will be like to be free of that horrible English king."

My stays were cutting into my side. I had laced them too straight that morning. I wiggled in my chair to find a more comfortable position. "I think that freedom must be a bit like taking off your stays," I said.

Annetje laughed. "Yes, it is good but at the same time strange. You miss being laced, even though you are glad you are not."

Rachel said, "Your mama wears stays because she's English. Dutch women don't wear stays." Her tone suggested Dutch women were the greater judges of fashionable dress.

"Dutch women don't wear stays because they are stout," Annetje declared. "I don't know of a woman who is not stout who doesn't wear stays."

"The witch doesn't wear stays," cried Rachel.

"The woman who came to the church?" Laney asked. "People threw stones at her."

I felt blood rising to my cheeks as my heart beat more quickly. I'd vowed to defend Hulda. Here was the very instance. I swallowed, and said, "Hulda is different from most of us. She lives as she chooses. Maybe that's what true freedom is."

Annetje asked, "Do you know that woman, Sarah?"

Mama had the ears of a fox and I suspected she was in the next room with Brom. Doubtless she would hear my answer. I took a deep breath and pressed on. "I do know Hulda," I said. "On the Sabbath that she was attacked – *unmercifully and unjustly*," I added. "She'd come to offer her aid. She wanted to help us defend ourselves from such attacks as happened to Laney's family."

Annetje's and Laney's faces softened with understanding, even approval. Rachel's remained unmoved as a gravestone.

Annetje said, "It was terrible, how she was treated."

Laney shook her head. "Oh, that poor woman! To have people wish her gone. I know what that is like. Sarah is so brave to take up for her."

"Did you visit her, Sarah?" Rachel cut in.

"Yes, I did, some days after she... after her..." I strove to describe the scene at the church without laying blame on Hulda's assailants. "She has a head wound and difficulty walking. I helped her fetch some healing plants."

Laney's remark sent my heart skipping. "We all must be like Sarah." Her eyes misted as she contemplated her charitable intentions.

"Yes, we must take up for this Hulda," Annetje agreed. She brightened, thinking of the Dutch cure for all ills. "We could take her pies and *koekjes*. No. We must invite her to our homes. She can sit with us at church. When the cold and storms come, perhaps she could take shelter with some kind family."

Annetje and Laney were seventeen, three years my elders. Their opinions would have merit. If they rallied behind Hulda, many would surely follow. A bouquet of righteousness blossomed in my bosom. I, Sarah, would save Hulda from the dreadful fate of the outcast. Henceforth, she would be accepted, eventually, even beloved. I called to mind visions of a smiling Hulda at our table as Papa said the blessing. Mama's face loomed, dark with distaste. I banished it at once.

Of course, that did not end the matter. As the girls were taking their leave, Rachel said, "I see that Sarah's under the witch's influence, too."

Annetje and Laney were astonished, and I felt quite the fool. I should have known Rachel would not be undone by a few meek words uttered in Hulda's support.

Rachel simpered. "Have you not put it straight even now, Sarah?"

That I did not know what she was speaking of did not help my cause. Rachel counted upon someone inquiring what she meant. She could then assume the semblance of a martyr, the bad tidings pried from her mouth.

"The mill wheel," she explained reluctantly. "Brom's foot was caught and he nearly died. Even now, his life is a ruin."

"What had this woman to do with the mill wheel?" Annetje asked.

Rachel favoured her with the sort of bored sigh she usually reserved for me. "Jost Van Vliet," she said.

"But how?" Annetje persisted.

Laney studied her thumbnail.

"The mill wheel," she said again. "Jost Van Vliet." Her voice tolled in funereal tones as it had on the day at her house when she accused me of raining evil down upon her mousy-brown head.

Rachel's invented sorrow galled me. She was lying in wait for a question about the witch and the mill wheel. Annetje provided it.

"Jost walked by the witch's house," Rachel explained. "Straight after, he was dragged to his death on the mill wheel. The witch knew when he was near her house, of course, and she cursed him. Unto death. Brom didn't go by her house, so his life was spared, praise the Lord."

I bristled. This narrative would soon come round to me.

"Why would the witch wish Brom harm?" Annetje asked.

"Sarah, of course. Sarah's been poking round the witch's house. She breathed in the evil air."

Laney was perplexed. "*Sarah* made the mill wheel turn?"

As Rachel shook her head in counterfeit woe, I found my voice at last.

"*Your brother* made the wheel turn, Rachel! It was Dan!" My breath came hard and I knew my face was crimson. "He was standing next to the lever when the gate opened. It was Dan who brought about Brom's accident – and it was no accident."

I supposed that Rachel would be shocked that I had at last confronted her, and struck silent by hearing the truth spoken. In fact, Rachel was little aggrieved by my accusation. As ever, she had the Holy Writ for a bludgeon: "The Lord has opened the mouth of the ass," she proclaimed, glaring at me.

"Your mouth!" I retorted. "Your brother opened the water gate and my brother ended up a cripple." I had spoken up. I was as shocked as Rachel. Blood raced through my veins like a creek swollen with melted snow.

Once more, Rachel sought rebuttal in Scripture. "Your mouth is full of cursing and deceit and fraud!" she shrilled. "Your heart is full of mean malice!"

At that instant Mama strode into the sitting room. Gone was the sweet-tempered mum of apple-peel prophecy. Hearing of injury done to her beloved son, her British blood was set to boiling. Indeed, that day Mama was a veritable Britannia, the warrior goddess who symbolised England's pride and power. Mama lacked Britannia's helmet and shield, but her eyes burned black with righteous fire and her arm, raised to point the way to the door, seemed to be brandishing Britannia's trident. She uttered not a single word, yet in a trice, she astonished Annetje, terrified Laney and cowed Rachel as she bade them go.

Mama lowered her defences only after the girls had disappeared down the lane.

"Dan," she said to me, and her eyes were pleading. "Was it Dan who brought Brom's ruin?"

– Chapter Nineteen –

A t first, I thought that Mama hadn't overheard my admission to the girls that I'd visited Hulda. Then I thought she'd forgot after my revelation that Dan had caused Brom's accident. Alas, I'd given her short shrift. She'd seemingly folded away that day's conversation into a corner of her mind, for she'd not spoken of it. Most assuredly, though, she had not forgotten.

To be truthful, I entertained a grudging admiration for Mama, for she had devised an ingenious way to keep watch over me: she set me to tending Thomas. He would notice and report my smallest misdeed.

On a grey morning a fortnight later, Mama told me to take Thomas outside. Brom needed rest, she said, but I thought it was also to give her respite from the irksome, impudent tyke. In my view, she should have considered the likelihood that Thomas would be querulous, shrill and thoroughly bothersome before she'd given birth to him. But that was Mama's custom, dropping unpleasant outcomes into another's lap. The lap most frequently dumped upon, of course, was mine.

Thomas danced round me, pulling on my skirts. "I want to go in the barn!" he shrieked. "I *command* you to let me go in the barn."

I said wearily, "You can't go in the barn. Papa keeps sharp blades there and he doesn't want you to get hurt."

"I want to see the owl."

"The owl is sleeping."

"You scared of the owl."

I sent evil thoughts in the direction of Brom. He was always telling the story about how the owl had frightened me years ago. Thomas hit me with the stout oak branch he used as a sceptre. I wrested the stick from his hand, marched into the barn and put it on a shelf out of his reach.

"Give me back my sceptre, minion! I command you!" he shrieked.

"I took it because you used it to hurt me."

"I'm the king."

"And I'm the colonies," I shot back. "I'm bigger than you and I won't endure your rude manner."

I could see Thomas' mind go round. First, he studied the shelf and the baskets he must climb to reach it. Then he stared at Papa's scythes, which were resting in a corner. I wondered whether he connected the scythes with the "Off with your head!" he was fond of shouting.

"I'm going to tell Mama," he said at last.

"Tell Mama that I took your stick away because you hit me."

"I'll tell her you let me go in the barn."

Maybe Hulda knew of a potion that would finish him. But I had nimble wits, as well.

"Tell her we went in the barn to fetch a basket," I said. "We're going to the orchard to pick peaches."

Papa was devoted to the cultivation of his apple trees. He and *Oom* Willem could debate for hours whether the pippin was superior to the *guelderleng*. Nobody paid mind to our score of peach trees, or our plum and cherry trees, either. They were in the far part of the orchard by the Albany Post Road.

I set Thomas to work picking peaches from the branches he could reach.

"This one's yet a bit hard. We should leave it to pick next time," I told him.

"I decide."

"As you wish, Your Majesty." I was pleased to have found a task that turned his mind from his royal duty to torment me.

"Who are they?" Thomas pointed at the Post Road.

Three men were coming toward us on foot. They looked to be younger than Papa, and their dress told me they were common folk, not gentlemen. As they passed a tree near the road, one of them bent a bough and picked a peach. He gave us a rakish grin.

Fruit was so plentiful in summer that no one cared if passers-by helped themselves, but the men had seen us. It would have been polite to ask.

The fellow who was eating our peach had a pack, so I concluded that he was a traveller. His companion had sunken eyes and a broken nose, and appeared to be half-starved. A knife handle protruded from the waistband of his breeches.

The third man had a red beard and a black hat with a wide brim and he carried a musket. He stopped and looked us over. "This here the road to Tarrytown?" he asked.

I nodded and pointed south in the direction of the village.

"The mill this way?"

I nodded again. I didn't want to talk to these fellows.

The man with the red beard looked round. "You near the North River here?"

These men must be strangers to these parts, or they would have known that it was called Hudson's River now. Travellers walked or rode the Post Road every day, but I was altogether revolted by these rakeshames. I wondered if Papa were close by.

Red-Beard jerked his chin in the direction of the big river. "You seen *Rose*?"

"I don't know Rose," I said, gathering up the basket.

The man with the pack spat the peach stone. "She don't know *Rose*," he mimicked. "He means the man-o'-war, stupid wench."

I was not stupid and I was a young lady, not a wench. I took Thomas by the hand and turned to go.

"That your brother?"

I pulled Thomas along. We needed to get away from these ruffians.

"Why's he got a bowl on his head? Keep his brains in?" The others laughed at Red-Beard's jest.

Thomas drew himself up in his most regal manner. "I'm a king," he told them.

Red-Beard burst into a laugh that wheezed like a saw severing a tree branch. The skinny fellow watched with gaunt, hollow eyes.

"A king, eh? This here a damned Royalist family?" Red-Beard asked.

"We're farmers. We're Dutch. Come along, Thomas."

"Except for the brat. He's a king." A new round of merriment began.

Thomas pulled away from me and faced the men. "I command you to go," he said.

At once the laughter stopped. "Command us, eh?" said Red-Beard. "I'm damned. Lad's barely out of clouts and he's commanding us."

"No king's commanding me," said Peach-Eater. "Not the old fool in England and not this imp, neither."

"Teach both them kings a lesson." The skinny man had spoken so softly that I wasn't sure what he had said. I put my hand in my pocket to touch my prism.

"What's that you got there?" Red-Beard pointed. "There. In your skirts. You're hiding something."

Blood rushed to my cheeks. My heart pounded.

"Let's see." The skinny man came toward me. I stepped back but I was too slow. He seized my elbow and tried to wrest my hand from my pocket. Likely he'd worn that stained brown shirt for a fortnight. I turned my head away.

His fingernails cut into my arm. "Fighting, are ye now?" He pulled me closer.

The skinny man reeked of wet leaves, old fires and the salty odour of sweat. He called to my mind a beast, a wounded, starving beast. Papa said they were the most dangerous.

I began to shiver. I willed myself to be still, but my body would not obey.

The skinny man gripped my chin with callused fingers. Before I turned my face away, I glimpsed stained brown teeth, several missing altogether. His breath smelled of fish. I tried not to retch as a bile humour rose in my throat.

His eyes were yellow like his teeth and they flickered for an instant. They fell to my neck and bosom. He grunted in satisfaction.

"What's she got in her hand?" Red-Beard called.

The skinny man made no reply. He put his arm round my shoulder and pulled me to him. I kicked his leg but I was thrown off balance with the effort. I fell backwards and he fell with me. Pain seared my arm as I hit a rock and I cried out.

For one so bony and slight, the man was surprisingly strong. He grunted again as he twisted my arm behind my back. I caught sight of my torn sleeve marked with blood. My pocket ripped open but my prism was still inside. I felt the round, hard weight as my leg pressed against it. The man raised his body to pull out his knife. In an instant, he was holding it to my throat. I could barely breathe. The open wound on my elbow throbbed.

He grasped the knife as if to stab me. Instead, he sliced open my green linen bodice. With a second, firmer slash, he split my stays and shift in two. He wrenched them from me and tossed them aside.

The knife had left a thread of blood from my breasts to my belly. Thomas stared at my exposed flesh; his brown eyes were round as copper coins. Red-Beard inched closer. Peach-Eater grinned. I fought to cover myself with my arms, but the skinny man held me fast.

He groped about his breeches. For an instant I thought he had stashed away another knife. Then he ripped open the buttons with his free hand and threw himself upon me. I felt his hot flesh against mine. Red-Beard and Peach-Eater backed away.

The skinny man strove to rip away my skirts, to little avail. Perhaps he would use his knife to slash me again. The stench of his body and breath caused me to gag.

He rose to his knees, eyes gleaming. I saw the bodily parts between his legs. I held a sob in my mouth.

Of a sudden I glimpsed Thomas hovering above us. "Leave my sister alone!" he shouted. "Don't you harm her, minion!" With a swift lunge of his head, he found the man's ear and bit it hard. The man screamed in pain. Thomas' pewter crown rattled as it hit the ground, and Red-Beard and Peach-Eater turned to look.

Thomas wheeled round and was racing away through the peach trees. The man cursed and jumped to his feet. "Damned brat bit me!" he exclaimed.

My attacker abandoned a clumsy attempt to button his breeches. He seized his knife from the grass and set out in pursuit. Thomas' calico-apron robe caught on a limb and tore, but he ran on, weaving under the low branches until he was out of view. I tried to rise, but my elbow bent beneath me like a broken branch. I rolled to my side and once more felt the prism hard against my leg. Without thinking,

I tried to take hold of it, although my hand trembled so I could hardly will it to move.

I didn't see the blow coming but I couldn't have dodged it anyway. Red-Beard was standing over me with his musket. "Now you're going to show us what you got in your pocket, wench," he said. "Give it up." He prodded me in the shoulder with the gun.

I could not obey. My arm would not move even if my mind had told it to.

Red-Beard wrested my hand out of my pocket and pried back my fingers. He tore the prism from me, held it to the light and turned it round. It was a sunless day, but shards of colours whirled inside the glass.

They were silent for a moment. Then Peach-Eater exclaimed, "Bloody hell! What's that?"

Red-Beard turned it in his hand. "Nothing like this in Connecticut," he observed.

"Why was you trying to hide it?" He cuffed me on the side of my head. "Asked you a question. Why was you hiding it?"

"I don't know. I..."

He took another swipe but my head was bowed. "Didn't want us to have it, eh? Damned Dutch butter-bags. Keeping it all for themselves."

Peach-Eater took the prism and held it to the light again. "They won't keep this. I'll take it for Susannah. She'll fancy it, for sure."

I pleaded, "No! Please don't! My Papa gave it to me! I..."

Peach-Eater kicked my ankle. "This here glass, it's magic, ain't it? Bring you luck?"

What was happening just then was no doubt the worst luck I'd ever had. "No!" I cried.

The skinny man emerged from the orchard. I marked that his breeches were buttoned and I felt a pinprick of relief. Thomas must have escaped him. Surely Papa would be here in an instant.

I managed to say, "It's not m-magic. It's a, a bauble. It's nothing. Tr-truly."

Red-Beard sneered. "Then why you all in a temper over us taking it?"

The skinny man peered back through the orchard in the direction of our house. "We'd best be getting on," he said.

Peach-Eater agreed. "Had enough of these damned Dutch. He helped himself to a peach from our basket as the three men headed off down the Post Road. My prism was in his pocket.

– Chapter Twenty –

I would find those thieves, the one with the red beard and the one who ate our peaches. I would run them to ground and get back my prism. Then I would tie their hands and feet and throw them in our root cellar. I would stuff mouldy potatoes in their mouths till they gagged on their pleas for mercy.

For that evil, foul-smelling beast who forced himself upon me, the root cellar was too kind a fate. I would bind big stones round his ankles and push him into Hudson's River. No, I would throw him in the water, and let him plead until the tide came in and drowned him. No, I would stuff a mouldy potato into his mouth, too, so he couldn't plead. He would choke, bit by bit, as the water rose. A quick death was too kind for him.

I was in my bed with blue-and-white-checked pillow-bears propped behind me. Mama had found an old shift for me to wear. I sipped a tea of pennyroyal leaves and rested my elbow, which Mama had washed and bound with clean linen.

Mama picked up my stays, which drooped in her hands like some battle-weary piece of armour. She frowned as she inspected the severed laces.

"Sarah," she said, and I knew she was altogether reluctant to speak. "Did these men, these scoundrels... did they harm you?"

"They took my prism!"

"I meant, did they...?" Mama had an abhorrence of mentioning carnal matters.

"No!" I shouted before she could finish. I ducked under my quilted counterpane and pulled a pillow over my head.

Mama took a breath. "Sarah, I know this is most difficult for you, but appears they... unclothed you, and..." She came near the bed and loomed above over me. I knew she was there although I couldn't see her. "...And did any of them...?"

I had a brief vision of the skinny man's exposed parts. "No!" I cried again.

"Are you certain?"

I recalled Amy saying that the act of love involved "people fastened together." I surely was not "fastened" with that wretch. He never truly touched me. Or did I just not know it?

It was bad enough to have undergone the ordeal. Telling of it to Mama was entirely too much to endure. I burrowed deeper into the pillows.

"Surely you know what I'm speaking of."

Just as surely Mama must have known that I was loath to speak of it with her. Of course, as a country girl I'd observed the mating of livestock. I confess as well that, in the company of Amy, I'd conjured amorous trysts with Tom Buckhout. I'd not known of the sight, the odour, the very beastliness of it.

"Sarah, there is blood on your petticoats."

"My elbow bled a lot."

"Answer me at once. Did those men...?"

Would the Grand Inquisitor never cease? I came out from the pillows, my cap askew.

"One of them sought to..." I told her. "But Thomas bit him."

At that recollection, at Mama's horrified face, I began to laugh. "Thomas bit him. On the ear. Then he ran off and the man got up and chased him." Mama's countenance—mouth ajar and eyebrows soaring over her spectacles—made me laugh harder still.

"And then the other man..." I paused to get my breath. "The other man, the one who stole our peaches, he took my prism. He took my prism!" My bosom heaved and the sounds I made were between a gasp, a bitter laugh and a wail.

Papa tapped at my chamber door. "How is Sarah?"

He stepped hesitantly into the room, and I smelled his familiar scent of cut hay, leather and earth as he wrapped me in his arms. He crooned little nonsense sounds and patted my back as he held me close.

"Ouch! My head!"

At once Papa pulled away my cap. His rough fingers parted my hair and touched my bruised temple. "What is this?"

"The man with the red beard hit me. With his musket... and then he... he took my prism!" My outrage gathered steam. "He took my prism and he wouldn't give it back. The man who ate our peaches..."

"All she can babble about is that prism," Mama said.

Brom and Thomas had come into the room. Brom leaned on Papa's shoulder to inspect my elbow. "Where did the men go?" Brom asked.

"Could you get back my prism?"

Brom said, "I'll find those Tory scallywags and..." His face crumpled as he realized his utter impotence. He thumped the floor with the heavy stick he used for a crutch.

As Papa left my room, he said, "Abraham, these men are *schurks*. We must not go after them."

"They went to the mill," Thomas said.

"The mill? Are you certain?" Brom was bewildered.

"They said they were looking for *Rose*, the British man-o'-war," I added.

"Were they soldiers?" Brom asked.

"No, they were just common men."

Mama sniffed. "They were common outlaws. His Majesty's men would never harm innocent…"

"His Majesty's soldiers burned Laney's house," Brom interrupted.

"I hurt, too," Thomas announced.

Mama gathered him in her arms and brushed his arm with her lips. "There now. That will make it well, Your Majesty."

"I'm not 'Your Majesty.'" Thomas stamped his foot.

"You're a very brave king, indeed. Where is your crown?"

"It was in the orchard," Papa told her. "Mary, you must tend to Sarah now. She must have a cloth for her arm to rest in."

Mama rummaged in my chest of drawers. The tea must have made me drowsy, for I hardly started when she held up the cloth Hulda had used for Elizabeth's clout.

Mama said, "I've not seen this before. These embroidered flowers are quite cunning. Wherever did it come from?"

"Hulda the Witch gave it to me," I said. I lay back on my pillows and closed my eyes. At once I realised my shocking revelation and sat up. Mama's face was a jumble of suspicion that I'd spoken the truth and concern that I had turned utterly daft.

"You must rest now, *Puffertje*," Papa said.

I slept until dusk and was awakened by voices drifting up to my bedchamber.

Papa was saying, "Children should not know of such *kwaad*."

Mama responded, "Evil occurs when ruffians are free to terrorize the countryside. If Lord Philipse were here…"

"Who drove out Lord Philipse? The *zots* who were taken in by the writings of some English *zot* who never leaves his *parlour*." Papa uttered the English word with bitterness.

Mama paused before she answered, "Some of the English zots, as you call them, are themselves suffering. My family…"

"Our children are your family, Mary. I am your family." Papa added, "Our family was hurt. This is not some rebel nonsense from one of your books." There was a pause.

"I will look in on Sarah."

In the light of the candle that Papa had brought, I noticed the grey in his hair and beard. He sat on the edge of my bed when he saw I was awake.

"You are not sleeping," he said regretfully. He knew I'd overheard the quarrel. He told me, "Your mama and I both love you, and Brom and Thomas and Elizabeth, too."

"You and Mama are different," I said.

Papa smiled for the first time that day. "*Ja*, we are different. We are *verschillend*."

At once a question came to me, one startling because it was so obvious and also because I'd not thought of it before.

"Papa, where did you and Mama meet?"

The bedstead creaked as Papa shifted his weight. He replied, "It was in the southern part of the county, at Lord Philipse's hall. It was at the time of Pinkster."

"Is that the feast Mama calls Pentecost?"

Papa nodded. "In those days, Pinkster was a great celebration. We put flowers on our wagons and went visiting our neighbours."

"Did you visit Lord and Lady Philipse's house?"

Papa looked surprised. "Why, no, *Puffertje*. We Van Tassels were common folk.

On the Philipse grounds there was a *fes-ti-val*." Papa spoke the word in the Dutch way. "There were booths selling cider and gingerbread, and the Negroes had great fun. For a whole week, they sang and danced in the way of Africa."

"Did you dance?"

"*Ja! Hi-a-bomba-bomba-bomba!*" Papa twisted his shoulders and clapped his hands.

"Was Mama dancing?"

"Ladies did not dance with those like me." Papa took a breath. "Your mother had dark hair and eyes and she was slender like a willow branch. Not one other was like her. As I danced, she smiled at me, who was only a *zot*."

"Was she with Grandmother Seabury?"

Papa's countenance at once turned solemn. "No, *Puffertje*."

"Did you talk to her?"

"What could I say to a lady of such station?"

"After the dancing ended, your mama was walking among the people. Something fell from her hand to the ground, a small fine cloth of linen and lace."

"A handkerchief?"

"Just so. I had not ever seen a thing so beautiful." He took a breath. "At first I thought to keep it so that I would always have a bit of that lady whom I thought never to see again. Then I thought she would feel sad if it went missing."

"What happened, Papa?"

"I carried it to her. My tongue was stuck fast in my mouth but your mama said, 'I am Mary Seabury.' I had never before done such a thing, but I bowed as if I myself were a gentleman. I said, 'I am Peter Van Tassel.'

"The world has turned since then," he said, and I saw the sadness in his eyes as surely as I'd seen Mr Underhill's that day that the church. "Now it is time for sleep, *Puffertje*. You must have dreams that are *zoet*." He kissed me on the cheek and arranged the counterpane round me before he left my bedchamber.

It was a time before I did sleep, for I was pondering the story. Indeed, the tale had raised a number of questions.

Had Mama meant to drop her handkerchief? Could that solemn, snappish woman ever have been a coquette? How could she have known that Papa would retrieve it?

Who had been Mama's companion that day? Papa's smile had vanished as I asked that question. Was it that man, Mr Underhill, who rode up to the church the day that Hulda was attacked? He was English and a Tory and he'd called Mama "Mary."

Then there was the most troubling: It was a very long way, not in time and distance only, from the Philipses' aristocratic hall to this gabled Dutch farmhouse where Van Tassels had lived for nearly a century. How in Heaven's name had Mama come to make that journey?

I thought of Papa's words, "The world has turned since then," and I began to understand a great truth: you could move forward or perchance stay still, but you could never go back. In those instances where your life went whirling off its course, you had no warning. That was the injustice of it: You didn't know then when some trifling, impetuous act would set you on a new path entirely.

Papa could not return to the Pinkster Festival and leave the fallen handkerchief on the ground. Brom could not heed the warnings about the mill wheel, and I could not take Thomas to the river instead of the peach orchard.

– Chapter Twenty One –

It had been a fortnight since the… I knew not how to think of, let alone speak of the occurrence. I'd remained abed, refusing all nourishment but *suppan*, the Indian corn mush thought to have comforting, if not healing, properties.

I heard Mama and Papa in the room below:

"Mary, you must go to her. This is work for a woman, for her mother. Sarah must not stay an invalid forever." He paused. "Are you certain that she was not… *schenden*?"

It took me a moment to translate Papa's Dutch: "*Defiled.*" That was the sole concern of everyone, even Papa. Did they not know that none of this was my doing? I wouldn't have gone to the orchard save for Mama's telling me to mind Thomas. It was her fault.

I could veritably see Mama's dark, doleful countenance, although floorboards and ceiling separated us. "She insists not. Her arm was cut. The blood on her skirts could have come from her arm.

"Oh, no, Peter," she added. "She had her monthly purgation a few days after."

Had they thought that I was…? A new surge of horror coursed through me. Then it came to me: With a belly or not, ravaged or not, I was still *schenden*. People would learn what happened and they would magnify and turn it all round. No one would marry me save for some bald, toothless widower with a houseful of brats.

Or I could die. I could die and be buried next to the three babies. I'd have a headstone, a bit bigger than the others, and Mama would sweep snow off my grave, too. I recalled Brom's remark that she favoured her dead children over us living ones. No doubt Mama would regard me more kindly after I'd died, especially when she had to fend for herself with Thomas. Tom Buckhout would visit every day – no, thrice weekly would suffice – and each time he would bring flowers for my grave.

I heard the thumping of Brom's stick on the stairs.

"You could help me pick corn," he offered, as soon as he'd knocked and I'd admitted him to my bedchamber.

Of course, I saw this for what it was: a barefaced ploy to get me out of bed.

Brom added, "Papa said there's a big storm coming. His toe aches."

Papa insisted – with great accuracy, I must say – that when his big toe hurt, bad weather was sure to follow.

"He wants to bring the corn in before it is harmed by the wind and rain. I can't do it alone." Brom smiled ruefully. "The corn's in the field hard by the river," he added. "No one will ... see you there."

"We're a capital pair," I said. "The lame and the wounded."

Brom's countenance was at once hurt, angry and resigned, but he didn't chide me.

In the last weeks, the cornstalks had grown taller than I. They caught the timid breeze and held it fast among their pointed green leaves. Sunlight blazed off the river and bored through the straw of my hat.

Brom twisted an ear of corn from the stalk. He leaned on his walking stick as he handed it to me. I tossed it into the bushel basket with my good arm. The other was still in the sling made of Hulda's cotton. I ran my finger over the embroidery and wondered if I would ever see her again. Those days when I walked the Post Road and made my way through Hulda's hollow were gone. I would never go anywhere. I would pass the rest of my days on our farm and after a time, no one would know I was there. Even Tom would forget me.

Brom heard my small sniffle. He asked, "Sarah, why mustn't you tell secrets in a cornfield?"

I took off my hat and fanned myself with it. "I don't know."

"Because the corn has ears." Brom chuckled at the feeble jest, and I realized that he'd meant to coax me to a jolly humour.

I missed the Brom who delivered tirades and taunts in equal measure. That Brom was gone as surely as the vestige of a carefree Sarah. My nostrils burned. To prevent Brom from marking another incidence of crying, I pulled back the cornstalks to gaze at Hudson's River, flat as glass that afternoon. *HMS Rose* was stealing across the Tappan Zee in the direction of Nyack. Her white sails flapped in an idle search for a breeze. I didn't see her larger companion, *HMS Phoenix*. The ship out of view was the more fearsome, I thought.

"Those ships are a thorn in my flesh," I complained. "Why doesn't General Washington do something about them?"

Brom answered, "General Washington has formed a navy."

"A navy! Why, he's barely raised an army," I exclaimed.

Brom abandoned all pretext of picking corn. He hobbled to the great sycamore and sank down in its shade. He gratefully accepted the tin cup of water I scooped from our drinking bucket.

He said, "We've had a navy for nigh a year. When General Washington was in Massachusetts he found that many of his men were seafarers. So he set them to stopping British ships and confiscating arms and provisions he found." He held out the cup for more water.

"What has that to do with us?"

"When the British fleet came to New York, our men followed."

"I think those scoundrels who took my prism were 'our men'," I said. My words lodged in my throat. I waited for Brom to rebuke me but he didn't.

"Sarah, those men shouldn't have stolen your trinket. But the British have been plundering the New England coast. Do you know who the worst of them is?" He pointed at the black-hulled ship bobbing aimlessly on unseen currents. "Captain James Wallace of *HMS Rose*."

I began to say that a second criminal act did not justify the first but I spotted Dan ambling round the far edge of the field. I jumped to my feet. Dan was hard enough to tolerate under any circumstances. That day, I could not endure him for a single instant. I ducked between the tall cornstalks and stood still.

"Picking corn?" Dan was skilled in remarking upon the obvious.

"Just resting a bit," Brom answered with equal facility.

"Thought I saw your sister." Dan never referred to me by name. I wasn't certain whether that was gratifying or galling.

"She was here a bit ago," Brom said vaguely. He pointed at the river. "Look, there's *Rose*."

There was a silence. I knew Dan was squinting at the river.

Brom asked, "Any news from the mill?"

Dan replied, "No use to tell you. You're a helpless cripple."

After a pause, Brom said, "I could shoot a gun. I'll warrant I can ride a horse."

Outrage made me quite forget I had no wish to see Dan. I shoved aside the cornstalks and strode out of the field.

"Who caused Brom to be a helpless cripple?" I shouted. "You did, Dan."

Brom began, "Sarah, is this...?"

Dan was more nimble of wit than I'd allowed. He countered, "Where'd you see that? In your witchcraft glass?"

"I saw it with my very eyes. You were standing hard by the lever when the water wheel began to turn."

Brom's eyes held a grievous hurt as he asked, "Sarah, is this true?"

"It is true," I declared. "I saw it."

Papa's toe had once more been right: a mighty storm was advancing up Hudson's River. The trees quaked and the branches of the old wisteria vine clawed against the windows like a cat begging to come in.

"The *Heer* will send his storm ship out tonight," Papa said, peering out our kitchen door at the darkening sky. As with his family, indeed, with most of our Dutch neighbours, Papa claimed fierce storms to be the work of *The Heer of Dunderberg*, the Lord of Thunder Mountain. This was a great craggy mound set at an elbow bend in Hudson's River some fifteen miles to the north. From Dunderberg the *Heer* was said to direct a phantom ship in the very midst of a terrible tempest to visit ruin upon the unwise and unwary.

The storm that night was remembered for years as one of the Heer's most monstrous achievements. Lightning struck a cottage in Nyack; two days after and three miles away across the river, we could see smoke from its ruins. At Cortlandt Manor, a farmer was killed as he ran to his barn to calm his livestock. His body was said to be reduced to a cinder, charred and ashen.

Isaac Martling claimed that the coins in his pocket were melted to silver lumps. Those who knew Isaac doubted that the coins lingered long enough in his pocket to draw lightning; any money he possessed was straightaway turned over to the tavern-keeper, they said.

That night my thoughts turned to Hulda in her rude hut. I

wondered if the wind would tear it down, or if a great tree would topple and crush her. I wondered if she missed me. I wondered if I could ever lift that great burden that I carried like an iron yoke on my shoulders.

The next day, of course, was the fairest of the season. Perhaps the *Heer* was remorseful for his devilish behaviour the night before. Except for a good-sized oak branch across our lane, our home was not disturbed.

I was on my way back from feeding the chickens – one of the few tasks I could perform with one arm – when I spied Amy cantering up our lane on her sorrel mare. My first thought was that she had best not be abroad without the protection of at least one of her brothers. My second thought was that I had no wish to see her or any other soul ever again, and the third was that she bore bad news.

"Oh, nononononono!" she responded to my query, dismounting her horse in a cascade of red calico skirts. "All are well, although a farmer down in Hastings had his barn burned by lightning." She looked about. "And how is Brom faring?"

I could not help but warm to Amy's presence. She alone was not fickle in her affections for Brom. Of course, she didn't know of my calamity, and I knew not to tell her. Amy was a veritable magpie, although one who never meant harm.

"Oh!" she cried, spying my bound arm. I hastily delivered the story I had prepared: That I'd slipped and hit my elbow on a rock. That was not far from the truth.

"What a *jolie...* cloth," she exclaimed, examining my sling. "Those little flowers are certain to make you well."

My mind flashed to Hulda, of course, and then to the unintentional truth uttered by Amy. A sling of cloth that Hulda had given me would indeed make me feel better. In fact, I was in sunnier spirits already. Amy was such a cheerful body.

"There is to be a picnic," Amy confided as we walked toward the house. "This will be at Teller's Point."

"It would be a long journey," I said, frowning. Neither Brom nor I could ride a horse, I was thinking. Teller's Point, a small, wooded nose of land jutting into Hudson's River north of Sing Sing Village, could be reached by land only on the rough paths of its much larger cousin, Croton Point. That of course accounted for its popularity.

"Your *Oom* Jan said you and Brom can sail with him and your *Tante* Margaret on *Zomer Wind*. They are going with us to make sure we don't get into mischief," she added, suggesting with a show of dimples that mischief could nonetheless be readily come by.

"A picnic would be a boon for Brom's spirits," I said. "Some of your mischief would be altogether welcome. Why, did I say something wrong?"

Amy was looking quite as if I had just pinched her without cause: bewildered, hurt and a bit defiant.

"It has been so tedious for him, staying at home," I explained. "I'm sure he's mightily pleased that you came to see him. Let's go indoors and I'll bring out some cold cider..."

Amy gripped my arm as if she were about to reveal that she had some fatal illness. "You must know first," she said. She blushed, and this time I did not find it endearing. "I have a new beau."

I stared at her, mouth agape. The notion that events had moved with unseemly haste ran through my mind. Why, it had been but a few weeks since...

"Well, who is he?" I managed to ask.

Amy tossed her curls, but I was unmoved by her affectations.

"Dan," she said.

- Chapter Twenty Two -

The spirits of those of us in the wagon were as melancholy as they had been that Sabbath when Hulda was attacked at the church. In Mama's absence, Brom provided the gloom. I sat on the wooden seat beside Papa, whose joviality appeared to be entirely invented.

"You will enjoy this frolic," he told us. "Long ago, when I was a *jongeling*, these picnics were great fun. And a picnic at Teller's Point..."

Slouching in the back of the wagon, Brom couldn't see the roll of Papa's eyes, suggesting all manner of saucy delights. I rolled my eyes as well, pursed my lips and fixed my eyes upon the Post Road.

There was no escaping this horrid picnic. I suspected that Papa had had a hand in the planning. He thought Brom and I had brooded far too long and that we needed the society of other *jongelings*. Even Mama, a foe of loose Dutch revelries, did naught to discourage our attendance. I didn't fancy being jerked round like a puppet. I was furious.

Old Pegasus came to a stop outside Philipse's Mill. Papa had arranged for *Oom* Jan and *Tante* Margaret to take us to the picnic in *Zomer Wind*, *Oom* Jan's market sloop. They would stay to "chaperone."

I stepped down from the wagon and handed Brom his crutch. I trudged and he hobbled down to the pier. Papa followed with a picnic basket, his old fowling piece and a small bag of birdshot. Brom had spent hours mastering the procedure of shooting a gun while propped on his crutch. He'd announced that he would not attend the frolic unless he could take the gun to bring down a duck for our supper. Papa had yielded.

"Oh, Sarah, you look especially fetching today!" From *Tante* Margaret's first words, I knew that she had been told what had happened. The necessity of beguiling me into a lighter humour had been impressed upon her. I was altogether nettled at the way everybody was tiptoeing round as if I were a porcelain vase teetering at the edge of a shelf.

Tante Margaret proclaimed how my peach linen gown went so well with my colouring, how cunning was the lace on the sleeves and how I was in store for a jolly time. I wondered what other ploys had been devised to cheer me.

Tante Margaret took her perch atop the cabin and resumed her usual pensive mien. Before her marriage two years ago, she had occupied the station that Laney held now: of the unrivalled and much imitated *coquette*. A scant three months after their vows were spoken, the local folk began to whisper about a baby to crown the blessings of this copper-tressed beauty and her well-favoured husband. By now, the subject was stale as a week-old crust.

Brom and I sat slumped like sacks of wheat on the deck of *Zomer Wind*. We watched silently as *Oom* Jan loosened the line that bound the mainsail and hoisted the weathered canvas up the mast. That was my customary duty. Raising the anchor was Brom's. As my arm mended, I'd be able to raise the mainsail once more, but Brom would never again haul the heavy chain hand over hand to lift the anchor. That task required two arms and now Brom employed one to steady himself.

Who else knew of my plight and what had they been told? Once the tale of my –defilement–slipped out, my life would be as finished as Brom's. Everyone would know. Everyone would shun me. Tears blurred my view of the red cliffs on the river's western bank. I stared at them and hoped that no one would remark upon my crying.

"Why are we anchoring so far from shore?" Brom asked *Oom* Jan as the sloop glided into the tranquil bay embraced by Croton Point. Teller's Point was the sandy spit stretching south from Croton Point.

"Tide's going out," he replied. "You don't want to be left high and dry, do you, *Zomer*?" He patted the transom. "It's a scant half-fathom deep here," he said.

"The water's so wide it seems a warship might anchor here," I said, choking back a sniffle. "It's a *trompe l'oeil* river."

Tante Margaret and *Oom* Jan started quite as if I had just uttered an astounding revelation. They each beamed with encouragement.

"*Trompe loo-ee?*" *Oom* Jan asked, so I explained, "Mama said that in France people might paint ivy on a wall to look as if real ivy was growing. *Trompe l'oeil* means "fool the eye" in French."

Oom Jan frowned. "Why wouldn't they just grow real ivy?"

Tante Margaret leapt to take my part. "Maybe the wall was in-doors, Jan. People would think that real ivy was growing in a house. If the artist were very good, that is."

Oom Jan shook his head at such folly, and Brom snickered. At least one frivolous jest had elicited a chuckle. I couldn't recall the last time Brom had even smiled.

Zomer Wind joined three other small boats at anchor in the bay. I wondered who else had come to the picnic. I didn't see Dan or Rachel and I let out a small, and no doubt unwarranted, breath of relief. Amy was picking her way along the water's edge, marked now by a line of brown seaweed that had washed up after the big storm. "Come on in!" she cried.

"We've a rowboat," *Tante* Margaret called back, indicating the small wooden dinghy tied to *Zomer's* stern. "But we are four, with a picnic basket. Perhaps Tom can fetch Sarah."

Tom! In my anguish about the picnic, I'd not thought of him once. Had I foreseen this calamity, I'd have thrown myself off the heights of *Kykuit*. I could still fall over the transom and drown. But *Oom* Jan had said it was shallow here. I'd merely spoil my gown.

Tom's skiff was so small it could barely hold the two of us. It lurched as he rose to help me in.

"Now, Tom, mind Sarah's arm. She's still favouring it," *Tante* Margaret said.

A truly terrifying thought crossed my mind. Tom knew! Somebody had told him, and doubtless they'd admonished him to treat me kindly. It was no happenstance that he was idling round Croton Bay with a boat. The Sarah-and-Brom marionette show, it appeared, was an elaborate production.

Tom made a few choppy efforts to pull the oars through the water. I could see he had little familiarity with boats, but his long legs – rather, my long legs – also hindered him. Our knees bumped as we sat facing each other. Yet it wouldn't help if I sat with my knees turned to one side. The boat was simply too small. Rather, I was much too tall. Why couldn't I have been of medium stature, like Papa?

"How'd you hurt your arm?" Tom raised his hazel eyes to mine. I recalled how handsome I'd once thought he was, and I realized I should have thought of something to say first. When someone had a conspicuous bandage, the first thing people asked was how they'd been hurt.

"I fell," I told him.

"Fell? Where?"

I took a deep draught of air. "In our orchard."

"How'd you fall, to break your arm in that manner?"

A vision of the skinny man sped through my mind. "I slipped on a rock," I told him.

"A rock?" His hazel eyes appeared to be muddied, and I recalled Mama saying that the eyes mirrored the man.

"There are rocks in the orchard," I answered, trying not to sound exasperated. "You know the land here. All manner of rocks jut from the ground."

"Did you trip?"

Perhaps Tom was in apprenticeship to Mama for the role of Grand Inquisitor.

"No, I fell backward." This was far more than I wanted to disclose. I must find another topic to converse about. "How many times have you rowed a boat?"

It was Tom's turn to look perplexed, then defensive. "You don't think I row good?"

Straightaway I was back in the fire. Asking about rowing was the last thing I should have done. "No, no," I offered hastily. "It's just that..." I tried to pick my words so I'd not insult him. He seemed a mite wranglesome.

"Just what?"

"I don't regard you as being a man of the water."

"Man of the water?" His eyes were now a clouded brown.

Once more I considered tumbling overboard. Doubtless that would provide a change of topic.

"You know, I believe you have a greater association with land." What an utterly addlepated remark. Except for boatmen like *Oom* Jan, everyone had a greater association with land. I was such a fool.

"Not that that's bad," I added.

A silence ensued that seemed to last a fortnight, at least. Tom knit his brow as he struggled to keep the oars even. I studied the stern rock face of High Tor across the river. Tom used an oar to pole our way the last few feet to shore. The skiff scraped the sand and came to a stop.

Tom stepped onto the sand at water's edge. He helped me to

my feet. The boat lurched as I stepped out. As Tom steadied me, I breathed in the scent of salt and leather that I recalled as I stood close to him at church.

"Sarah," he said, and I noticed that his face was flushed. "I was going to ask you, do you want to look for Captain Kidd's treasure this afternoon?"

Captain Kidd's treasure! I'd forgot that it was said to be buried on Croton Point, more notorious than even the Hollow for secluded trysting sites. What was I to say? How could I stumble through thickets with only one good arm? What if Tom tried to kiss me? Of course he'd try to kiss me. I should just refuse to go. But then Tom might ask Laney or Amy. Enduring boys was altogether exhausting. I was miserable.

Samuel Youngs and Jemima's cousin Isaac van Wart had gathered branches to make a cooking fire after someone had caught fish or brought down a pigeon. Amy and Laney were looking for oyster beds in the shallows. Annetje was with them. Rachel and Jemima were weaving branches to make a shelter. Jemima waved, but Rachel chose to be absorbed in her task. I didn't see Dan, and I wondered briefly if he were sick. Then Amy might resume her affections for Brom.

Oom Jan and *Tante* Margaret appeared with a fishing pole, their basket of food and a smaller basket with *Tante* Margaret's sewing. He leaned Papa's gun against a tree.

Oom Jan asked me, "Are you going to help me land a big fish, Mate?"

"I don't know." I'd not considered such a thing. Other than gathering oysters, which I didn't much favour, I'd thought fishing was for men.

Oom Jan baited a wicked-looking hook at the end of a long line. "Try your hand," he said, handing the pole to me.

"How should I drop the hook in the water?"

"Toss it, like so."

I did, and the hook travelled a small distance.

"You caught seaweed, Sarah," Brom pointed out.

The retort, "Why don't you try?" was on my tongue. Then I spied his crutch.

Oom Jan suggested, "Perhaps we should go to the end of the point."

"I thought we were at the end of the point," I said.

"There's a sandbar that goes out for a furlong, at the least," *Oom* Jan replied. He grinned at me. "*Trompe loo-ee.*"

Tante Margaret pulled on *Oom* Jan's sleeve. "Sarah must fish with Tom," she said. She sounded altogether snappish.

"Ah, yes," *Oom* Jan replied. "Tom has a boat. It is far better to fish from a boat."

Tom dragged over the little skiff. I stepped in and he pushed the boat through the slimy brown clumps of sea grass drifting at the water's edge. "Ugh! What's this rubbish?" he asked.

I told him, "Flotsam or jetsam. I can't think which is which."

Tom frowned. "Huh?"

I tried again. "It's sea grass. The great storm must have churned up the river bed."

"The river *bed*?"

"Why, yes," I answered. As I spoke I realized that I had sounded quite as if I thought my knowledge to be superior. I tried to soften my tone. "The river bottom."

Tom uttered a sound that was a cross between "Huh" and "Um."

I said, "How odd it must be, that grass grows at the bottom of the river. There's an entire world down there that we never see. What do you suppose it's like?"

"Wouldn't want to know. Only time I'd be down there was if I drowned."

I glanced down at the tarnished brass oarlock. I thought of King Midas as he found that even his bread turned to gold at his touch. A prize I'd sought desperately had turned out to have a terrible flaw.

I laughed nervously. "Tell me about Captain Kidd's treasure."

Tom chuckled. He stopped rowing, and I was pleased, for I thought that we were far enough from land in such a small vessel. He said, "It's buried close by."

"How do you know?" I sounded altogether quarrelsome.

Tom took the fishing pole, attached a protesting worm to the hook and cast the line overboard. "Everybody knows," he said.

I wondered if that was what boys said when they wanted to remind girls that theirs was the superior intellect. Maybe I should coddle him.

"Did you bring a shovel?" I asked.

Tom looked at me with half-closed eyes. He turned his attention back to fishing. I flushed with shame as I understood. Tom hadn't meant that we should go digging up Captain Kidd's treasure. It was merely an excuse to be alone with me so he could kiss me. I had thought Tom to be slow of wit, but I was so stupid that he would never take me to look for the treasure. He would probably take Amy. *She* wouldn't ask foolish questions.

I cleared my throat. "Well, I have heard that Captain Kidd passed time in these parts. His crew was from upriver, I believe."

Tom nodded.

"What would you do if we found the treasure? I mean, would you spend it? What would you spend it for?"

Tom turned his attention from the fishing pole. "Never thought about it. What would you spend it for?"

My reply surprised both of us. "Oh, I'd get a boat," I said. "A boat, a bit bigger than *Zomer Wind*, but not so big as *Phoenix* or *Rose*."

Tom appeared to be altogether astounded, although he didn't seem to think I was a zot. "What would you do with a boat?"

"I'd sail it, of course."

"By yourself?"

"I might have a crew," I conceded.

"Where would you sail? Across the river?"

"Much farther. Perhaps even across the sea."

Tom's smile was almost even. "You're bold, Sarah," he said.

Did he mean that I was bold as in brazen, or bold as in brave? Luckily, Tom expanded on the topic.

"You don't shy from standing apart from the others. You make your own way."

Tom thought I was courageous! I gave him a radiant smile.

"You're..." he searched for the right word. "You're independent." He blushed again. "Guess Brom's like that, too."

"We have the same mama and papa," I pointed out. I smoothed my skirts and looked out over the water. I gasped.

Phoenix and *Rose* were creeping toward us. For an instant I thought they were apparitions. They'd come round Verplanck's Point, heading downriver. They were three miles away at the least, but they loomed large and fearsome against the gentle green hills surrounding Haverstraw Bay. Clouds scurried across the sun and suddenly I was cold.

"Let's go back," I said to Tom.

– Chapter Twenty Three –

"**C**an they see us?" Laney peered at *Phoenix* and *Rose* from behind a sapling pine at the river's edge.

Jemima blinked nervously. "They can see Sarah's gaily-coloured gown," she said.

I hastened to step back into the underbrush, yet I was fixed upon the sight of the warships. There was hardly a whisper of wind, and their sails drooped. Their square black gun ports stared and their spars and sprits were bare as bones. Yet they advanced, as relentlessly as a plague.

"Tide's carrying them," said *Oom* Jan.

I marked the shock on Brom's face as Dan put his arm round Amy's shoulder, and drew her to him. Dan chuckled. "Keeping to the other side of the river. They're scared of us."

"Channel's on the west side," *Oom* Jan told him. "They'll be turning this way soon."

A man's shout travelled over the water. I couldn't discern the words but they sounded like a command. Men bustled about on *Phoenix's* deck. Her sails swung round and her bowsprit pointed straight at us. *Rose* followed. Sails swelled as the great ships caught a puff of wind.

"They're heading for us!" Laney wailed.

"Coming about," said *Oom* Jan.

"We durst not leave now," *Tante* Margaret said. "They surely see us. They'll think we've ill intentions."

"Best lie low." *Oom* Jan gathered the picnic baskets, abandoned shoes and fishing gear and set them in the shelter.

Amy pouted. "They have spoiled our frolic."

What a fickle jade Amy was. Scarcely a month past, she'd been claiming she'd invite the British to dinner.

Laney began to cry. "Must we stay here? They'll take us away."

Despite his crutch, Brom was swift in reaching Laney's side. "They'll not trouble us," he assured her, "I'll keep you safe."

HMS Rose was advancing upon us. Straight on, the ship resembled nothing so much as a grim, dark face with heavy jowls and a very long nose stuck in the air.

Oom Jan warned, "Get in the shelter until they've passed."

Isaac van Wart drained his mug. His complexion was usually of a ruddy hue, but today it was veritably crimson, visible even through the scant whiskers I supposed to be a beard. "Why should we hide from them? We've a right to a picnic," he declared in a voice thick with small beer.

Samuel scoffed. "The only rights we have are to lick the boots of Royal George and the jackanapes he sends to conquer us."

"Here's a thing for those blackguards to see!" Brom hobbled briskly to our picnic basket and pulled out a cloth of red-and-white striped linen. I could see a snake and the words, "Don't Tread On Me."

"Where'd you get that flag?" I demanded, wondering how he had contrived to slip it out of the house unobserved.

"Elijah," Brom answered. He limped to the water's edge and struggled to unfurl the flag.

"Brom, take shelter," *Oom* Jan said. "Don't taunt the Lion now."

Alas, Brom looked to be intent upon impressing Laney with his revolutionary zeal. Perhaps he sought to regain Amy's affections as well, I thought sourly. He turned a deaf ear to *Oom* Jan's warning.

Samuel loped to Brom's side, his spectacles glittering in the afternoon sun. He and Brom each took a corner of the flag and held it high. "Halloooo, King George!" Brom cried.

"Brom, no!" cried *Tante* Margaret. "You must not anger them."

The ships had set a course for Sing Sing. Like Tarrytown, the village was perched on a hillside by the river. I could see a row of brick houses. Smoke curled from a chimney and a woman was drawing water from a well. I wondered if I could warn her.

Of a sudden, Brom was brandishing Papa's gun. "Perchance they'll pay mind to this." He raised it to his shoulder. "Got 'em in my sights!" he cried.

"Don't waste the shot," Samuel advised him. "Wait until they come closer."

The gun made a hollow, cracking sound as Brom fired. A sailor at *Rose's* rail trained his spyglass on Teller's Point. The ships were nigh upon us, and slowing. Another shout, "Stand by to..." drifted across the water.

Men climbed the masts and inched their way out along the spars. They gathered in the sails.

"They're coming to capture us," Jemima cried.

A rowboat with a half-dozen men slipped from behind *Phoenix's* hull.

Laney screamed. "They're coming for us! They're going to..."

Brom grasped her hand. "Laney, they'll not hurt you. I won't let them."

I was not at all sure how Brom would keep that vow, since fully one half of his person was given to the task of getting himself about.

I shaded my eyes. "They're not rowing any more."

Tom stood behind me. He said, "They're dangling some kind of rope over the edge. They're fishing."

"They're taking the water depth," *Oom* Jan told him. They'll be staying,"

Phoenix's great anchor chain thundered as it spewed from her bow.

We huddled inside the leafy hut that Rachel and Jemima had made of sapling branches. Although the ships were out of view, those uninvited guests loomed large and fearsome. Every so often, Samuel or Isaac got up to have a look at them.

I was gratified that Tom had seated himself by me. Perhaps he would ask me to go walking again. Of course I'd go. Perchance he would try to kiss me. I supposed that I would allow him.

Tom himself interrupted my pleasant reverie. He handed me a pewter plate and favoured me with his crooked grin.

"Oysters," he said.

I managed a weak smile. I'd never fancied oysters, yet Tom was watching me expectantly. I took one and put it in my mouth. It was the same salty, slippery wad as oysters I'd eaten before. As he turned away, I spat it discreetly into my hand and tossed it into the under-brush outside.

"How was it?" he inquired, turning to me.

"The oyster?"

Of course Tom meant the oyster. I was such a fool. I'd been parsing our conversations that day. Our exchanges were awkward. Our words collided. Indeed, they often sped past each other entirely. What was amiss? Plainly, some failing of mine.

Yet Tom wasn't put off when I babbled about having my own ship and sailing the seas. In fact, he said I was bold and independent. A dark thought consumed me: perhaps he thought I was a loose girl. In Mama's view, promiscuity ranked with blasphemy and murder among the greatest transgressions. Yet that was because Mama was English. Everyone considered Amy to be loose. It enhanced her popularity altogether.

I vowed to increase my efforts to be a more pleasing companion. I would not comment on how Tom rowed a boat. I would not introduce topics he knew little of, like flotsam and jetsam. I would never reveal that I disliked oysters.

"Oh, the oyster was most tasty," I assured him.

"Have another," he urged.

I smiled demurely. "They are so savoury, you must have one. But I would enjoy a taste of that cider that Annetje brought."

Brom hobbled up to the shelter and began the task of fitting his ungainly frame through the opening. "Ships are still there," he reported, as he sank to the ground beside Laney.

"They'll attack us," Jemima predicted mournfully.

Samuel shook his head. "They are paying us no mind."

"They think we're too puny to bother with." Brom was altogether aggrieved that the British had ignored his flaunting of the "Don't Tread on Me" flag, not to mention his firing upon them.

"They'll attack at daybreak," Dan suggested.

I said, "If they would attack us, they'd have done by now. The British don't steal round like..."

"You mean like our militia?" Dan sounded quite as if he were accusing me of standing up for the British.

I swallowed. "No, I mean that the British have by far the greater might. Why, if they had wished it, they'd have shot their cannons and brought an end to us all."

The sun had dropped behind the tall red cliffs on the western bank. A cool breeze shilly-shallied up Hudson's River, rippling random patches of the wide water. Fireflies' golden lamps twinkled.

Would we stay the night at this inhospitable site? What would happen come sunrise? It would be a brief battle, picnickers with a flag and three fowling pieces versus two of His Majesty's warships.

I fought a mighty urge to run from the shelter and plunge into Croton Bay. *Oom* Jan had said it was shallow, but the tide was rising. I could never haul anchor or raise the sails. I would drown and my body would wash out to the ocean and no one would ever know what became of me. Perhaps Tom would try to rescue me. Yet he had little acquaintance with the water. Hadn't I just remarked upon that very thing?

Oom Jan had walked to the water's edge. "No steady wind," he reported as he ducked his head into the shelter. "Might blow in the small hours."

"Can we go home then?" Jemima sounded as miserable as I.

"We must pass the night here." Amy's zeal for amorous escapades seemed to have deserted her.

"We could walk back," Annetje offered in a quavering voice.

"Where is your lantern, Jan?" *Tante* Margaret asked.

"Aboard," *Oom* Jan replied ruefully. "The two we have here won't give light for more than an hour."

Samuel shook his head. "We could never follow those footpaths round the bogs. They can scarcely be marked in full daylight."

"What would become of our boats?" asked Jemima's cousin, Isaac. He stroked the reddish whiskers on his chin.

"They'll take us captive," Jemima predicted.

I said, "We're captives now. We might as lief be chained in their stinking holds."

Laney choked and pushed away her untouched plate. At once, every eye was fixed upon her as she began to weep. I marked a few reproving glances aimed at me for mentioning "hold," where her father was said to be imprisoned.

Everyone thronged round Laney to console her. I'd suffered a calamity like hers, no doubt one more grievous. Nobody minced round distasteful topics in my presence. No one sought to lift my spirits.

"Our families will be alarmed if we don't return soon," said Annetje.

A frantic round of speculation followed. Would someone come looking for us? Would they see the great ships and turn back? A rescue party might wait till morning, but by then, we could take our own leave. Would the British attack our little fleet whilst we sought to leave Croton Bay? Brom's flaunting the flag was now seen as perilous folly. People had been imprisoned or shot for less.

Tante Margaret tallied the contents of the picnic baskets. "Our food will sustain us through midday tomorrow," she said.

"They'll have killed us by them," said Jemima. Her face, customarily of a pale hue, was even whiter in the firelight.

Brom gulped the last of his rum punch. He studied the pewter cup for an instant before he hurled it against the shelter's frame. He said, "Those redcoats have no right to come here where nobody wants them."

Samuel stretched his long, lank arms. "Tories want them here," he said, yawning.

"Like your mama's chum Nathaniel Underhill," Dan said to Brom.

"And Sarah's chum the witch," added Rachel.

The talk had turned so quickly that I was taken unawares. Nonetheless. I answered promptly, "There's not a shred of proof that Hulda..."

Dan leaned forward, the better to place his smug, pallid face within my view. "There's proof. That woman talks witch-talk with soldiers."

My cheeks began to burn. "Where? When?"

Isaac answered. "Saw them with my own eyes. They were up in the hollow where she lives, gabbling like geese. One thing is sure: she understood them and they understood her. Then they all went off together."

"The soldiers that burned our house were talking witch-talk," said Laney.

I tried to understand these accusations. "How can that be?"

"It was witch-talk," Laney insisted. For an instant I thought she might melt into tears once more. Then she set her small jaw and hardened her eyes.

Tom drew ciphers in the dust with a stick. No doubt he was showing prudence in remaining silent.

I took a breath. "What about the time you came to visit, Annetje? We talked about Hulda. You said we should treat her kindly."

Annetje blinked and looked down. "That was before I knew."

"Knew what?" I sounded shrill and desperate.

"She talks witch-talk with the soldiers." Annetje's gaze remained fixed on her hands in her lap. "The soldiers sent her to spy upon us."

"Hulda was here many years before the soldiers," I retorted.

"Many years ago, she knew the British were coming. In fact, the British sent her here," said Dan.

My heart was pounding, but I pushed on. "Jemima, you said she brought you tea when you had measles. It helped you to heal."

Jemima studied her shoes.

I turned to Tom once more. He was resting his head on his folded elbows, so he didn't mark my silent entreaty.

Still, it was possible that Tom didn't know much of Hulda. How would he learn of a reclusive woman who lived in the woods? Perhaps the one time he had seen her was that horrid day at the church.

"Perhaps she does make the *magique*," Amy mused. "If she can make a drink to cure a person, she could also..."

Dan cut in. "Tell the British of our plans."

Rachel hadn't reminded us even once that Hulda had caused the snake to bite her. She said, "So of course they're not afraid of us."

Isaac snapped his fingers as a mighty revelation came upon him.

"That's why the redcoats are so brazen. They're in league with the witch. She tells them who we are. She tells them what we are about to do."

Rachel was warming to the topic. "The witch knew we would be having a frolic here. She told the ships to come and spy upon us."

Jemima added, "She tells them what we're about to do. She knows even before it comes to our minds."

I made an entirely inadequate effort to scoff. "Oh, truly..."

Amy's eyes were huge dark circles. "That half-breed boy who does her bidding comes to find us in the night. He places evil thoughts in our heads. Like so." She plucked scraps of "evil" from the air round her.

"There's no such creature," I declared stoutly.

Rachel added, "She gave Brom the notion to wave the flag. She means to have the British send us to our deaths."

Oom Jan wrinkled his brow. "Why would she do that?"

"She wants to bring her vile viciousness upon us." Rachel said blithely.

Tante Margaret asked, "Is this the same woman from the church...?"

"The witch!" cried Rachel. "And Sarah is her cohort. The witch taught Sarah to invent evil spells and..." Rachel paused to collect her thoughts. "...And she taught Sarah to make herself disappear. Now Sarah comes prowling round our houses..."

"You said Sarah could fly," Jemima reminded her. "You said she can pass through closed doors."

At once Laney chimed in, "Sarah came one night to my bedchamber whilst I was sleeping..."

Samuel, plainly sceptical, pursed his lips. "But your bedchamber was burned with the rest of your house."

"I am staying with Rachel now," Laney told him. "It was her bedchamber."

"Were you not asleep, Laney?" Samuel persisted. "It must have been a dream."

Of course Rachel had been veritably panting to seize control of the conversation. She said, "It was no dream. I saw her, too. Sarah appeared as a phantom. Her form was wispy, like smoke. I could see straight through her."

Eyes bulging and mouths ajar, the small audience was in Rachel's thrall. Tom shifted his weight to put distance between us.

I looked down at my gown. A wet grey stain, remains of the oyster, marred the peach linen. I picked at it with my thumb. But at the next words, my heart rose to my throat and rendered me utterly mute.

Dan said, "Sarah was with the witch one day. The witch was telling her what leaves to pick…"

Everyone looked at me.

Dan went on, "And that's but a whit of their evil. Sarah and the witch were talking about soldiers as they gathered the leaves. They were making up a spell to curse us and help the British."

"It w-wasn't British soldiers," I stammered, and at once realized my terrible mistake. Tears burned my eyes and I loathed myself for crying.

Tante Margaret was staring at me quite as if she'd seen a spectre. She said, "Sarah, is this…?"

"She just confessed," said Dan.

For an instant my eyes met Brom's. He looked away hastily.

Of course I tried to set them straight, and of course my words were a tangle of truth and logic. Needless to say, my audience was not at all disposed to hear it.

"Hulda was telling me a tale about Indians in the hollow where she lives," I began.

Samuel gave me a stern stare. "Are Indians helping the British?"

"These were Indians of long ago. They're sleeping – *dead* – now."

"Until they've life breathed back into them by the witch," said Dan, "Perchance she changes them to British soldiers."

"Sarah makes a spell to raise the dead from their graves," Jemima declared.

"How can you speak such an untruth?" I cried.

"I saw you in the graveyard," Jemima said. "*Spooks* were dancing round you."

"Why are you...?" My face was red and my hands were slimy with sweat. My heart thumped in my bosom.

"Because you're a Tory," Rachel proclaimed. She turned to the assembly. "Sarah and the witch want the British to drive us from our homes."

This argument was entirely like a swarm of hornets. It darted, buzzed and stung, and was therefore impossible to swat down. The best rebuttal was silence, to let everyone know that their accusations were so absurd I need not answer them. Yet I must say something to defend myself.

"The Sabbath at the church," Brom recalled. "The witch said she'd seen soldiers and..." He strove to embellish the tale but he was no Rachel.

I tried to set him straight. "Hulda didn't say she had seen soldiers. She said they were going to come here."

Rachel said, "She made them burn Laney's house. She was angry at us for turning her away from the church that Sabbath."

Laney began to weep once more. "She... burned... my house."

"Your house was burned before Hulda came to the church."

No one was at all moved by my revelation of the truth.

Brom took Laney's small, white hand. "We'll burn her house then. We'll drive her far from here," he assured her.

"Sarah," added Isaac. "If the witch learns of this, we'll know who told her."

– Chapter Twenty Four –

Mama was at the desk in her closet. I perched warily on the edge of her worn blue brocade chair.

Surely she wanted to know why our party of picnickers hadn't returned until the morning after. But I thought it a trifling misdeed. Mama's closet was reserved for talks about truly terrible offences, like the time Brom and I locked Isaac in the smokehouse.

I said, "We had to wait until sun-up to come home. The moon was new and we couldn't see in the dark." I added, "*Oom* Jan and *Tante* Margaret were with us through the night."

Mama's eyebrows soared in disbelief and her nose appeared to extend another two inches, at the least.

She said, "I am told that two of His Majesty's ships..."

Somehow Mama had heard of Brom's flag and his shooting at the ships. She should be lecturing him, not me. I struggled inwardly to decide how much of Brom's folly I should reveal.

"They lay at anchor off Sing Sing," I said. "We were frightened..."

"And why was that?" The Grand Inquisitor's trap was poised to snap shut.

"The ships are very large," I offered lamely.

"His Majesty's ships are here to protect his subjects. His *loyal* subjects."

Mama was about to say that Brom had acted in a rash manner. She had no right to know everything, and it wasn't fair to try to make me betray Brom.

The brass-and-rosewood clock on the parlour mantel chimed. In the sitting room, Verkenner snored peacefully.

Mama favoured me with her through-the-spectacles stare. "I have heard disturbing news, Sarah. You continue to take up for that unfortunate woman despite..."

I was utterly astounded. How she had learned of occurrences at the picnic, I had no notion. Brom must have betrayed me. He was a very rapscallion.

To gain vengeance, I began the story of Brom's taunting, indeed firing, upon *Phoenix* and *Rose*.

Mama was not distracted. "There is even talk that you may have visited her."

"They're going to burn her house! They might kill her!"

I swung my leg and my ankle struck the tapestry footstool with a thump.

"That is not your concern," she said.

"What will happen to Hulda is the same that befell your Cousin Samuel. A mob ransacked his house and carried him off." I paused, thinking that most likely Hulda would fare far worse at the hands of a mob than an Anglican clergyman.

Mama sniffed. "I'd hardly compare anyone in my family with that wretched..."

"They're exactly the same!" I cried. "Don't you see, Mama? Don't you see?"

The sun shone through locust leaves, casting dappled patterns on my rock by Hudson's River. Brom found a stone and tossed it into the water.

"You're a fool, standing up for that witch," he said.

I retorted, "You are the greater fool, firing on His Majesty's ships. If you weren't so intent on gaining favour with Laney, you'd get your wits about you."

To my satisfaction, Brom looked worried. "Did you tell Mama about that?"

"I did not," I answered, thinking that in light of his betrayal I certainly should have. "And I don't appreciate your tattling to Mama."

"I didn't tell her anything."

"How did she find out, then?"

Brom shrugged. "*Tante* Margaret, I'd guess. She thinks you shouldn't keep company with a witch and a spy. You'll be thought to be a witch and spy, as well. In truth, you already are."

To hide the tears forming in my eyes, I leaned forward to gaze upriver. *Phoenix* and *Rose* were still lying at anchor off Sing Sing.

Brom put aside his crutch and lowered himself next to me.

"We have to rid ourselves of such tyrants," he explained, nodding toward the ships.

"Hulda is hardly a tyrant."

"She's in league with tyrants, and that's why she must go."

"Go?" I exclaimed. "There's not a shred of evidence she's a tyrant. Or a witch, either."

"Smoke in the chimney means fire on the hearth."

"What gives you the right to pass judgment on someone else?"

"This is war," Brom declared. "We need do whatever we must. We're fighting to be free."

"Is that what our Declaration of Independence says? That your freedom is more important than hers? That you have leave to destroy her to protect yourself?"

Brom gazed at the river for a time. When he spoke, his answer wasn't truly an answer. He said, "You must be a witch, just like that woman. That's what Dan thinks."

∞

"*Puffertje*, your heart is kind. But these are matters that we must leave alone."

Papa and I were in the barn. He was sharpening scythes for the coming harvest.

He said, "I know you want to help this woman but you cannot. You must leave her to God."

"Didn't God command us to love our neighbours?"

Dusty sunlight filtered through gaps in the barn's wooden planks. The scents of hay and cattle mingled in an earthy perfume. The blade scraped against the whetstone.

∞

Hulda picked a withered marigold. She split it open and little white-tipped splinters spilled into her hand. "The new flower," she said, shaking the seeds into a small leather pouch.

I knelt beside her in her garden. "They're going to burn your house! They're going to kill you!

"People are telling monstrous lies about you," I went on. "They said you were talking with British soldiers."

"I talk the soldiers." Hulda picked another marigold.

"No, they think you were…" I wasn't certain how to explain spying. "…Helping the soldiers."

"I help the soldier. He have the hurt here." She tapped her head.

"But people don't understand. They're coming to attack you."

"Who comes?"

"My cousin Dan, for one. And others."

Hulda leaned on her knee and pushed herself to her feet. "They have the fear. Like the snake. It bite because it have the fear."

I'd pondered that puzzling remark since I'd first heard it uttered. It was on the day I met Hulda, that day with Rachel and the rattlesnake.

Hulda made her way down a row of hollyhocks and I followed her. The pink and white blossoms were so weighty that the stalks bent over the path. Hulda lifted them aside gently so we could pass.

I said, "They're afraid of the British because they're so much mightier. I don't know why they're afraid of you."

"*Ach, Liebchen!* They have the fear of me because I do as I will." Hulda stopped before a bed of kitchen herbs. She frowned at a leaf with a brown edge, and plucked it off.

"They're afraid of you because you're free?"

"*Ja.* They have also the fear of you, *Liebchen.*"

"I'm not free!" Hulda should pass some time with Mama.

"You come here," she pointed out, moving on to the feathery green dill.

"Why does that make people afraid?"

Hulda stood and faced me. I could see the red line on her head where she'd been wounded. Her hair, light brown with silver strands, was growing back, but it was not yet long enough to draw away from her face.

She said, "With you they see brave. You show them how they could be. They have the fear to be as brave as you. They do not like to know that."

"Why don't they allow me to go my own way? I do them no ill."

Hulda surveyed her garden. "People not like flowers," she said. "You see this rosemary? This bay leaf?"

I nodded.

"They grow here and here." She meant next to each other. "Rosemary have no wish to be bay leaf. Bay leaf not angry that rosemary have needles, not leaves."

"And I'll warrant it's not vexed that the bay leaf isn't another rosemary," I commented.

"*Ja, Liebchen.* You see."

"But what about people?"

"People like birds," she said. "Birds see chick that is not like others, they push from nest."

"But then the little bird will die!" I exclaimed.

Hulda brought her face close to mine. She pushed a finger into my bosom. "You not die. You strong. Go own way."

I strove to understand. "But what of Brom? Brom is my brother," I explained. "He's going to attack you and the only reason is that he wants to gain favour with that ninny Laney van Tassel. Or that flighty Amy, who..."

Hulda frowned. "The Laney house have the fire?"

"That's right. Soldiers burned her house and so..." I tried to make sense of this absurdity but I could not.

"The brother need love. We make the charm."

"A love charm? How will that help?"

"He will not have the fear that Laney and Amy not love him." Hulda pinched off a sprig of dill, examined it and nodded. "This one keep away the bad."

"What's that you're picking now?"

"For the happy."

"It smells like sweet marjoram," I told her.

"*Ja.* And this." She plucked a stalk of rosemary. "This so the brother remember."

She tapped her head.

I had no notion what Brom was supposed to remember. He should forget the foolish thought that attacking Hulda would aid the cause of independence.

"This one for the brave." She tried to pick some thyme but it didn't yield.

"You see, *Liebchen*, this plant brave." She took a small-pearl-handled knife from her pocket and made a deft cut. "Now we find the bag."

I followed her into her dim, cave-like dwelling and watched as she opened a drawer of the big walnut chest in the corner.

"Why, that's a Bible," I exclaimed as she lifted a book from the drawer and laid it carefully on the tree stump that served as her table.

Hulda gave me a searching look.

"I mean…it's such a lovely old volume." I ran my hand over the black-leather cover with worn gilded lettering. "You must have had this for a long time. Did it come from across the sea?"

"*Ja*. See, *Liebchen*." She opened the Bible to a yellowed page with names writ in black ink in a stilted hand. Some of the letters had dots above them. "The family. The Hulda family."

She closed the book and returned it to the chest. "Here now is the charm for the brother," she said briskly, and I suspected she didn't fancy speaking of sentimental matters.

It came to me that I also needed help in finding my way through the maze of travails I'd encountered of late. "Could I have a charm, too?"

"You have the happy, the love and the brave."

"I care naught for love," I said, thinking of that dolt, Tom. "But I would like someone who would take my part once or twice."

"You have also the glass."

"I don't have the glass. It was stolen by some horrid men who…" My remaining words were lost in a sob. "I suppose you were right, you cannot possess a thing forever," I added.

She pondered for a moment. "*Liebchen*, you keep a thing forever. Many things. Here." She tapped her brow. "Others, too. You see with your own eyes. People look at same thing, but not see what you see."

As Hulda embraced me, I realized with amazement that she was the shorter of us. I'd always seen her as being of my stature, if not greater. She had to raise her arms to put them round my shoulders, and her head lay on my bosom.

I wept and wept, for no reason or perchance for every reason. She patted me and made little clucking noises I supposed were meant to comfort me.

I was comforted, somehow. It was quite as if I'd shed the cloak of sorrow that had been wrapped round me for a long time. I no longer needed to hide in its dark folds. I could stand in the summer air and flourish like a flower.

There was a boom in the distance, and another. I'd not heard the sound but I knew *Phoenix* and *Rose* were firing their big guns. That hollow thunder hadn't come from the north, from Sing Sing. It had come from the south, where our farm lay.

I stuffed Brom's love charm into my pocket and bade Hulda a hasty farewell.

"The glass come back," she called after me.

– Chapter Twenty Five –

As I reached my rock by Hudson's River, I came upon a truly astonishing sight: *Phoenix* had run hard aground. She perched on a shoal near Kidd's Rock like a grand lady atop an entirely inadequate footstool. *Rose* had set anchor. Four smaller British vessels crowded round like anxious children.

Seamen from *Phoenix* had rowed out into the river. Their silhouettes were black against the sunlight glittering on the water. As I watched, they heaved an anchor overboard. I supposed that, lacking wind, their intentions were to pull the great ship into deeper water. The seamen should have spared themselves their labour, I thought. *Phoenix* would float when the tide came back in.

I shaded my eyes with my hand to watch her crew's endeavours. There was great scurrying round. *Phoenix* was withdrawing her cannons. One disappeared from its square porthole, then another. Great rumblings came from the ship's belly.

Was the warship signalling surrender? That seemed unlikely.

After a time I marked that *Phoenix's* stern had risen a bit. Shouts of elation came from the ship. It seemed that the cannons were being moved forward to put more weight on *Phoenix's* bow. Perhaps then the ship would float more quickly.

Of course the ship's woes had not escaped notice. A dozen men and boys had gathered at the mouth of the Pocantico. I saw Brom's fair hair amidst the darker heads, and I made my way along the rocky bank to join them.

"The British fired their cannons. What happened?" I asked Brom.

Dan answered for him. "Some *zots* were firing at the ships and *Phoenix* shot back. Now they know we're coming for them."

"Coming for them? Who is coming?" I asked.

"Those *zots* may prove to be a diversion," Brom said.

Oom Jan gazed downriver. "Tide's turned. *Phoenix* will be back afloat soon."

I was utterly puzzled, and peeved as well. Why did no one answer me?

Samuel Youngs came loping swiftly along the rocky bank. "They're in sight!" he cried.

About a half-dozen awkward vessels, scarcely larger than market sloops, were advancing up the river. Blue pennants streamed and white sails jutted at a rakish angle from their twin masts. A line of oars, at least a dozen on either side, was pulling them towards us, and they looked for all the world like great wooden grasshoppers with crooked wings. I had never seen the like.

Oom Jan pointed at the water flowing north past Kidd's Rock. "Let's not tarry," he said.

He started up the path to the mill, and the others followed. It came to me that *Zomer Wind* must be at the mill pier.

"You can't be thinking of... attacking *Phoenix* and *Rose*? Why, that would be utter folly," I cried.

Samuel answered, "*Phoenix* and *Rose* are geese on a pond. We shall cook them."

"Armed geese," I retorted.

The tide was flowing briskly now. *Phoenix*, the mythical bird that rose back to life from ashes, was proving to be true to her name. She wobbled and swayed, and uttered a great moan as she rose unsteadily from the rock. She was afloat.

The odd little boats were coming closer. Their sails sagged on that windless day, but their oars dipped rhythmically into the water and propelled them closer.

Zomer Wind slipped past as she sailed out of the Pocantico into Hudson's River.

Oom Jan called, "Stand by to come about." Brom, seated on the transom, loosened the lines holding the foresail. *Oom* Jan pushed the tiller as far to the left – *larboard* – as it would go. The boom swung with a great thunk and Samuel hauled in the lines on the other side. *Zomer Wind's* bowsprit nosed eagerly into Hudson's River.

They were indeed going to attack the British ships. *Zomer* called to my mind a toy boat that Papa had whittled for Thomas: a tiny craft bobbing haplessly in a large tub of water.

The larger boats had almost reached *Phoenix* and *Rose*. I shouted to *Oom* Jan but the wind swallowed my warning. I raced up the path to the mill. The pier was deserted, but Ceaser appeared at a window when I called.

"*Oom* Jan and Brom went out to fight the warships, but they'll be blown to pieces! Some other boats are coming," I cried.

"Be calm, Missy Sarah." Ceaser disappeared and in a moment joined me on the pier. We looked down the Pocantico toward Hudson's River, but willows at the water's edge blocked our view.

Ceaser searched in his pockets. He held out empty hands to show he had no sweetmeats. "Do these boats come from downriver?" he asked. "Those are boats of the American navy. They will help Jan and Brom."

"The boats have oars," I told him.

"They are row galleys. In a battle, often the wind does not help."

"How did they learn of *Phoenix's* distress?"

"Elijah rode to tell them. He made great haste, for when the tide turns the big ships will get back their advantage."

The sound of cannon firing roared up the Pocantico.

"Go home, Missy Sarah," Ceaser told me. "With the shooting there is no place for you."

I nodded and ran back to see what was happening.

It appeared that at first the British had paid no mind to *Zomer Wind* or the other trifling sloops on the river. But the galleys swarmed round them now.

Those scoundrels who attacked me had said something about *Rose*. Likely they had intended to join the American navy. Perhaps my prism was on one of those boats. I squinted to see if I could spy the man in a black hat who had stolen it from me.

The next blast fairly deafened me. I covered my ears as a puff of smoke drifted from one of *Phoenix's* square eyes. Shots from a galley answered the British fire. I heard a low whistle as an iron ball sped toward *Phoenix*, and then the creaking sound of timbers breaking. I could hardly see, but I thought the Americans had landed a shot in the warship's bow.

Three galleys formed an unsteady line facing *Phoenix* and *Rose*. They were close enough now to fire smaller ammunition. The galleys' crews were loading canvas bags of grapeshot into the guns on their decks. As they returned fire, I noted with dismay the great wall of cannon facing them. *Phoenix* and *Rose* were veritable fortresses, as forbidding as any of the stone castles I'd seen in Mama's books. The guns on *Phoenix's* lower deck alone were greater than the guns on all six galleys.

The galleys pitched in and out of view in the smoke that shrouded the river. Oarsmen struggled to steady the little craft, but the tide, rising smartly now, had turned the galleys broadside to the warships. The full destructive might of His Majesty's Navy rained upon them.

Galleys' hulls were ripped open, their oars reduced to splinters. One galley's bow gun was cut cleanly in two.

The masts of *Phoenix* and *Rose* protruded from the pall of smoke. The ships themselves were nigh invisible. *Zomer Wind* had disappeared altogether. My eyes watered and I fairly choked with the bitter smell and vapour.

An iron ball the size of a cherry slammed into the rock I was standing on. A sharp pebble stung my shoulder and I staggered and fell. Another shot flew past me into the underbrush. I lay still for a long moment, praying that with the noise and smoke of battle they couldn't hear my rasping breath or see my trembling arms and legs. After a long while, I crawled to hide amongst the willows and tall grasses on the river's bank. Ceaser was right: a battle was indeed no place for chance observers. Yet I couldn't summon the resolve to leave.

For an instant the smoke cleared. I could see a half-dozen places on *Phoenix* where American guns had shot holes in the huge hull. One shot had hit a spar on *Phoenix's* foremast. The wooden pole was nearly broken in two. It dangled perilously above the deck. Seamen strove in vain to clear away the canvas that drooped from the spar shrouding the deck.

A sailor had climbed the foremast. Clutching the spar and searching with his bare toes for a foothold amongst the lines, he inched his way out toward the place where it had broken.

Zomer Wind was hard by *Phoenix's* massive hull, her mast bobbing before the gun ports. Brom was in the bow. He had Papa's gun. The boat lurched in the roiling waters, and Brom made several tries to steady himself on his crutch.

The sailor reached the tangled sails. He took out a knife and began to cut them loose. An officer on deck was shouting orders. Brom raised the old fowling piece, aimed and fired.

The sailor screamed. His arms flailed as he tumbled into the river. Several men leaned over the deck rail, calling to him as he floundered round.

Brom was sprawled on *Zomer's* deck, exhausted, I supposed, from the effort of standing and firing the heavy gun. Nonetheless, he saw the musket on *Phoenix* raised and pointed at him. He scrambled round the lowered jib and vanished in its folds. Samuel saw the musket, too, and dove for cover. I saw *Oom* Jan crouch, all the while holding fast to the tiller.

Brom tumbled overboard. Perchance he had meant to, as he'd leaned back off the transom, clutching the gun. For a long moment I couldn't see him, and I wondered if the British had shot him. Then his head appeared behind *Zomer's* broad wooden rudder. I wondered if the river was shallow enough for him to stand, and then I had a pleasing revelation: in water, Brom's crippled leg was not the encumbrance it was on land. In fact, he could move the more freely.

The sailor thrashed about. I called to mind a triviality that Mama had once told me: Sailors did not know how to swim. If they had the ill fortune to fall overboard, their drowning would be easier, she said. That seemed to me to be small consolation. I wondered if the sailor had yet realized that the water was in fact quite shallow. If he could make his way to the bank he needn't drown.

A musket ball whined as it sped toward *Zomer Wind*. The soldiers were aiming at her once more. Brom ducked behind the rudder as grapeshot pelted the little sloop.

Fire spat from one of *Phoenix's* cannons. There was a blast, and a great creaking groan. *Zomer Wind* had surely been hit. A cloud of smoke surrounded her. Her rudder had been sheared away.

There was another blast. *Zomer Wind's* mast snapped and toppled over. Someone screamed as the boom came crashing down.

Crumpled sails covered *Zomer's* deck as well. It came to me that the little boat looked entirely like a laundry basket tossing helplessly in the angry waters. Samuel floundered round, but I couldn't see *Oom*

Jan. I scanned the waters round *Zomer's* stern, but there was no sign of Brom. Had the shot that took away the rudder struck him also?

The sailor was drifting upriver. Likely, he was dead. Perhaps his mates on board *Phoenix* had put an end to his suffering. Great splinters of wood – broken oars, a section of a mast – were strewn across the water. An American galley, the one with the flag, had a wide hole where her bow had been. I could see her curved timber ribs and the barrels in her hold. One galley seemed to be attempting to retreat. Her single gun had been shot away and her sails were in tatters. A third vessel was listing so far to starboard that her sails nearly touched the water. Water rushed through a wide breach in her hull. One by one, the wounded galleys turned from the battle. With scarce wind and against the tide, they set a course downriver.

Zomer Wind – or what remained of her – was wallowing in the waves stirred up by the battle. She had drifted so close to *Phoenix* that they must collide. I wondered if the British would set fire to her. There was no trace of *Oom* Jan or Samuel. Brom hadn't been aboard when the boat was hit, so perhaps he wasn't harmed. I squinted and shaded my eyes as I scanned the river for a wet blond head amid the drifting rubble. The water lapped higher on the rocks.

I had to go home to tell Mama and Papa. They had surely heard the terrible tumult of the battle. Possibly Brom had been spared. Perhaps he'd made his way to shore and was hiding amongst the rushes at the water's edge. I took one more look before I turned to make my way home.

As I came near our farm, I saw two vultures wheeling silently above the cornfield. Their wide black wings raked the sky. I supposed they had found a dead animal, for they flapped to the ground beneath the sycamore tree.

Under the tree was a crumpled mound of blue and white. I walked closer to this oddity and the vultures raised their horrid fleshy red heads to stare at me. They flew reluctantly to a dead branch as I approached.

I was but a scant rod away when the pile appeared to move. A bare leg emerged and then an arm. The sailor Brom had shot rolled toward me and sat up. I should have fled at that very instant, but I merely stared, astonished.

"'Ey there! You!" He struggled to stand. I'd thought him badly wounded, at the least. It appeared he'd not only survived both being shot and falling into the river, but he was on his feet coming after me.

I darted into the cornfield. Weeds pulled at my feet and leaves snatched my sleeves. Clouds of gnats, annoyed that I'd disturbed them, flew in my face. I heard swishing and snapping behind me as cornstalks bent and broke. The sailor had followed me into the field. I could hear his rasping breath.

I could see only stalks and leaves. Our barn must be somewhere to the right. If I could reach it, Papa would save me. A vine caught my foot as I turned and I stumbled.

At once I could see the sky, a deep summer blue mottled with the smoke of battle. I'd reached the gully that ran through the field; the corn growing near the muddy ditch was scarcely as high as my waist. Across the gully was the sailor. He was not ten paces away.

I plunged back into the higher corn. The sailor came clumping after me. He could see and hear the stalks move as I ran, so he could follow me with little effort. I crouched and pressed my hands against my stays to quiet my fevered breathing.

I saw his bare legs pass a few rows away. They stopped and turned. The sailor stood over me. He seized my arm and pulled me to my feet.

- Chapter Twenty Six -

The sailor was so slight of stature, he was no bigger than Tom Buckhout's ten-year-old brother, but he was weathered as an old boot. Indeed, his skin was the colour of leather – a coppery tan – and it was etched with deep furrows. Black specks of gunpowder, traces of blood and a hole the size of a sixpence marked the left shoulder of his loose-fitting blue shirt. This was the very wretch that Brom had shot.

"Ye're a lass, by Jove!" the sailor exclaimed. "Ye're tall for a gal. Thought ye might be a lad in gal's dress. When we saw ye watching the row, we thought ye was sending signals to the rebels in the sloop." His eyes were the colour of a musket barrel. "Was ye?"

I shook my head.

"Why was ye there then?"

I couldn't say that my brother had shot him. I couldn't say that *Zomer Wind* was my uncle's boat. I could say the battle, the *row*, took place near our farm, but I didn't want this fellow to know where I lived.

"I-I heard the shooting," I told him. I pulled a burr from my skirt. I willed my hands to stop shaking but they didn't.

"Acquainted with the 'ealing woman, are ye?"

"The eeling woman?"

"Don't be saucy now. I don't favour saucy gals."

"I don't understand what you said."

"I said the 'ealing woman."

"The *healing* woman?" He meant Hulda. This wretch had just fallen off a British ship and he knew about Hulda.

"Got 'it in the shoulder by some damned rebel," he complained. "'Urts like the divvil."

I eyed him warily.

"Know the 'ealing woman, do ye? Ye'll take me to her. Come on then."

"But..." I protested.

"This may set yer resolve."

He pulled a knife from his belt and spun me round. His knife was at my back as he marched me out of the cornfield. I looked about desperately for Papa or Mama or even Thomas. But the sailor steered me away from our house and barn.

"Where's this road go?" He peered at the Post Road but kept his knife pointed between my shoulders.

"North and south." I could utter no more than a few words between fitful breaths.

"And which way to the 'ealing woman?"

"That way." I pointed south.

In an instant he had his knife at my throat. "That way's the mill wot's a 'ideout for rebels."

I was startled to learn that Philipse's Mill had such notoriety. I took a deep breath and said, "To reach her home, we need pass the mill. We turn at the church and go north through a little hollow. That's where she lives."

The sailor came close. He had the rotted smell of river water and dried blood. "One trick and I'll slice ye up and use ye fer bait."

The sailor was favouring his injured shoulder, but I could see the muscles in his arms. He was strong. He must be quick as well, from climbing ships' rigging. Once I'd led him to Hulda, what would he do with me? It wasn't likely he would let me go free. He would kill me, or worse, take me back to *Phoenix*. Then they'd put me on a prison ship in New York harbour. Perhaps Brom would be locked in the same putrid hold. No one would ever know what had become of either of us.

I bit my lip so I wouldn't cry but a sniffle escaped.

"Don't start tunin' yer pipes now." As both his arms were engaged in restraining me, he pointed with his chin. "That's the mill, is it?"

Someone was standing by the milldam watching water pour into the pond below. I gasped as I recognized his brown hat. It was Dan.

The sailor asked, "Know that feller?"

"He's my cousin."

In an instant, the sailor shifted his knife to his left hand and put his right arm round me to restrain me from waving my hands to signal.

Dan peered at us. Like Rachel, he was short-sighted. Perchance he couldn't see me. He took a few steps toward us and called, "Hallo, Sarah the Spy!"

"'E say something about a spy?" The knife worked its way through my stays.

"Halloo, Spy!" Dan shouted again.

I conjured a gratifying scene of Dan roasting amidst the fiery coals of Hell.

He called, "What happened to your brother after he shot the sailor?"

The sailor's knife pierced my stays. "'Twas *your brother* shot me?"

"No! No! You misunderstand." I managed to squirm away from the knifepoint.

Dan ambled up the hill towards us and I quickened the pace. I had hoped that someone at the mill would come to my aid, but with my accursed luck, I'd encountered the one blackguard who would send me to my doom.

Dan called, "Who's your redcoat chum there? Paying a visit to the witch?"

The sailor jabbed me again. "You rebels is bloody clever, you is. 'Ow's he know that?"

I shook my arm free from the sailor's grip and called to Dan, "He's a fellow from Cortlandt Manor. He wants to know the way to the Romers' place."

Fortune had not abandoned me altogether. At that instant a man's voice called from the mill, "Dan, help me with these wheat sacks."

"Here's where we turn," I told the sailor. I hurried him down the path past the graveyard and into the hollow. The sailor looked round at the mossy rock walls and silent hemlocks.

"Can't see why 'Is Majesty is keen on keeping this bloody wilderness. Not a proper pub. Gals wot are giants and..." he gestured toward the graveyard, now out of view. "A land not fit for the living."

"It's said this hollow is haunted," I told him.

"'Aunted, you say? What sort of 'aunts?"

"There's an old Indian chief."

He looked about nervously. "An Injun? With one of them 'atchets wot peels off yer 'air like a potato skin?"

There was a rustling sound.

"Wot?"

"I heard something."

"Don't tell me it's that old Injun now. I'm losin' me patience."

There it was again. A footfall and a branch snapping. Up on the ridge. Someone was following us. Whoever it was, he would surely know that the sailor wasn't from Cortlandt Manor. Nobody in this colony said "po-tye-to" or "pye-shunce." He would realize that I was aiding the enemy. He would know we were going to Hulda's. He would have proof that I was a traitor. I was sure I'd spied a flash of brown in the brush where the noise came from. Dan's hat was brown.

"Bloody 'ell!" The sailor slipped on wet moss. He snatched at the air as he tumbled down the rocky bank and landed in the stream. He thrashed about in the shallow water.

"Something pushed me foot," he complained. "Been walking wet decks since I was a babe." He winced as he tried to get to his feet. "Zounds, me shoulder!"

"Hush, now!" I snapped. "You make such a din, you'll wake the others."

The sailor's eyes were as large as pewter plates. "Wot others?"

"The other Indians. There's a whole tribe. If their sleep is disturbed, they'll be in a foul temper, for certain." I was beginning to relish having the upper hand. "Sssh!"

"Wot now?"

"I think I heard them. Up there." I pointed in the direction of the rustling. To my surprise and gratification, the bushes crackled once more.

The sailor struggled to rise. "Me foot's gone crooked," he complained.

"The old chief pushed you down," I told him. "He doesn't favour scapegraces in his domain." I was seized with inspiration. "And he doesn't favour knives. We'd best give him this one."

I picked up the sailor's knife. I drew my arm back and threw the knife as far as I could. It sailed past a sapling maple, over the tangled laurels and out of sight amongst the thorny underbrush.

The sailor shivered. "'Elp me now, there's a lass. Don't leave me 'ere with them bloody Injuns!"

"I will help you," I said in a voice I didn't recognise as mine. "But the old chief is watching. Unless you want to stay here for all time, you'd best be meek. And very quiet."

I stepped down the bank and extended a hand to him.

∞

Hulda burst out laughing when she saw me with the sailor. "You have here *Der Gefangener*," she said as she motioned for us to come in.

"The what?"

"The... catch." Hulda brought her hands together as if she were clasping them in a trap.

"Prisoner? But he captured me. I'm his prisoner."

"*Nein, Liebchen.*" She chuckled as she led the sailor to the light and pulled his arm from his shirtsleeve.

"Owww, me arm! Don't cut off me arm!"

Hulda probed his shoulder. "*Nichts.* No bad hurt. The shot will come out like so."

She made pincers with her fingers and clasped them together. "Who is this... prisoner?"

"I'm a sailor wot's on *Phoenix*. This gal stole me knife after 'er brother shot me clean out of the rigging. Nearly died, I did." He sank onto the blanket-covered bench by the wall.

Hulda regarded him severely. "You have the knife?"

"I did until that gal threw it to the old Injun after 'e pushed me into the water."

"You make the scare for Sarah?"

I sat down opposite the sailor. "He came ashore and chased me down in our field and stuck a knife in my back and made me lead him to you. I'm not certain how he knew that you..."

"She 'elps us," the sailor chimed in. "Tended to that 'Essian wot got 'it in the 'ead with a shovel by a serving gal and..."

My jaw dropped nearly to the floor. "Were there *Hessians* on a British ship?"

"Boatload of 'em," the sailor told me.

"Hessians? Aren't they German?"

Hulda had followed this exchange. "*Ja*, from Hesse. Not far from *mein* home."

"So they speak German?"

The sailor snorted. "Don't speak the King's English. I'll vouch for that."

The soldiers that had attacked Laney's farm weren't British. They were Hessian. They spoke in the same tongue as Hulda. That was why Laney claimed that they talked witch-talk.

"Them 'Essians is nasty devils, they is," the sailor allowed. "Wouldn't fancy 'aving one look down a musket barrel at me."

Hulda pulled a pair of small pincers and a curved metal hook from the pot where she had set them to boiling. She laid them on the clean linen cloth she'd placed on her stump-table.

She turned to me. "No need you stay."

The sailor wailed, "'Ow's I'm going to get back to me ship? Don't cotton to this bloody wilderness."

"The ball now," Hulda said briskly. She lifted the sailor's arm and pulled away the sleeve of his torn, bloody shirt.

– Chapter Twenty Seven –

Dawn's grey light seeped into my bedchamber and the mocking-bird's morning song drifted into my dreams: "Be wary wary wary."

The trilling stopped and Verkenner began to bark. A horse was pounding up our lane. I blinked awake and sat up as the rider jumped down and banged on our door.

Likely everyone else was asleep, too. It was a long moment before I heard Papa's voice. The top half of the door swung open. I jumped from my bed and threw open the shutters, but could see naught but that the rider was a man with brown breeches. A wide-brimmed hat concealed his face.

"The British have put ashore. They're searching for Brom," he said.

There was a high keening sound and I knew Mama had heard. I ran into the boys' bedchamber. "Brom! Wake up! The British are coming to take you away."

Brom groaned and rolled over, but Thomas leaped from his bed in a trice. He'd been General Washington for nearly a fortnight. The stick that had served as a royal sceptre had become his sword.

"Muster the troops!" Thomas shrieked.

I hurried to the top of the stairs and called down, "How long before they get here?"

"They've passed the church."

I ran back to the chamber. Brom slumped on the edge of the bed, rubbing his crippled forearm. His cheek was marked with a purple bruise, acquired, I supposed, during yesterday's battle.

"You've less than five minutes to run," I told him as it came to me that Brom could manage no speedier gait than a hobble. I threw his breeches and stockings at him and hurried back to my chamber. I tightened my stays so quickly the laces nearly broke. As I pulled on the blue calico skirts I'd worn the day before, a small cloth bag fell to the floor. It was the charm that Hulda had fashioned for Brom. I ran back to his chamber.

"Brom, I've something for you." I held out the little bag.

Balancing with his crutch under one arm, Brom was making a clumsy attempt to button his breeches. He waved the charm aside.

"Hurry! They're coming! They're coming here!"

Brom looked up at me. "How will they know to come here? You and your chum the witch tell them?"

I was utterly confounded, not in the least because Brom's remark contained a nugget of truth. Thanks to Dan, the sailor knew my brother was the one who'd shot him. He knew where we lived. But what had happened to the sailor? He didn't know the way back to the ships. He'd allowed as much. Perchance he'd passed the night at Hulda's.

"They're coming this way. Ours is the first farm they'll pass," I told him, silently congratulating myself for the prompt and altogether logical reply.

Brom hobbled down the stairs, wincing with each footfall. I wondered what new injuries he had acquired yesterday and also how he could ever elude determined and seasoned pursuers.

Papa was pacing the floor and Mama was searching for her spectacles. Thomas peered out the window. "They're here," he shrilled. "Stand and fight!"

Mama went into her closet and pushed open a window by her desk. "You must get away," she told Brom. "Sarah, you and Thomas go outside to greet them."

"Greet them?"

"Why, yes," she responded, as if welcoming a party of enemy soldiers were quite the custom. "Take a bucket. Go to the well. Offer them water. Thomas, you are not to speak of General Washington."

Mama's plan was artful indeed. We were to delay the soldiers at least until Brom could hide. If we appeared to be frightened or surly, the soldiers would know that if Brom did not live there, other rebels surely did. If we played our parts well, perchance they would go away.

I realized I was still holding Brom's charm. I stuffed it into my pocket, took up the water bucket and stepped outside. A half-dozen of redcoats were advancing up our lane.

These were no Hessian witch-soldiers. They wore not only scarlet jackets with gold trim on their shoulders, but bright red waistcoats as well. I'd not seen such hats ever. They were leather caps with crowns and the letters "GR" etched on the high peaks in front. I supposed they were intended to make the soldiers appear bigger and more fearsome, but their muskets – nearly as tall as the men and fitted with sharp three-sided bayonets – were dreadful enough.

I spied the sailor, although I had but an instant to think on his treachery.

"You there, girl. Put down the bucket and come here," one soldier ordered. I took him to be an officer, for his hat was laced with gold and bore a black cockade.

I walked toward them, scowling at the sailor. I was pleased to see that he looked sheepish.

The officer asked, "Is this your house?"

I wondered why he thought I'd be drawing water from the well if I didn't live here. I realised that he took me for a serving girl, and I flushed with anger. The British had no right to set foot on our farm

quite as if they owned it. They had no reason for their arrogant behaviour.

The sailor spoke up. "What 'e wants to know is, where's the chap
with the yellow 'air? 'E's your brother, right? That clown wot shot
me?"

Thomas had taken refuge behind my skirts. "This is my brother," I told them.

Thomas' dark eyes were enormous as he took in the sight. "Why
does it say 'GR' on your hats?" he asked.

"It's for 'George Rex,' my lad. 'Rex' means king. George is your
king," one soldier explained.

Thomas frowned. "There's another George. He's a general.
General Wash'tun."

I tried to pinch him inconspicuously.

The soldiers snickered.

"General Washtub, you say? Ho, that's rich! We'll give him a
scrubbing right enough."

The officer silenced them with a stern look. "You have no other
brothers?" he inquired.

I looked downcast and bit my lip. "There." I pointed to the three
small gravestones under the beech tree.

"Two brothers," Thomas said mournfully. "And a sister. They
died."

Mama came hurrying out of the house. She was veritably aglow
with cordiality.

"And she's our mother," Isaac told the soldiers.

"I am so relieved to see His Majesty's troops!" Mama exclaimed.
"Those rebels have been most disagreeable, I fear."

The officer made a slight bow. "That's quite true, Ma'am," he
answered. "We're after one in particular, a young fellow with fair
hair. Have you seen...?"

"I have indeed," said Mama, as I gulped and Thomas gawked.

"Have you inquired at the mill? I'm quite certain he's been there."

Mama had just said, "bean," and she'd said "they-ah" in the best Seabury-Royalist manner.

"We've just come from the mill, Ma'am. Begging your pardon, we must have a look round now. We hope not to trouble you."

I marked the slight waver before Mama responded. "Not at all," she said. "In fact, I do hope you'll take some refreshment. Sarah, could you put the tea kettle on, please?"

I took it that she was telling me to go inside to hide away evidence that Brom lived there. But what was I to do about his bed? Rachel had said that the first thing soldiers did when they raided a house was to count the beds. That was how they knew how many people lived there.

Providence intervened in the unlikely person of the sailor. He looked at the ground and shifted his weight from the foot he'd twisted yesterday in the stream. He cleared his throat. "'Ere now, perhaps I 'ave myde a mistyke. Must have been another 'ouse what 'as a yellow-'aired rebel. No rebels 'ere."

"I'm certain you're right," the officer told him. "We'll be on our way then. We regret to have troubled you, Ma'am."

"Now there's a proper English lady," I heard him remark as they withdrew. "Not like those contrary wenches in Boston."

Mama bent over the kitchen table, her head in her hands. Isaac nestled beside her.

"Stop shaking, Mama. You mustn't be 'fraid. You're as brave as General Wash'tun."

Mama smiled ruefully. "I fear I am a bit frayed. That was most harrowing."

"We tricked the bad soldiers," Thomas pointed out.

I sat on the bench across from her. "Yes, Mama, that was *trompe l'oeil*. You fooled their eyes."

"I suppose the art is to make people believe what they see," Mama mused. "It's like that cunning little glass that your Papa...oh, wait! With all the ado, I'd forgot."

She rose and went to the cupboard. She opened the door and took out my prism.

The prism had been in a dozen hands, at the least, judging from the fingerprints that smudged it, but it was surely the same round glass with triangular facets. As Hulda had foreseen, the glass had indeed come back to me. I cradled it in my palm, feeling its weight, admiring its airy rainbow as it caught the sunlight.

Mama rose to stir the fire. She said, "That fellow who brought it by is the one who was here this morning. He's your brother's friend from the mill. Elijah."

"Elijah? I've not met him."

Mama turned to me. "He said he saw you yesterday."

- Chapter Twenty Eight -

In the sitting room, Mama and I tended to the mending, Elizabeth dozed in her cradle and Thomas played on the floor. The only sound was the clap as he landed the small wooden ball in the cup on the stick he held. The toy had once been Brom's.

We did not speak of them, but Papa and Brom infused the very air with their absence. Brom had tried to flee by squeezing through a window in Mama's closet. His crutch had fallen to the ground. Then Papa had gone first and helped Brom as he struggled over the sill. Mama did not tarry. She shut the window behind them and went outside to join Isaac and me as we faced the soldiers. That was the last any of us had seen of Brom or Papa.

Just before midday, we heard a clamour on the Albany Post Road. Surely, this portended good news. Perhaps Brom was among them, recounting with relish how he had eluded the redcoats. Papa would be there, too. I wondered briefly why they had not come home first but I banished the troublesome thought.

"I'm going to go see..." I told Mama, who blinked at me through her spectacles like an appalled owl. "Mama, I'll be well. No one is shooting."

I ran upstairs to my bedchamber and set my prism on the washstand. No one would take it from me ever again. I tied on my straw hat and hurried out the door.

The redcoats were marching north on the Post Road in tidy rows, bearing their muskets on their shoulders. The six who had been at our house this morning had multiplied to a score, at the least. Right foot, left foot. Their legs, with white stockings and dark gaiters, swung forward at exactly the same pace. Their scarlet coats brightened and faded as they marched in and out of the sunshine under the elm trees along the road. Their bayonets gleamed.

An equal party of our neighbours trailed the soldiers. There was a grim and angry air about them. Brom and Papa were not amongst them.

Across the road I saw Jemima's ginger-haired cousin Isaac, Amy's brother Gabriel and James Romer, who carried a fowling gun slung over his shoulder. Samuel Youngs was gesturing with his long, ungainly arms as he spoke to them. His father Joseph was pointing at the redcoats and shouting something about tyranny.

Isaac Martling was there, of course. Tom Buckhout's little brother Jake was balancing atop the stone wall at the edge of our orchard, his arms outstretched. Dan was with him and Tom. He grabbed a fistful of cherries from a low-hanging branch as he passed. Amy and Rachel were walking beside a tall, bearded young man I'd not seen before.

The third faction surprised me, because it included those who customarily avoided a fray. *Mevrouw* Frena Romer had climbed a small way up an embankment, the better to see, I supposed. *Tante* Gertje was beside her.

I started as *Oom* Willem came up to me and took my arm. "Is there word of Abraham?"

"Brom got out of the house this morning just as the soldiers were coming up our lane. I don't know what became of him."

In the silence that followed, I could tell *Oom* Willem did know, and was pondering whether to tell me. At last, he said bitterly, "The soldiers hunted him down like a rabbit. They locked him in chains and broke his crutch to bits. When he could not walk, they kicked him as he crawled."

My hand flew to my mouth as I envisioned this horrifying scene. "Where is he now?" I asked.

Oom Willem said, "He is their prisoner."

After a moment I asked, "And what of Papa? Did you see him?"

It was his turn to be shocked. "Peter is gone, as well?"

"He was helping Brom."

Oom Willem stood in silence, his head bowed. At length he said, "Did the soldiers burn or steal? Are the little ones…?"

"We are well." I choked on the words. "How is *Oom* Jan? Brom said *Zomer Wind's* boom knocked him senseless as it fell."

"Margaret is tending to him. He must not move his head," *Oom* Willem answered.

Dan sauntered over. "Who was the Tory you were cosying with yesterday?" he asked me.

"Why, you are the villain…" I began.

Oom Willem said, "Daniel, you must not vex your cousin. Our family has many troubles."

"And your son is the very cause!" I shouted.

Dan's smug countenance turned to one of surprise.

I was hardly gratified. "That was indeed a British sailor you saw me with yesterday. He was holding me at knifepoint," I said.

Oom Willem's look of concern was just like Papa's: bushy eyebrows furrowed over worried blue eyes. He asked, "You were the captive of a British sailor, Sarah?"

Dan scoffed. "He knew Sarah is a spy. Likely she was taking him to see her chum the witch." He marked that I drew my breath in sharply at his unwitting truth.

Oom Willem knit his brows once more. "What was the reason he took you prisoner? Be silent, Daniel. I will hear from Sarah."

"The sailor was aboard *Phoenix*. He was aloft trying to repair the rigging and Brom shot him. He fell into the river but his wound was trifling and..."

"Abraham *shot* a British seaman?"

"He was aboard *Zomer Wind* with *Oom* Jan and Samuel Youngs, I marked your absence, Dan," I added acidly.

Oom Willem ignored my jibe. Doubtless he thought his son's cowardice to be the wiser choice. "And how did this sailor come to capture you, Sarah?"

"He got out of the river and made his way up the bank to our farm. He was but lightly wounded. He threatened to stab me and then he forced me to take him..."

"To the witch!" cried Daniel.

I decided to turn the tables. "And you were the very fool who babbled that it was Brom who had shot him. He knew where Brom lived..." I noted uneasily that I'd spoken of Brom in the past tense "...so he led the soldiers directly to our house this morning."

The hubbub rose sharply, and we moved closer to see. The redcoats were still in formation, but their pace had slowed. Isaac Martling was strutting alongside the soldiers. He wagged his head and swung his arm with exaggerated precision.

"That man has not missed a brawl since his cradle days," *Oom* Willem said.

Isaac stopped marching and turned to the crowd. "Are these good fellows lost?" he demanded, scratching his head in mock puzzlement. "I believe they're going in the wrong direction."

As Isaac had intended, there was laughter from the crowd. James Romer pointed toward the east. "England's that way!" he shouted.

Several others began to chant, "Go back to Eng-land! Go back to Eng-land!"

Samuel hastened over to us. "Do you think...?" he began.

Alas, my hackles had remained staunchly upright. Having revealed one dark truth about Dan I decided to disclose the larger evil that I knew he had done.

I shouted, "And Dan is the very cause of Brom's falling from the mill wheel..."

Dan's face was the scarlet of the soldiers' coats. I suspected he was horrified at having his treachery revealed.

"Daniel, this cannot be," *Oom* Willem said. He turned to me. "Was Rachel there? Did she see this...?"

In the scene I remembered – Dan's trying and failing to climb onto the mill wheel with Brom, jealousy of his better-favoured cousin, and his cruel and senseless revenge – Rachel had not been a witness. But that would not prevent her from providing dramatic testimony. That her words would discredit me would be spice for an already savoury dish.

I forged ahead. "I saw you, Dan. You were hard by the lever when the water gate was opened. You opened the gate to start the mill going round. You meant to cripple Brom, if not kill him."

Samuel shook his head with so much vigour his spectacles bobbed on his ample nose. "No, Sarah. No. Dan did not open the mill gate."

"I saw him," I insisted.

Dan yelled, "You didn't see it because I didn't do it."

I scoffed, "Well, *somebody*..."

"Isaac Martling," said Samuel. "He was in his cups."

Oom Willem put in, "That man is always in his cups. Are you saying, Samuel, that Isaac is at fault for Brom's *ongeval*?"

"Brom's... *accident*?" Samuel translated the Dutch word correctly.

"It was no accident!" I put in.

"Sarah, it was," Samuel said gently. "Isaac stumbled into Dan."

"Did he cause Dan to hit the lever...?" I sought to salvage some scrap of my theory.

Samuel wrinkled his brow. "No, I believe that Isaac himself caused the gate to open. He'd stumbled into Dan and sent him sprawling."

Dan added, "Then Isaac tripped over me. That was when he fell against the lever."

Before I had the time to sort out these appalling revelations, someone fired a rifle from behind our orchard wall. We turned to see.

The British officer, the same one who had thought Mama a fine English lady, shouted, "Company halt!"

The troops came to a stop and the officer turned to the crowd. "Disperse at once, I command you, "Disperse at once!"

Isaac swaggered up behind the officer. "About face!" he ordered. "Return to England at once, I com-mahnd you."

"This is our country, not yours!" someone yelled.

The officer shouted, "These colonies belong to His Majesty King George. Now stand down..."

"Here's a rock for King George!" Someone hit a redcoat square-ly between the shoulders.

"This one's from Brom Van Tassel," someone shouted as he and several others pelted the soldiers with rocks, whilst Isaac whooped with glee. He cried, "That's the way, boys. We'll see which is harder, a British pate or a Westchester boulder."

Oom Willem said, "This is dangerous. We must take cover."

I scrambled up the embankment. I would not be caught in a battle again, nor did I want the soldiers to recall that I was the rebel's sister. Panic seized me by the throat and fairly choked me. I cowered behind a big oak tree.

"Stand by to fire!" the officer barked. "Prime and load."

To a man, the soldiers dropped to one knee. They readied their muskets.

"Pre-sent!" the officer called out. His men raised their muskets and aimed at the thickets where people were scurrying to hide.

Tom's younger brother darted across the orchard. A soldier caught the movement from the corner of his eye. He whirled and fired. Little Jake screamed and clutched his arm. He tumbled to the ground.

For a moment everything was silent and still. I saw Amy's green gown, the young man's beard and Isaac Martling's mouth agape in astonishment. Then a shot whistled from behind the stone wall. The soldier fell to his knees. He pitched forward, clutching his chest. His musket clattered onto the road beside him.

Another shot rang out. It had come from the woods hard by me. The officer threw up his arms and reeled backwards. One of his men tried to catch him but the officer sagged to the ground. His pointed leather cap was tilted over one ear. A dark stain spread across his scarlet coat.

Everyone looked to see who had fired the shot. It was Hulda. Her bonnet had slipped off her head and hung round her neck. I could see – everybody could – the pink and white scar etched on her head and the jagged clumps of hair round it. She opened her pouch to re-load her rifle. She looked as calm as if she were about to bag a pigeon.

More shots came from behind the wall and the soldiers fired back. A familiar pall of bitter-smelling gunpowder smoke gathered over the road and orchard. I coughed and wiped my eyes. My heart was beating so hard I could feel the pulse in my ears. I crouched behind the tree and longed to be at home.

Hulda aimed and fired again, and another soldier crumpled to the ground.

Someone cried, "Up there! That woman!"

Several soldiers began to make their way toward her. Their muskets scraped the rocks as they climbed. One soldier grabbed at the bushes to pull himself up and cursed as the thorns tore his hands.

What would I do if they should see me? This oak tree was no place to hide. The soldiers were close enough now that I caught the salty smell of sweat on their woollen uniforms. I could hear them panting. I could see their flushed faces and wild eyes. They fumbled with their muskets. I knew I must warn Hulda but if I spoke out the soldiers would surely find me. They might come after me instead of Hulda. I shrank behind the tree.

Hulda paid the soldiers no mind. She poured gunpowder down her rifle barrel and jammed a wad of linen after it. She was reaching into her pouch for gunpowder as the first shot hit her. She staggered but she tried to tap the powder into the pan. She was raising her rifle once more as a hail of musket balls drove her back against a tree. I closed my eyes as I heard her fall.

A long moment passed before I peeked out from behind the tree where I was hiding. Hulda was struggling to reach her rifle.

A heavy foot stamped on her wrist. "You'll not need that where you're going," the soldier told her. He seized the rifle and tossed it into the underbrush.

The soldiers circled round her. One raised his musket. "Why must we wait to finish this rebel scum?" he asked. He ran his bayonet deep into her chest.

I could not bear the deep sigh that Hulda gave as the bayonet ran her through. It was as if her very life were leaving her. I couldn't look but somehow, I did. She reached toward me and made a little coughing noise.

Her rifle had fallen a small distance from me. I looked at her once more. Then I was on my feet. I slipped from behind the tree and seized her rifle. I shoved my way through the ring of soldiers. I stood between them and Hulda.

"Stand back!" I ordered.

The soldiers looked me over. "Colonial wenches are a feisty lot," one observed. "Take one down and straightaway another pops up."

Another soldier aimed his bayonet at Hulda. "Mark how King George deals with rebels, girl. You'll be next."

I swung the rifle so the barrel clashed with the steel bayonet and pushed it aside.

"Let her die in peace," I said.

The soldier paused. "Is this the lass from the farm?"

"The one with the English mum?"

"The one with the traitor brother."

One soldier chuckled. "Is this wretch your kin, too?"

"Indeed she is." My eyes met his and did not blink. "We Americans do not tolerate rule by tyranny or by bayonet. That makes us all kin, and you had best remember it."

The soldiers eyed me uneasily. "These people are mad," one muttered. Slowly they began to back away. They turned and vanished into the woods.

Hulda's gown had a dozen dark holes the size of blueberries and a slash the width of my finger. That must have been where the bayonet had pierced her. There was not much blood. I wondered if my eyes had deceived me. Perhaps the soldier had not stabbed her, after all.

I sank to the ground beside her. I found her hand and took it. Her flesh was cold but I could feel her heart beating. It was very, very fast, like a woodpecker drumming on a tree. I leaned over her and searched her face.

"Do you see me?" I asked.

Hulda was trembling. With each breath her face creased in pain. Her eyes moved slowly and settled on me. A sound in her chest was like her heart turning over.

"*Ja,*" I thought she said. Maybe it was only another breath.

Around her mouth and nose her skin was turning blue. The great vein in the side of her neck bulged. It was blue as well. Her eyelids drooped.

Hulda made a rasping sound. As her mouth fell open, I saw where the blood was. I remembered the blood on her teeth the day I'd first seen her and I turned my head away. I hoped she would not see me cry. A trace of pink bubbles dribbled from her mouth and I wiped it away with the hem of my gown.

Hulda's eyes opened wide, and I believed that she might be about to speak. She looked past me, up through the trembling leaves to a patch of sky. She raised her hand and called out a joyous greeting.

Then I saw. I saw clearly. Hulda the Witch was passing through the Gates of Paradise.

– Chapter Twenty Nine –

The underbrush rustled, the bushes parted and Dan emerged. The tall young man I'd noticed with Amy and Rachel was with him.

"What happened?" Dan was staring quite as if he'd not seen me before.

The young man's eyes travelled to Hulda's rifle on the ground next to me. "Your cousin put the British Army to flight," he said. He seemed altogether amused. I was irked.

Dan took a step toward Hulda's body and peered at her. "That's the witch," he announced.

I'd closed Hulda's eyes. The wonder and joy in their sightless stare were for another world. I'd folded her arms across her bosom to conceal the red-rimmed slashes of the soldiers' bayonets. I'd tied her bonnet back on her head and I'd struggled to smooth her hair to cover the scar. It came to me that I should have left it so the people who were now making their way toward us would call to mind their cruelty to her.

I cried, "She wasn't a witch! She was kind and good and..." I saw my skirts were smeared with the blood I'd wiped from her face. "The soldiers killed her."

"Then you sent them packing, Sarah Van Tassel." This chap acted quite as if he knew me. He asked, "Did you tell the soldiers that the old Indian was going to cast a spell on them?"

I took measure of him. He appeared to be older than Brom or Dan but younger than *Oom* Jan. Mama would say he was well favoured. His curly brown hair was captured in a cue, and his beard was trimmed neatly. He wore brown breeches. This was the very rascal who yesterday had followed the sailor and me in the hollow! I jumped to my feet and straightened my hat.

"You let that sailor terrify me!" I cried.

He grinned. "Looked to me to be the other way round."

"You could have helped me!"

He raised his hands in a gesture of surrender. "I am truly sorry," he said. "I will not make that mistake again."

I was considering a retort as Samuel Youngs and his father Joseph appeared. They were followed by remnants of the crowd.

"We gave notice to the bloody British," Joseph said grimly. "They won't haste to meddle with us again."

"Scant revenge for beating Brom like a stray dog," Samuel replied.

They started as they saw me, and again as they saw Hulda's body on the ground beside me.

"That's the woman who was shooting at the soldiers," Samuel said. He bent over her body, took her wrist and put his thumb against it. "She's dead."

"That is...*was* Hulda..." I began.

"The witch!" Rachel interrupted.

"The spy," Dan added.

Samuel told him, "If she were a spy, Dan, she hid it well. She killed two British soldiers. One was the very scoundrel who thrashed Brom."

The utterance of Brom's name at once had a beneficent effect on the gathering: Jaws tightened and eyes hardened with patriotic resolve. Pitying glances were directed at me. Their regard of Hulda was the more remarkable: Heads were cocked to view her from an angle. I heard a few murmurs of "brave woman" and "poor soul."

Of course, *Tante* Gertje was a dissident. Her eyes veritably disappeared into her face as she squinted at Hulda. "An evil spirit is ever troubled. Yea, even unto death," she pronounced.

Mevrouw Romer was still gasping from the effort of hauling herself up the embankment. "Are *you* possessed of an evil spirit, Gertje? This good woman defended us. Why, look at her!"

I'd not seen Hulda in a manner of repose. In fact, I'd never seen her when she wasn't bustling about with purpose and vigour. Her strong, callused hands seemed ill at ease lying still upon her breast.

"Now, good dames, let us not argue." Joseph cleared his throat. "Let us bind up our wounds and bury our dead..."

Joseph's entreaty, intended no doubt to calm the passions Hulda seemed always to have stirred, in fact had the effect of roiling them further.

Tante Gertje cried, "Bury her? We should set a torch to her."

Mevrouw Romer turned to the others. "This woman has given her life in our defence. I say she has earned a resting place worthy of her heroism."

Tante Gertje gasped. "You cannot mean ... the churchyard. You may not bury a witch in Christian ground. That is contrary to God's will."

"You are no more fit to discern God's will than the rest of us, Gertje," *Mevrouw* Romer snapped.

"*Dominie* Ritzema is at the church now. Let us ask him," *Oom* Willem suggested.

The good pastor arrived soon after, panting and red-faced from his haste to attend to this ecclesiastical crisis.

Tante Gertje snatched his sleeve. "Hear me, *Dominie*!" she shouted, as if it were possible to do otherwise. "If that... *schepsel* is buried near my kin, they won't wait until Judgment Day to rise from the ground."

Dominie Ritzema tried to free himself from *Tante* Gertje's grip, and I suspected he had been called upon before to settle such quarrels. He stared sternly over the tops of his spectacles as the assembly waited for The Lord's Judgment to be dispensed.

"Now, you claim that this woman was a witch. Have you proof?" he inquired of *Tante* Gertje.

"She had no kin." *Tante* Gertje's jowls trembled.

"She spoke in strange tongues." Jemima's stepmother *Mevrouw* Van Wart offered timidly. "She concocted malicious potions."

The *dominie* nodded gravely. "Did this woman ever call upon the Lord?"

Tante Gertje snuffled loudly. "She was never in attendance at services."

"The Lord himself opens the Kingdom of Heaven to all who believe in him, even those who do so at the last," the *dominie* intoned. "But without proof that this woman was a believer..." He shook his head sorrowfully.

"Hulda has a Bible," I said, almost to myself.

The *dominie* came close. "What's that, my child? Speak up."

"Hulda has a Bible," I said more loudly. "It's inscribed with her name, *Dominie*. It's at her home."

Tante Gertje shouted, "My Rachel swears that this one is a witch like the dead one. Tell them, Rachel!"

At that command, I was terrified. A goodly number took *Tante* Gertje's Scripture-soaked tirades with a pinch of salt. Yet I supposed that most people had not learned of her daughter's similar inclinations.

Rachel's head was bowed. She seemed to be intent on studying the grass.

Tante Gertje prompted her. "Tell how Sarah lured you into that nest of snakes. How she held you fast so the witch could bite you."

I waited for a torrent of falsehood to spill from Rachel's mouth. But she only stammered. "Sarah... Sarah and the witch..."

Tante Gertje shook her fist in my face. "See how this one has cursed my daughter. Even now she strikes her dumb, *Dominie!*" She paused to think of something bad enough to say about me. "She is a very instrument of Satan."

The *dominie* frowned as he turned to me. "Have you kept company with that woman?"

Dan answered before I could. "She goes to the witch's dwelling."

"Is that true, child?"

I took a breath. "Yes I did go..." I began.

"And for what purpose?" The *dominie* was considerably more stern.

The young man with the beard and brown breeches stepped forward. "Sarah went to her home with me."

I tried not to look as astonished as everyone else.

Tante Gertje exclaimed, "I've not seen *you* before!"

"I'm Elijah, the third son of Joshua Lent of Van Cortlandt's Manor, near Peek's Kill. I've been working at the mill. I... I... cut my hand and it needed care. Ceaser mentioned the curing woman and Sarah offered to guide me to her home..."

The *dominie* looked stern. "So Sarah knew where this woman lived?"

Tante Gertje shouted, "And she is a very partner of the witch! She..."

Elijah accomplished the not inconsequential feat of silencing her. "Sarah said she believed that the woman lived deep in the hollow behind the church. Brom went with us, of course."

At the mention of the suddenly-sainted Brom, the assembly murmured in approval. *Tante* Gertje continued, although in milder tones. "Since you are a stranger here, you must not know this woman was a witch. In fact, she may have tricked us with her death. Even now, the witch possesses this girl..." *Tante* Gertje shook a hammy fist at me. "The witch may have changed into another being altogether."

Isaac Martling, that trusty weathervane of public opinion, had at last divined which way sentiments were blowing. He sidled up to Elijah. "Now, sir or madam, as the case may be," he began. "Since you must be the new witch of Philipsburgh Manor, I beg you to cast a spell on Gertje Van Tassel. Let no more prattle come from her mouth, let no more..."

Everyone laughed but *Tante* Gertje. "This one admits he's a stranger here," she shouted, pointing to Elijah. "How would he know of this demon's Bible? Answer me that."

Elijah turned to the *dominie*. "Hulda was my kin," he declared stoutly. "Of my grandmother's people, I believe. Of course I can bring you her Bible." He paused. "I'm not certain how to reach her home from here. Perhaps Sarah could guide me."

Elijah looked at me. He raised his eyebrows and inclined his head just a bit, as if to say, "There. You see." I thought I was the only one who noticed.

Tante Gertje seized Rachel by the arm. "Let us go! I cannot abide the thought of that demon spending Eternity in the company of my family."

Isaac pointed to the sky with his remaining hand. "Look! There's the witch!" he cried. "Hallo-o! Do you see any of Gertje Van Tassel's kin up there? What's that you say? Her family's not there? Then I reckon it's safe for you to go on in."

Even *Dominie* Ritzema couldn't hide a smile. "We'll go to the churchyard and choose a spot for her grave," he said. He nodded toward Dan, Samuel and Tom Buckhout. "You must bring shovels to prepare the ground."

Tom took my arm as I turned to go. He seemed bent on telling me something, yet altogether ill at ease about it. "S-Sarah," he began.

For an instant, I wondered why I'd ever seen him as naught but a bumpkin, and a tongue-tied one at that. I eyed him inquiringly.

"You're... you're very brave," he stammered and promptly fled.

Mevrouw Romer called out, "James, in my chest at home is that linen cloth I brought from Switzerland. Fetch it, please. It will make a shroud worthy of this woman Hulda."

That was the first time I had ever heard anyone call Hulda by her name. As I looked once more upon her, I could have vouched that Hulda's lips had twisted into an expression of wry amusement.

– Chapter Thirty –

Elijah and I cast slanting shadows across the Post Road in the afternoon sun. His legs were long, and I saw that he was shortening his stride to match mine. When he caught me looking up at him, he smiled.

"Sarah Van Tassel," he said. I thought he savoured the speaking of my name.

How strange it was that this fellow had been in my life for some time, hovering just out of view. We'd been at the same places, and the people we had seen had seen each of us. Like Brom. *Brom*!

"What of Br-rom?" My voice broke as I asked.

"The bloody lobsterbacks took him prisoner."

"What became of him?"

"I'll warrant they took him to *Phoenix* or *Rose*."

"Is that as bad as…" I swallowed "…as a prison ship?"

"Bad enough," he said.

I strove to put the scene together in my mind. "Papa was with him!" I exclaimed. "Did they take Papa?"

He shook his head. "No."

"Did-did they kill him?"

"No. Your papa set upon the soldiers who had seized Brom. One of them clubbed him with the butt of his musket. Your papa was knocked senseless."

I let out a small, wounded cry.

"That was good fortune, in a way," Elijah went on. "As the soldiers were shackling Brom, two of them tried to revive your papa so they could take him prisoner, too."

"*Revive* him?"

"They kicked him and prodded him with their muskets. They spat in his face, to no avail. So they left him in the road."

"Where is he now?"

"I helped Ceaser to move him under a tree. He was beginning to come round as I left."

As we neared the mill, I asked, "Why were you following the sailor and me?"

He looked thoughtful. "I was curious about a girl who would have a prism."

"Oh, forgive me! I forgot to thank you for getting it back for me. How ever did you...?"

I thought he blushed. "I'm lucky at cards," he allowed.

"Lucky at cards, unlucky at love," Mama said. I tried to recall what I knew of Elijah: Papa had said he was a *zot* because he wanted to put to sea. Amy said he was a rogue because of some misfortune with a girl.

"Are you Hulda's kin?" I asked.

"The same as you," he answered.

"I'm not..."

"You did know her."

I frowned. "How do you know that?"

"You said she was kind and good. How do you know that?"

"Those were the first words you spoke when Dan and I came upon you today. Here's the way to her home."

I stopped walking. "You said you didn't know where she lived!"

He blushed once more, and I understood: He wanted to be with me. I didn't think he was a zot, for he was quick of wit, and I didn't think he was a rogue. A rogue wouldn't have blushed whilst talking to a younger girl.

We followed the path along the tumbling river. There was the mossy rock where the sailor had slipped. There was the thicket where I'd thrown his knife. I wondered if anyone would ever find it.

Elijah said, "It must have been a gift that Hulda had, looking beyond what most folks notice. You have that gift as well. What did you see about her?"

I thought for a moment. "I saw things that shouldn't have been there but they were. The first time I saw her, when Rachel was bitten by a rattlesnake and Hulda helped her, I thought her strange and a bit frightening. Then she smiled, and she looked, well, she looked kind.

"People like *Tante* Gertje saw only that she was strange. Then they turned it a bit to make Hulda evil. But I'd seen her smile. Once I saw that, I thought of her as good."

Elijah watched me intently. His eyes were the colour of very deep water.

The hut was in a state of dishevelment that I'd not seen before. Blankets were in a heap on the floor. A wooden bowl and spoon on the tree-stump table had dried scraps of something that appeared to have been *suppan*, the Indian corn porridge much relished by the Dutch. Beneath the iron cooking pot, embers still glowed.

I turned to Elijah. "Hulda would never have allowed this disorder. Someone else has been here."

Elijah stroked his beard thoughtfully. "I cannot think that word of her death would have spread so swiftly and I'll wager most folks have no notion where her home was. Besides," he added, pointing to the tall chest of walnut wood. "There's a *kas*. It's not been touched. Is that where she kept her Bible?"

The tears I'd held back for so long came flooding forth. Elijah murmured that I'd been so brave, it was fitting that I should cry now.

"I'm not brave! That time in the churchyard, when people attacked her, she came over to me and her head was bleeding..." I caught my breath. "...As she looked at me she was begging for help although she didn't say anything, and I was such a coward that I acted as if I didn't know her."

"And today you stood down an army to defend her." Elijah took me by the shoulders. He looked into my face quite as if he were searching for some revelation there. He flushed with embarrassment and took his hands away.

I went to the chest, opened the top drawer and took out the Bible. "There's a note inside," I told Elijah. "It's written in her hand, I think. It's in German."

He unfolded the yellowed paper. "I believe it's her will."

"Can you read it?"

"A little. Now, here it says... *gelt*... gold, money. She wants to leave her money to... to help the women made... widows by war. We must find the gold and take it to the *dominie*." I suspect it's somewhere in this *kas*."

Elijah laid the will back in the Bible. His eyes met mine for a long moment. He looked away and cleared his throat.

I couldn't understand what I'd just seen. In Elijah's face were surprise and joy, and the discovery of something he'd been waiting a long time to see. It was the light I had seen in Hulda's eyes at the last. In bewilderment, I slipped my hand into my pocket. There, my fingers closed round Hulda's love charm.

The second drawer we searched yielded a small brown leather bag. I opened it and counted out fourteen gold pieces. Eight bore the likeness of King George the Second, the present king's father. Six pieces had the profile of King Frederick of Spain, whose double chin was his most prominent feature. I wondered how Hulda might have come into possession of the latter. I would never know.

I folded Hulda's blankets and banked her fire. The embers glowed more dimly now. In a day, they would be cold and ashen.

"I must return her home to her standard of order," I explained to Elijah.

He didn't ask why, and I was gratified, for I could not have told him.

I gathered the bowl and spoon and looked about for a way to wash them.

"I'll fetch water," he said, picking up the battered wooden bucket.

I glanced up as he ducked under the narrow little portal. Hulda's garden was in glorious array. Who would tend it now? It came to me that I could. I could live in this solitary sphere Hulda had created.

It would be my snug and simple world, mine alone. I would live on my terms, as she had. I could decide with whom I would pass time. I'd never again set eyes on Rachel or Dan or *Tante* Gertje. I might see Mama, but only for tea. I would not have charge of Thomas any more.

I'd return to our house, but only to collect clothing and my prism. Likely I could carry my featherbed, as well. The wooden bench that had served as Hulda's sleeping pallet was hard and narrow.

But how would I occupy myself each day? I doubted that Mama would lend me her books. Would people shun me as they had Hulda? My pearl had at its core a speck of grit. I rose slowly to my feet and followed Elijah out into the garden.

Elijah's back was turned to me, and he appeared to have frozen in mid-stride. The bucket dangled from his hand. Behind him, pink and white hollyhocks were in shadow.

"Get back, Sarah," he said.

At that instant a boy came into view. I judged him to be of perhaps twelve years. He was garbed as a savage, with a bare chest and deerskin tied round his waist with a thong to cover his lower parts. His head had been stripped of hair save for a lock in the middle that appeared to have been smeared with some sort of dark-coloured grease. Red dots adorned his cheeks. His skin was of a dusky hue, but I'd seen his blue eyes before. They were Hulda's.

He stared at Elijah in an altogether hostile manner, and I wondered if he possessed some weapon to accompany his fierce demeanour. When he turned his gaze to me, his eyes softened. He'd seen me before.

My head spun with queries: How much time did he pass with Hulda? I called to mind the bare footprint in the mud. He must have been the one who made it. Why had she never spoken of him? Where did he live? A native village deep in the northern hills, I supposed. I'd heard rumours of such a place. He must have been the one who'd rumpled the blankets and eaten the suppan. Could he converse in even basic English? And how was I to tell him that his mother was dead?

The boy spared us the burden of imparting the dreadful news, for he turned and vanished into the woods. Elijah and I stared at each other.

At length he said, "We said we'd bring her Bible to the *dominie*. But what about the gold? Perchance her son should have it?"

"No," I said, rankled that Elijah had named the boy as Hulda's son. "She made it plain she wanted the gold to go to war widows."

The companionable quiet we'd shared on the way to Hulda's cottage turned to a discomfiting void as we made our way back. I thought bitterly that barely an hour before, I'd been full of sorrow, yes, but also gratified that Hulda would have a dignified burial. I'd been the source of that reconciliation.

She had deceived me.

There had been talk of a half-breed boy. Perhaps everyone else had long known of it and that was why Hulda had been cast out. I felt the fool for taking her part.

Elijah looked at me and I knew he knew my thoughts. He asked, "How does this change the way you see her?"

"Why, it changes everything," I blurted. "I had no notion that this primitive existed, much less that he is plainly of her flesh."

"Does it make her the less kind?"

I replied in a haughty tone. "That... savage... was an aspect of her that I'd not known."

"You didn't answer."

I didn't want to talk about this shocking occurrence. I needed time to set my thoughts in order. The truth of it was, I'd believed myself to be her sole companion, the only one she regarded with affection. I'd thought she needed, indeed craved, my company and friendship. I'd seen myself to her as she had been to me: a treasure that was mine alone.

That had been an illusion. A half-breed bastard claimed a closer bond with her.

"How did this ... this ... creature come into being?" I demanded.

"Clearly, his mother coupled with a native."

"But how... how could she? They are so...".

"Do you think perhaps it was not her choice?"

My heart raced and my breath quickened as I recalled the skinny man in the orchard. Suppose he had... accomplished his intention? Had it become known, I might have been rejected as Hulda was. Suppose a child had come into being? Could I have borne such a shameful burden, and provided it with nurture, even love? I glanced furtively at Elijah. I wondered if he knew about the skinny man.

A great void yawned before me, of all the things I didn't know and never would, of questions that could be answered one way or another and both could be right and both wrong. The earlier revelation, that Isaac Martling, not Dan, had been the cause for Brom's accident, sprang to my mind. I had been mistaken. I had seen a *trompe l'oeil* conjured from my own beliefs, experiences and prejudices.

Elijah was not to let me go unchallenged. "Does it change that she helped your cousin after the snakebite?"

"No," I admitted sullenly.

"Does it change that she gave her life for the very neighbours who shunned her? That she must have given it willingly?"

Elijah knew the answer. I kicked a pebble on the path.

"Appears to me," he said, "That you saw things that shouldn't have been there, but they were."

I was angry to have my very words turned back on me. That they were true annoyed me further. We walked in silence along Pocantico's mossy embankment.

The grave was ready by the time Elijah and I arrived back at the churchyard. The *dominie* had chosen a site by the northeast corner of the old stone church.

Elijah said, "See how her grave is at a distance from the others. Your aunt's kin can rest undisturbed."

"Hulda does favour solitude," I allowed.

The women had done a fine job of tidying Hulda. Her hair had been smoothed beneath her bonnet and her arms were folded on her bosom. Her gown was clean, although wet in spots where someone had scrubbed out the bloodstains. As I was thinking that her serene aspect might also be sly, James Romer hurried up with the cloth for her shroud.

Dominie Ritzema examined Hulda's Bible and the will, and pronounced them both to be genuine. I opened her small leather bag and counted out the fourteen gold pieces. The assembly of mourners murmured with amazement and approval. People were always impressed by large sums of money, I thought bitterly. Hulda had now purchased the esteem she'd not had in her lifetime.

The *dominie* inspected the earthen bed where Hulda would rest. "She shall face the East, so that on Judgment Day the Rising Sun will greet her," he said.

We gathered round as the *dominie* read from the Book of Job: "Man that is born of woman is of few days and full of trouble."

I suspected that *Dominie* Ritzema read those words at every funeral. Nonetheless, I bowed my head and folded my hands. Elijah did the same.

"*My kinfolk have failed, and my familiar friends have forgotten me,*" the *dominie* intoned, rocking back on his heels and raising his eyes to Heaven.

I fidgeted, and saw Elijah take note of it.

"*...And they whom I loved are turned against me.*"

The Job of countless travails, or the *dominie*, at least, were uttering the very words Hulda might rightly have spoken. I looked upon her. She had been *overleden* but a few hours, yet the serene countenance I'd seen earlier had vanished entirely. The corners of her mouth had turned down, her nose had lengthened by an inch, at the least, and behind her closed eyelids I suspected she was glaring fiercely.

Perhaps she was angry. Yet I couldn't recall an instance when Hulda had uttered a wrathful word. The closest she had come was snapping at the British sailor I'd led to her home. She'd thought he had harmed me.

In this matter of the bastard boy, no doubt she had expected differently from me. Yet she knew I'd shown naught but failure and forgetting when she was attacked that day at the church. And what had happened? Hulda had not held me to account for it. If she'd been hurt or resentful of my cowardice, I hadn't seen it. She'd overlooked my very obvious flaws.

The truth of it was, I wanted to see only the facet of Hulda that aligned with my own views. That was why, I supposed, that I'd held her to be a treasure that I alone possessed. But our friendship had in fact been but one plane of a faceted globe. I saw her in one way and others in their own ways. It did not diminish my friendship with her, that others viewed her from a different angle. Of course they would.

I joined our little group of mourners in reciting: "*For I know that my redeemer liveth, and that he shall stand at the latter day upon the earth: And though after my skin worms destroy this body, yet in my flesh shall I see God.*" My voice quavered.

"This day we gather to honour one who is *overleden*," the *dominie* said, using the Dutch word for "dead." "Our sister, er…"

"Hulda," Elijah whispered.

"Hulda. She was a fitting example of God's command to Love Thy Neighbour."

The group shifted uncomfortably. Everyone knew well how much they had loved her.

Dominie Ritzema continued, "In life, our sister loved her neighbours by making medicines to heal them of their bodily distresses."

Mevrouw Romer murmured in agreement, and I suspected she was the one who had told this to the *dominie*.

"In death, it seems, her love abides." The *dominie* produced the bag that I had found in Hulda's *kas* and shook it so the coins jingled.

"She has left her earthly treasure to help other languishing souls. Her kin here…" the *dominie* nodded toward Elijah. "Her kin here produced her will which instructs that this money be used to ease the plight of women left alone to face the woes of life."

Some amidst the mourners glanced about with puzzlement. Of whom had the *vreemdeling* written? Hulda herself was the only outcast they could call to mind.

Elijah explained, "She intended that the money go to women

made widows by war."

Joseph Youngs cried out, "This woman gave her own life to save ours. We must use the money to build her a monument so that she may live forever as an example of..." He cleared his throat as he sought to recall a virtue Hulda exemplified.

"My kinswoman never put store in earthly things," Elijah broke in. "She wanted her money to go to widows, and we should respect her wishes."

The mourners shifted about, grateful that the bag of gold was not to be squandered on a memorial that would ever remind them of their own shortcomings.

"All Hulda would want is for flowers to mark her grave," I added. Heads nodded and words of approval grew louder.

As *Mevrouw* Romer unfolded the length of fine Swiss linen that would serve as her shroud, *Dominie* Ritzema tried to set Hulda's Bible upon her bosom. Her crossed arms prevented him.

"See, the witch is refusing the Bible," I heard a woman whisper. "She cannot take it with her to hell."

"Perhaps we should give the Bible to her kin," suggested Joseph, nodding toward Elijah.

Most in the group agreed.

Elijah protested. "Oh, no, I may not take it," he said. "I'm but a distant cousin. Her Bible must go with her to Eternity." He looked at me to help him.

I found myself saying, "Why, I believe she has much closer family. "There's the boy. Her...her *son*. He should have his mother's Bible."

Elijah's eyes widened in amazement. "Oh, yes," he managed to say. "Why, that is a fine idea." He took the Bible *Mevrouw* Romer proffered and said to the *dominie*, "We shall see that the lad is given the Bible. Now, we need gather flowers for Hulda's grave."

Elijah and I emptied the nearby meadows of daisies, cornflowers and Queen Anne's lace.

A Note on Characters

Hulda the Witch was a real person. The circumstances of her life and death are told in Edgar Mayhew Bacon's "*Chronicles of Tarrytown and Sleepy Hollow*," published in 1916. She is buried in an unmarked grave at the Old Dutch Church of Sleepy Hollow.

The British attack on **Jacob Van Tassel's** home is described by Washington Irving in his story, "Wolfert's Roost." Irving bought the property in 1835, renamed it "Sunnyside," and lived there for many years.

Eleanor "Laney" Van Tassel, Jacob's daughter, is said to be Irving's inspiration for Katrina Van Tassel in "The Legend of Sleepy Hollow."

Ceaser and **Dimond** were listed among the slaves in a 1750 inventory of the estate of Adolph Philipse.

Isaac Martling was a local idler and jokester. The loss of one arm during the French and Indian War prevented him from seeking honest work, he said.

As head of the Dutch Church in New York, **Dominie Johannes Ritzema's** duties included supervision of the church on Philipsburgh Manor. In 1776 and 1777, Dominie Ritzema was probably in Tarrytown, as he signed several church documents during that time.

Frena Romer and her husband Jacob came to America as indentured servants. After years apart, they were reunited, married and had eight children, including James.

The Rev. Samuel Seabury was Anglican clergyman and outspoken Loyalist. He became the first bishop of the Episcopal Church in the United States.

Nathaniel Underhill was the mayor of Westchester and a prominent Tory.

Isaac van Wart became a national hero in 1780. With two other militia, he captured Major John Andre, the British officer who was carrying General Benedict Arnold's treasonous plans for the surrender of the American fortress at West Point NY.

Samuel Youngs was a Continental Army officer and Westchester Guide during the American Revolution. He later became a school teacher, and is believed to be the character model for Ichabod Crane in "The Legend of Sleepy Hollow."

Joseph Youngs, Samuel's father, was a prominent patriot. His farmhouse, in present-day Valhalla, served as headquarters for American troops during the Revolution.

Many of the fictional characters, including Sarah, belonged to families who lived in Tarrytown at the time of the Revolution: Van Tassel, Martling, Requa and Buckhout. The Lent family lived near Peek's Kill.

Foreign Words

DUTCH WORDS

Dominie - pastor

Genoeg - enough

Grootje - grandmother

Guelderleng - golden apple

Haasten zich - hurry up

Heer - lord

Idioot - idiot

Jongeling - youngster

Kas - chest

Koekje - cookie

Kwaad - evil

Kykuit - lookout place

Meisje - girl

Mevrouw - Mrs.

Mijnheer - Mr.

Niet spreken - be quiet

Olykoek - doughnut

Ongeval - accident

Oom - uncle

Overleden - deceased

Puffertje - little cinnamon cake

Schenden - defiled

Schepsel - creature, witch

Schurk - outlaw

Spook - ghost, phantom

Suppan - Indian corn porridge

Tante - aunt

Verdoemd - damned

Verschillend - different

Vreemdeling - foreigner

Vrouw - Dutch woman

Zieklijk - sickly

Zoet - sweet

Zomer Wind - Summer Wind

Zonderling - strange

Zot - fool

Zwijn - swine

ENGLISH WORDS

Addlepated - confused, stupid

At sixes and sevens - in a state of disarray and confusion

Bluestocking - intellectual or learned woman

Chary - suspicious

Chit - immature or impudent young woman

Closet - small, private room

Dissolute - lacking shame or good manners

Durst - dare

Fortnight - two weeks

Goody Bull - England

Harridan - bossy or belligerent old woman

Jackanapes - impudent or conceited person

Jade - worthless woman

Keen - to lament or complain

Lief - as happily

Macaroni - fop, dandy

Monthly purgation - menstruation

Patten - raised shoe or clog worn in wet or muddy places

Perchance - maybe

Pocket - pouch or bag tied round a woman's waist and used to hold small items

Puffed up - showing one's pride

Rakeshame - vile, immoral person

Rapscallion - mischievous person

Tresses - hair

Whey-faced - pale

Whit - very small amount

GERMAN WORDS

Ach! - oh!

Gefangener - prisoner

Gelt - gold

Glas - object made of glass

Heimatland - homeland

Ja - yes

Krank - sick

Liebchen - sweet one

Mein - my

Milch - milk

Nein - no

Nichts - nothing

Schlange - snake

Schwester - sister

Was ist los? - What's happening?

FRENCH WORDS

Beau - handsome

Coccinelle - ladybug

Coquette - flirtatious woman

Magique - magic

Taisez-vous - be quiet

Trompe l'oeil - visual illusion in art

Tu penses de trop - you think too much

About The Author

Journalist and historian **Marcia G. Moore** finds that what actually happened is invariably more interesting than any story a writer could invent. She began telling tales of Sleepy Hollow as a columnist and reporter for *The Tarrytown (New York) Daily News*. Later, she helped to publish a guidebook and she gave tours of the burying ground of The Old Dutch Church of Sleepy Hollow (New York), where many of the real-life characters of *The Turning Glass* — including Hulda the Witch — are buried.

Her articles have appeared in *The New York Times*, *SAIL* magazine and other publications. She was a contributor to *We Are One*, a collection of essays about the War of 1812 on the Chesapeake Bay. Her children's picture book, *Wind and Oyster Jack,* was published in 2017 by Schiffer Books.

She is a graduate of the Medill School of Journalism at Northwestern University and the Graduate School of Journalism at Columbia University.

Marcia and her husband Jack live on Maryland's Eastern Shore with five boats, two cats and a Labrador Retriever.

www.ingramcontent.com/pod-product-compliance
Lightning Source LLC
Chambersburg PA
CBHW060915250626
47159CB00008B/3011